FROZEN ANGELS

A Novel

Joanne Eagles Honeycutt

JOANNE EAGLES HONEYCUTT

BOOK 1 OF THE EDGECOMBE TRILOGY

simply francis publishing company
North Carolina

Copyright © 2023 Joanne Eagles Honeycutt. All Rights Reserved.

No part of this publication may be reproduced, stored in a retrieval system or transmitted, in any form or by any means-electronic, mechanical, photocopying, recording, or otherwise without the prior written permission from the publisher, except for the inclusion of brief quotations in a review.

All brand, product, and place names used in this book that are trademarks or service marks, registered trademarks, or trade names are the exclusive intellectual property of their respective holders and are mentioned here as a matter of fair and nominative use. To avoid confusion, *simply francis publishing company* publishes books solely and is not affiliated with the holder of any mark mentioned in this book.

This is a work of fiction. Any real persons depicted in the book have been fictionalized for dramatic purposes.

Written permission has been granted and or attribution given for the use of all photographs in this book not taken by the author.

Library of Congress Control Number: 2023906014
ISBN: 978-1-63062-048-6 (paperback)
ISBN: 978-1-63062-049-3 (e-book)
Printed in the United States of America
Cover and Interior Design: Christy King Meares

For information about this title or to order books and/or electronic media, contact the publisher:

simply francis publishing company
P.O. Box 329, Wrightsville Beach, NC 28480
www.simplyfrancispublishing.com
simplyfrancispublishing@gmail.com

Dedication

For my husband Rhett
and my wonderful family

Cast of Characters

Primary Characters
Willie – Willa Abigail Pridgen
Hap – Thomas Rolland Tyson
Caroline King Cromwell – daughter of Elijah and Sarah

Cromwell Family of Shiloh Plantation
Elijah Cromwell – Caroline's father
Sarah King Cromwell – Caroline's mother
William King Cromwell (Will) – Caroline's brother, son of Elijah and Sarah
Coeffield King (Coffie) – Sarah King Cromwell's father
Jacksie Thrash King – deceased wife of Coeffield King

Secondary Characters
Wendell Tyson – Hap's father
George Edmundson – overseer of Shiloh Plantation
Maggie Edmundson – housekeeper for Cromwell Hall
Fate Edmundson – George and Maggie's son, Will Cromwell's best friend
Shug Maples – Fate's girlfriend
Michael Collins – Caroline's tutor
Litchfield Jacob Bagley – a suitor for Caroline Cromwell
Doctor Rufus Knight – one of three doctors in the area
Miss Penelope Cromwell – (Miss Penny) Elijah's aunt

Prologue
1861

The slight figure peeked from behind the tree to see if life stirred in the cottage before her. The smidgen of moonlight played across her tear-stained face. Why had she chosen to sever herself from her own flesh and blood? Biting her lip with each moment, she fingered the woven basket handle. Whimpers clogged her throat.

Over and over she'd taken half steps around the tree, only to jerk back, pushing the rough bark into her shoulders.

Do it! her mind screamed.

Suddenly a numbness consumed her, and as if controlled by the unseen, she stole onto the porch and positioned her burden. She froze, then bent down, allowing her hand to slowly drag across the carefully folded cloths.

With a glistening, contorted face, she turned and flew off the porch, scampering into the pitch darkness. It was the wee hours of a warm April morning.

Chapter 1

1867

A NEW SON

Willa Abigail Pridgen's shanty sat at the end of Station House Road, a small dot lost behind towering oaks and a few Carolina pines. The woman never had visitors, but when the earth moved and her old hound dog howled, she knew someone was coming.

One spring morning Willie, as her parents called her, heard Old Blue struggle beneath the house, dragging himself out to scout a disturbance down the road. The scrawny hound circled the well-swept yard, his strained cry piercing the air. Dust stirred down the way as Willie saw a horse and rider loping toward her. Goose flesh pricked her skin. Quickly she latched the screen door, although why she thought this flimsy old door would protect her was beyond reason. Still, Willie needed some assurance between her and an intruder.

"Oh, my God," she mouthed, then squinted in disbelief, as dust from the rider settled in her front yard.

Wendell Tyson dismounted and pulled a child down from his saddle. He turned and rested his heavy boot on her porch step and looked up. His wide-brimmed hat flipped off with ease as he mopped his brow in the steamy heat. The last few days had been scorchers, even though summer still was a few weeks away.

"How you been, Willie?" he asked, his voice rolling off his tongue like molasses.

Wendell Tyson's muscles bulged beneath his shirt and pants. His strength frightened her, but his eyes showed no anger, no schemes. A slight guilty smile softened his creased face.

Her heart's thumping rang in her ears, as Willie Pridgen stood mute, staring at the man who'd almost raped her. With all the jugging that day, she knew he'd remembered nothing from his drunkenness, but why in God's name was he standing in front of her porch now, after all these years?

"Hey, Willie," a small voice sounded.

Willie jumped. She'd forgotten the child but now saw him peering from behind his daddy's pant leg. A smile flickered across her face, but her eyes quickly darted back to the rugged man before her.

"Willie, you know Hap here. You gotta take him. I swear, nobody wants the scamp. I can't handle him with all the other children. You been the only one who could get him to do anything since losing his momma. When I ask who he wants to live with, he says 'Willie.' Over and over. Please."

Wendell was begging.

The woman stared, perplexed, at this man who'd shown her so little mercy and compassion years before. She rubbed her arms unconsciously and remembered the dead weight of him on top of her, a man passed out from mourning the loss of his wife, a man too drunk to even know what he was about to do. It was a miracle that Willie squirmed out from under him and ran across the yard to reach the road. Where she was going, she had no idea, but six children on the man's porch, one a baby in his older sister's arms, stopped her in her tracks. How could she leave them? She couldn't, and she didn't.

Several years passed until one day she knew it was time to go home. But in Tarboro, Willie only knew loneliness. Both parents had died from malaria and no other family lived close by.

Slowly her insides stirred as she looked at the boy. For the first time in a long time, somebody needed her. But a white boy living with a black woman? In Tarboro, North Carolina? Nobody

Chapter 1

would care on Station House Road, but what about the townsfolk and even her people? Only one person in the county she could think of who wouldn't mind, but he was unreachable.

Suddenly, she smiled and said under her breath, "Lord Jesus, I got me a son."

She flung open the rickety screen door and her arms to the child. Hap Tyson ran, grabbing her waist, burying his head in her skirt, his fingers tightly clutching the folds of fabric.

Wendell Tyson watched a few moments, then nodded, as if convinced that he'd done the right thing for his child. He swung up in the saddle, its leather creaking under his weight.

"You mind Willie, boy."

His words sounded more like a threat than fatherly advice. His son could only smile, nodding as he clung to Willie, staring up at her face with hope. Willie and Hap looked at the disappearing figure riding slowly, neither realizing a tear-stained face moved slower down Station House Road than the determined one that had brought the boy.

* * *

That night, as she sat in her mother's old rocker, Willie's new son crawled up in her arms, his head on her shoulder in the crook of her neck. The popping and creaking of the chair seemed to soothe them both.

His question caught her by surprise.

"Willie, where's your baby?"

"What?" She stopped rocking.

"Sister told me about your baby."

She sighed, taking a deep breath, before she spoke.

"I had to find him a home, Hap, just like your daddy had to find one for you."

"Pap cried today. Did you?"

"Oh, yes, son, it was the hardest thing I ever did. It isn't easy giving up your own flesh and blood. So, I'm not surprised this is very hard on your daddy."

She rocked again and pulled him closer. She supposed he was thinking about his father, but his next questions surprised her even more than the first.

"Is it a boy like me?"

"Yes," she said hesitantly.

"Is he close by? Do you see him?"

She gritted her teeth and blinked several times.

"He's in and around Tarboro, but I only see him from afar. It's a secret."

"You mean like, 'Cross my heart. Hope to die' kind of secret?"

She laughed softly and kissed the top of his head.

"Yes."

She watched him as he leaned back in her arms, making the big "X" across his chest before he said, "Hope to die."

"Thank you, son. Now, I think it's time we both go to Napper's Town. It's late."

"Napper's Town? Where's that?"

"My daddy used to call going to bed, 'Napper's Town.'"

"Where am I going to sleep?"

"I'm giving you your very own room where my parents used to sleep. Would you like that?"

"Ohhhhh, Willie, I never had my own room. You remember we all had to sleep in two beds."

She remembered. When she discovered her condition, she'd fled across the county line with the help of her parents and found work with the Tysons. They were a rowdy houseful, but they'd welcomed her into their family. She'd cared for the children while Cora and Wendell worked the fields. Their small farm lay on the outskirts of Greenville down in Pitt County. When they found out that she was having a child, Cora Tyson held her hand through her difficult delivery.

"You scream if you need to, girl," Cora said more than once.

Chapter 1

Willie did.

"She's done," the midwife had whispered, shaking her head at Cora.

Willie Pridgen had given her baby up, secretly placing him on the porch of George and Maggie Edmundson in Tarboro. Maggie was barren; now Willie was, too. Neither would ever discuss this child. Only Willie would know the truth.

"Willie, what if I get scared, being all by myself?" Hap whispered as he stirred in her arms in the rocker.

"Well, we can fix that. Suppose I crawl up on the bed with you until you go to sleep?"

"Oh, will you, Willie?"

She hugged him closer. He was hers.

Chapter 2

1879

THE MEANEST SCOUNDREL

Two women leaned toward one another on a street corner in Tarboro, their heads almost touching.

"I swear that boy is the meanest scoundrel in all of Edgecombe County," one hissed.

"You talking 'bout Hap Tyson?"

"Course I am," the other scoffed.

Such was the scuttlebutt around the pot-bellied stoves and on many street corners in the village. The locals had lost count of all his scrapes with the law and his scraps with the citizens. Many agreed that trouble shadowed him from his first conscious day and probably would on his last. Surely Ole Scratch had etched Hap's crooked smile on his otherwise handsome face. And, being raised by that weird woman, Willa Abigail Pridgen, who lived at the end of Station House Road, did not strengthen his credentials one iota.

* * *

"I swear she's a witch."

"Naw. What makes you say that?"

"Remember Mister Cephas Jones? Well, he told my momma..." and over the years the stories would stretch further and further from the truth.

Time after time, packs of scamps would sneak down Station House Road to spy on the mysterious squatter. Many accepted the challenge to slip down the road, trying to figure if Mister Cephas Jones's claim was true. Rumor had it that the man delivered a jar of jam from his wife, but when he walked into the yard, he looked

Chapter 2

through the window and saw her sitting in a rocker by the fireplace, singing strange songs Mister Cephas had never heard. Then he saw the doll. She was sticking pins in it and smiling. A jackrabbit could not have scampered faster, according to the spy.

Old Blue's hackles would rise at each occasional interruption and give her warning that someone lurked outside the house. His low, muted growl never failed to announce an intrusion.

And year after year Willie would throw open the door, caught in the light from the interior of her house eerily darkening her body, yet shining through her long, wild shock of hair. Old Blue would hobble out on the porch and bay, nose in the air, jowls flapping. And how many times had she closed the door, biting her lip to smother her laughter? She'd sit on the floor with her old hound and shake for minutes on end. She'd enjoyed the joke on the sneaks, but after Hap came, she promised herself to put the witchcraft rumors to rest. Regretfully for her, the talk did not stop.

However, she continued to make her dolls for Carver's Mercantile. Even if she'd shouted from the roof of the store, even if the Carvers had also shouted, no one would have believed that she was only supporting herself with her craft and was not a witch.

* * *

The history of Station House Road where Willie lived revolved around an unusual story about two men who lost their lives by being kind to a lady of ill repute. A drunken mob lynched them on the Medusa Tree, a strange, snaky-looking tree a few miles from town. Its twisting limbs stretched heavenward and careened bodies and souls into the pit fire of hell or into the arms of their Maker.

One victim who swung on the tree had built the Station House, but after his death the building stood ghostly, falling in disrepair. Eventually, the county repossessed the man's property and auctioned off parcels on the steps of the Edgecombe County Courthouse. Houses sprang up along a road behind the Station House, but soon the turnover of owners branded the area as blighted with poor folks squatting in the few hovels left.

Being poor bonded these families. Their differences made no difference. Existence did.

A strange phenomenon evolved along that stretch: the farther down the road one traveled, the poorer the families were. Willa Abigail Pridgen lived at the very end of that pathway, with few folks making the U-turn at her shanty.

Willie suffered no birth pangs with Hap Tyson, but that child would put her through every other kind of pain she could ever imagine. What was it she'd heard once? "If you don't want pain in your life, don't have any children." She swore Hap lived on the edge and dared lightning bolts to strike.

How many times had she heard accusations from the sheriff?

Once he said, "Miz Pridgen, it's your boy."

Willie's eyes rolled skyward. "What now?"

He stood on her front porch with an air of despair. Old Blue's guttural sounds warned him to come no closer.

Squirming, the lawman said, "Well, Miz Grantham says that somebody, who certainly looked like Hap, turned her flower pots over on her front porch. She can't swear on the family Bible, but she thinks it was him."

Another time, he told her that somebody had clipped all Mrs. Prescott's prize roses before a contest.

On and on the stories flew.

Willie had lost count of these wild tales and accusations. One day she knew they would face a serious dilemma.

On the other hand, Hap could not understand why everybody wanted to blame him for everything that went awry. All of his life, he'd felt the weight of being accused.

Even at school, when a student lost a lock of hair as the children were playing catch, the boy had scanned the group and timidly pointed toward Hap.

"I guess he done it," the boy said.

Chapter 2

Guessed? Frantically, Hap whipped around for support. He received none, but the teacher still gave him several strokes with her willow switch.

"Why, Willie, why? Why is it always me?"

"I don't know, son. I guess everybody's got to have somebody to blame. You just seem like the best pick, but you and I know the truth, Hap. That's all that matters right now." She paused, reflecting on words of wisdom, if she had any, for her son. Hesitating, she finally spoke. "My dear boy, I am going to tell you a story...about me."

"You? I don't understand."

"You will, hopefully." Once more she reflected. "Remember back when you first came down Station House Road, you asked me about my child?"

"Yes, of course I do. Sister told me all she knew, and you answered my questions. I know he's a boy and lives here in Tarboro, but you said that it was a secret. He knows nothing about you."

"Yes, and you know how hard it was to give up my child, just as it was for your Pap to bring you to me." He nodded. "Well, that was the first big sadness in my life. The second was losing my parents. Hap, your Willie fell into a dark pit of grief. I was one miserable creature. I lay in that bed over there by the hour, hardly eating or sleeping. Then, one day, I felt the road shaking and I knew somebody was coming my way."

"Who was it?" Hap asked.

"My oldest and dearest friend, the Captain, and Miss Sarah was riding with him in their buggy."

"The Cromwells?"

"None other! But, I did not want to see them. I was a mess."

"What did you do?"

"At first, I didn't answer the door, but the Captain persisted by banging on it and calling, 'Willie, Willie, you open up, now!' I knew I had to face them. Slowly, I cracked open the door, and that man practically cried when he saw me."

"What happened?"

"Both he and Miss Sarah packed me up and took me to Shiloh, the place where I grew up and was the happiest. I don't think Miss Sarah cotton to the idea very much, but the Captain was not to be denied. I stayed in the little cabin where my parents and I lived when they worked the land. Slowly, I began to see that life was worth living. Miss Sarah even got me sewing and making dolls for Carver's Mercantile. I returned home, but rumors on Station House Road were flying that I was a witch."

"That was unfair, Willie, and not true."

"I know, son, but I played along with the scamps. Old Blue and I had fun. I'd open that door and look like a wild woman and Old Blue would howl up a storm."

"You two were quite a pair."

"We were, son. We were, but I wanted it to stop, especially when you came into my life. I am so, so thankful for the Captain and Miss Sarah. They saved me. Just think if I had stayed on that bed and died, I never would have had the joy of having you as my son.

Life will be bumpy at times, but those bumps will humble you and make you stronger. And, remember, Hap, people will be people. Some good and some not so good."

"You're right about that," he agreed.

"Let me tell you something else. My pain, my grief, pushed me into another direction, a better path, a better place. You asked the question 'Why me?' Well, what are you going to do with your pain, your grief? You have choices in this life, son, just like I did. Do you want to go backwards or forwards? It is up to you. Old Willie cannot make that choice for you."

"I know, I know," he murmured, his head bent down. Suddenly, he looked up, smiled, and said softly, "Come here, Willie." Standing, he towered over her.

She did as she was told, as his long arms enfolded her. When

Chapter 2

they pulled away from each other, their faces were wet with tears, not from sadness, but for joy.

Through all Hap's crises, Willie remained his best friend, spending countless afternoons with him in the woods, having picnics and watching the wildlife. In time Hap became an expert bow hunter and fisherman, but only by slipping over to the lower 40 on the nearby Shiloh plantation, where the pickings were plentiful. The lower 40 was timberland, unfit for crops or pasture but wonderfully fit for fish and fowl. The owner, Captain Elijah Cromwell, cared nothing for either since his family and the rest of the plantation demanded his time and interest.

One balmy day, Hap cast a line in a nearby creek. His pole never quivered.

"Rats! A whole hour and not one bite," he complained, pulling his pocket watch out.

Bored, he climbed the bank and wandered farther onto Shiloh than he'd ever been. His pulse raced. *Suppose someone catches me,* he thought.

Suddenly, he stopped. The most astonishing weeping willow he'd ever seen appeared ahead, a gentle breeze rippling its graceful branches as it stood on the edge of a creek nestled in a grove. It was a tree of great presence. Fascinated, he walked in and out of its thick leafy branches, which dragged the ground. They were so dense that he could not see in or out. He ventured farther onto a grassy mound, completely encircled by tall pines and hardwoods, securing it from all outsiders. The young man dropped down on a fallen log and bent to pluck a straw, popping one end into his mouth.

Hap claimed this spot of solitude as his right to sit and think, escaping the scrutiny of the folk across the Tar River who'd branded him the meanest scoundrel in all of Edgecombe County. This secret hideaway would hedge him in with no interference, no bother, and no fights. He could have peace here, but pounding hooves suddenly jarred his thoughts. *What peace?* He was not alone.

Diving for the willow, he fingered the greenery to catch a peek of the intruder. *Who would dare?* His mouth gaped as he spied the young mistress of Cromwell Hall, the Captain's daughter. She dismounted and sat on the very spot that he'd claimed. She wore a riding habit, the coat a winey red with a Tartan plaid skirt covering her petticoats, her leather buttoned boots dulled by the dusty road. She looked flushed from the ride.

Over and over again, she muttered, "They...just...do...not...understand...me." Her riding crop popped the log with every word while flying bark clung to her costume. She rose and paced the grassy knoll, talking to herself, never suspecting that someone else might be near.

"Come on, Nellie. Let's go or Mother and Maggie will be worried. Ha!" she said with sarcasm and scorn. Mounting her pony, she slapped Nellie's flank and raced back toward civilization.

Hap remained frozen behind the branches of the willow. His mouth never closed as he'd watched this breathtaking young woman. He swallowed, desperate to relieve his parched throat. He'd been so tempted to speak, but he dared not. He was on private land.

Hap's insides burned. He knew her as the privileged young woman of the plantation, but from what he could gather, she was as misunderstood as he. Quietly, he turned toward the creek bank.

"Willie'll be mad I'm late, but it was worth it," he said, punching the air.

He trotted through the woods, smiling in anticipation of her fussing, but he knew a kindred spirit on Shiloh would hear the same scorching words. Parental concern and scolding knew no class, of that he was certain. It pleased him that they were bonded, although the Captain's daughter did not know this yet.

Chapter 3
THE DRESDEN DOLL

*H*ap only knew Caroline Cromwell from afar. As children they'd seen each other around Tarboro, but surely she would not have remembered him out of the dozens of urchins who gawked at the finery and plenty of the moneyed families. Over the years he'd watched her riding down Station House Road with her mother and some of the church ladies to deliver clothing and shoes to the less fortunate. He'd seen her grow into a beauty.

"What you staring at, boy?" a voice once growled behind him, as he hid from the Cromwell carriage.

Hap wheeled around. He'd been caught at his post, spying on the ladies giving out their goodies. All the younger boys cowered in fear of this tough guy, but not Hap. He reared up to his full height and glared back at this bull of a man.

"Nothing," he snarled, his eyes narrowing to slits.

He walked quickly to the bridge, bumping the man's shoulder on his way past, worried that the Cromwell carriage would overtake him before he could hide again from view. Dropping down onto the river bank, Hap dreamed about the young mistress. How could anybody have such clear skin and such golden curls?

As a child, Caroline truly was the darling of the town, but nostrils flared with indignation as many women saw their husbands act foolishly over her. Her smile could peel years off the face of an elder.

"That little snip will cause Sarah Cromwell many a tear if you ask me," tongues wagged, as they watched the young girl blossom.

Caroline Cromwell had stolen the heart of every grown man

who saw her, first as a precocious child and later as a maturing young woman. She was small, blond, and delicate—truly a Dresden doll—but within her burned a strong, independent spirit. Early on both Sarah and Maggie Edmundson, the Cromwells' housekeeper, had sensed this child's desire not to be the doted-upon daughter of a prominent family in Edgecombe County. Sarah Cromwell was of two minds about her daughter. Although she recognized this spirited behavior as her own, when Caroline would disappear for hours on the plantation, her mother's eyes would lock with Maggie's in fear. Scolding had been rampant with pouts and pursed lips in response, as only the very spoiled can do.

Over time, her brother Will observed these lively exchanges between mother and daughter. He would stifle snorts behind his hands or shake his head in puzzlement.

Even Maggie would question her young mistress. "Miss Caroline, where have you been this time? You shouldn't be riding your pony off in those woods like that. Somebody is gonna git you."

Maggie's chest would tighten each time she'd see the disheveled woman-child, sitting astride Nellie, racing her pony with a devilish grin to the barn. Pulling a bandanna from her pocket, Maggie would mop her deeply furrowed brow and return to her chores, apprehensive that trouble certainly loomed for this family.

* * *

Every week, Willie Pridgen delegated duties for Hap, errands in town for one.

"Let's see, son. I need two more yards of this material from Carver's." She handed him a scrap. "Better get some pins and needles, too."

"Willie, why not come with me today?" he asked.

She hesitated, but shook her head. Even after a few years, the

Chapter 3

townspeople still stared and murmured at the odd couple. She just never could shake the stigma of her raising "that wicked white boy" at her Station House Road shanty. She often thought that Hap's youthful attitudes could handle these affronts better than she could.

He smiled his crooked smile. "Never mind. I'll take care of it," he said, kissing her forehead as he left the house.

Hap never minded her requests and actually relished any confrontation that required a defiant glare and his crooked smile.

* * *

Surprises disarm even the most confident rebels, and Hap catapulted toward just such a predicament that summer afternoon as he ran Willie's errands. He approached Carver's Mercantile. The store fascinated Hap, filled with all its displayed items from pins and needles to licorice. He loved rummaging through the packed counters and shelves.

Ezekial Carver had come south to Tarboro and was the first black shop owner on Main Street. Now, his son Moses carried the load of running the store. The Carvers favored no clientele, which was not always suiting to disgruntled folks who frequently bellyached about the success of others. The Carvers were hard workers and treated their customers equally and fairly, no matter what their station in life.

This particular day, the tall, strapping youth with a shock of brown hair slowly ambled toward the store's front, packages in hand. He chewed on the remnants of a licorice stick when the front door flew open with force. The door rattled and ricocheted toward him and hit his firmly planted foot. Caroline Cromwell was talking to her trailing, frustrated mother, and as she turned around, she was staring straight up into Hap Tyson's face. They were inches apart.

The bonding in that look was simultaneously all-knowing and all-confusing, as each seized and sized up the moment. Only seconds elapsed until the crooked grin spread across his handsome face.

Gathering her wits, Caroline gazed straight at his teeth and said, "The licorice must be good." She swept past him with the flare of a princess.

The smells of soaps and oils from her toiletry filled his nostrils. He thought he would die on the spot, until her jarring words sank in. Licorice always discolored his teeth. Clasping his hand over his mouth, his face flushed, but he didn't care. He'd practically touched the Dresden doll. His heart thumped. Grasping his packages, he reached for the door, catching snatches of conversation.

"I saw this fabric in the window and I like it. The Carvers can sell it to us just as easily as the Clarks down the street. You want me to go to Warrenton Academy. That's fine, but you need to consider some of my wants, and I want that fabric," Caroline retorted with a curled lip, pointing to the big bolt of material.

Evidently, the argument had been tiring and animated. Sarah Cromwell stood at the entrance to the Carvers' store. How could she leave gracefully without insulting these nice people? She succumbed, but she silently vowed that her daughter's contrariness would have to stop.

Closing the door, Hap shook his head and sighed as he walked up Main to the bridge. His dreams dissolved. Warrenton sounded miles and miles away.

I wonder if she remembers me from Station House Road? he thought.

Hap recalled running and hiding more than once when he did not want anyone, the church ladies or their daughters, to see him on the road. He did not know whether she'd ever spied him.

For the moment, Caroline's preoccupation with her mother in Carver's Mercantile blocked any thoughts of the young man that she'd practically run over, but then she did have a moment. She

Chapter 3

thought of that crooked smile that washed across his face whenever she saw him in town or on Station House Road. It fascinated her. How many times had she picked him out of the crowds, discreetly, cautiously, carefully, not to be caught eyeing this strange boy from the wrong side? She'd quiz her mother incessantly about Station House Road and Weird Willie and all the ragamuffins who would slink around corners every time the plantation folk and moneyed people of the town strolled on Main Street or the Town Common.

"Why such curiosity?" her mother always asked.

"I suppose I feel compassion for those who don't have as we do. That's why I always want to go with you when you hand out the clothes and food. I'm so fortunate and...they're not..."

Caroline seemed to defy convention for defiance's sake, for the least amount of snobbery disgusted her. Her family never really showed or allowed any blatant snobbishness as she saw it, but many of her father's associates did, especially in their parlor talk, overheard by the young mistress.

* * *

The Warrenton Academy enrollment lasted for only one year.

"I suggest a tutor for Mistress Cromwell," the headmaster said. "Would you like me to send a list?"

"That would be nice, sir. The Captain and I would like to further her education."

"Your daughter's marks are so high that we're afraid she's bored," the headmaster advised. "A tutor can challenge her, provide as much individual attention and discipline as possible."

Sarah Cromwell smiled at these words. They were the same words her own mother had heard. Only her mother never acted, and Sarah had slipped into the mode of preparing herself to become Mrs. Elijah Cromwell of Cromwell Hall on Shiloh plantation. She knew that it would not be long for women's issues to dominate the public domain. Education being one... Her mind drifted to the past.

* * *

Sarah King followed her parents into Calvary Episcopal Church one spring Sunday morning. Catching her breath, she saw the back of Elijah Cromwell's head as his family sat in the opposite pew from theirs. Just as they neared their pew, his head swiveled in time to catch her eye before she could cast her eyes downward. She blushed.

A custom had developed with the parishioners to have lunch on the Town Common after services to socialize and catch up with the news of the community. This gathering was also a time that the young people had a chance to socialize as well. Elijah had made a plan to ask Sarah King to "Walk the Green" with him, a signal that he was interested in her, and surely all eyes would be upon them. The chaperones were plentiful. He could hardly wait until the sermon was over, and finally the rector closed with, "In the name of the Father, and of the Son, and of the Holy Ghost." And the congregation said *Amen*.

The Town Common center section filled quickly after the service at Calvary. Lunch progressed with families and friends clustering to hear the latest news of the community. It was time for Elijah to make his move. He slipped away from family and found Sarah chatting and laughing with friends, but suddenly all of them went mute, leaving Sarah curiously looking at five silly grins that told her something was up. Slowly turning, she stared into Elijah Cromwell's face. Again, she blushed.

"Miss Sarah, would you 'Walk the Green' with me?" Five pairs of eyes bulged, but Sarah King did not hesitate to say yes. She knew that this young man had a kind gentle spirit, and if he wanted her to "Walk the Green," then he was a serious kind gentle spirit. As they walked, Elijah talked about the coming next few years. He'd made a bargain with his father Thaddeus Cromwell

Chapter 3

that he would enter the military through the Citadel, but upon returning from his military stint, he would take over running Shiloh. Rumors of war between the states had begun to rumble, and even the locals had formed militias in the county. Elijah's two older brothers were already in professions, one a lawyer, the other a doctor. Naturally, the father felt the youngest should be prepared to run Shiloh, but Elijah wanted the military first. So, they had agreed that if a war broke out and he got home after it ended, he would take over the duties for the plantation.

"Why are you telling me this, Elijah?" she asked. "I am confused."

"Miss Sarah, I want permission to court you until my time for the Citadel comes up in the fall. Would you be agreeable? May I speak to Mister King?"

"You are serious," she whispered.

He nodded and reached for her hand.

Love blossomed on these walks on the green. The eyes on the Town Common followed this courtship with great interest, and by the time Elijah left for the Citadel, they were engaged. After his first year, they married, with the understanding that she would live at Shiloh with the Cromwells, waiting for his return. Their first child was born as the second year began. Dedicated to finishing early, the young Captain transferred to Raleigh to train recruits for the war, which had begun. On his next leave, he regretfully came home to bury his mother. A new marble angel monument was added to the cemetery of angels. The one joy that came from that trip was Sarah getting pregnant with their second child, a daughter this time.

As the war ended, Captain Cromwell returned to Sarah, to two children, and a grieving father. Soon, Thaddeus died, some say of a broken heart. The Georgia marble merchants received another order for the angel statuary for the patriarch of the third generation of Cromwells to live in Cromwell Hall on Shiloh

Plantation. Elijah and Sarah bonded in a mighty way as they embraced the life of the land on their beloved Shiloh.

Sarah smiled through these sweet memories, realizing how fortunate she had been to walk the green with Elijah Cromwell, the Captain as many now called him. Her husband stood tall in Edgecombe County, Shiloh's own. He was carrying on the heritage of their generation, and she was proud to be a part of it.

* * *

Caroline returned to Shiloh in late spring with an abundance of energy, ready to embrace her homecoming.

"A luncheon at Mrs. DeBerry's? Mother, I'd prefer riding Nellie. With Father."

"Darling, you can't insult my friends, and what about your grandfather? And later we must talk about a tutor."

Caroline rolled her eyes. It's starting again, she thought, and, who would her mother come up with as her tutor? Some stodgy old maid–or worse, some stodgy old man? Good grief, how can one stand all this?

The Cromwell ladies set out by buggy for Tarboro for their luncheon, but as they swung out of the drive, Caroline craned left and saw the Medusa Tree standing off in the distance, alone and stark.

"Mother, tell me again about the first hangings on that tree," she said.

"Why would you be remotely interested in such a dreadful subject?" her mother answered. "We're going to lunch with some very nice people who certainly do not discuss such ungodly affairs." But Sarah knew the subject was not closed.

"I'm interested, Mother, and not afraid to discuss such matters."

Oh, yes, Sarah said to herself. *This moppet is my flesh.* She half smiled and sighed. "The woman's name was Delia Barlow..." She related the entire Constable history and story as she'd heard

Chapter 3

her father discuss this horrendous hanging with his colleagues in his study. "The case was never cleared and mars the legal history of Edgecombe County as Coffie sees it," Sarah concluded, just as the buggy passed the turnoff for Station House Road.

Hap saw her first and darted behind the ruins of the old Station House. His insides churned as he peeked to see the golden curls over the back of the buggy. School was out for the locals, and like many, he'd been on his way into town. Now, his reasons for going doubled and with great speed. He had no clue that Caroline was back in the county and certainly had no idea that she was home for good. He watched briefly as she looked down Main Street, waving at a strolling couple or a shopkeeper tidying up the walkway.

The young girl loved the downtown ride through Tarboro. She'd missed the gong of the old town clock at City Hall and the charming colonial-styled courthouse. Her grandfather's law office, a two-story brick building with a decorative crown over the front door, sat across the street, convenient for him and his clients.

Go see Coeffield King about your case, townspeople would say. *He practically lives in the courthouse.*

Sarah and her daughter knew the burgeoning caseload of the patriarch. The old barrister needed a young, new assistant to ease his schedule, which had become far too heavy for just the one man.

Caroline's head swiveled as she absorbed all the familiar sights of her childhood. It was good to be home. The carriage cut through the Town Common and swung left to Mrs. DeBerry's Tearoom. Caroline strained to look down the huge green to catch a glimpse of her grandfather's house. She knew their next stop would be there.

Using the side streets to avoid detection, Hap breathed heavily by the time he reached the Town Common. The towering oaks hid him well and allowed a closer view of the tearoom. The blond curls disappeared into the house. Slowly, he slid down the back side of the closest massive oak and fussed at himself for being so foolish. Suppose someone had seen him darting from tree to tree like a thief, when all he wanted was a glimpse of the Captain's daughter?

Dang.

Unbeknownst to Hap, someone *had* seen his unusual behavior. Maggie Edmundson, with the day off, had come out of Carver's Mercantile. She'd walked down Main Street to the Town Common. She, too, used the large trees to hide herself, but from Hap.

How very strange indeed, she thought.

She watched as Hap picked himself up, kicked the earth, and slowly trudged across the Commons, totally vulnerable to any eye. He was unaware that Caroline's seat in the tearoom gave her a direct view of his path across the grassy green.

Well, well, well, the boy with the crooked smile. How very strange indeed...

Her sentiments matched Maggie's.

Chapter 4

Michael Collins

Michael Collins had answered Sarah Cromwell's letter and requested an interview at Shiloh the following week. He'd graduated from the University of North Carolina and hankered to return down east to teach and live close to family in his hometown of Edenton. Tutoring several wealthy pupils appealed to him. He'd have time for his passion, writing poetry.

He pulled on the reins of his horse and looked in awe at Cromwell Hall, situated with the plantation acreage, stretching as far as his eye could see.

The old manse stood back from the road, majestic among magnolias with the traditional Southern pecan grove planted to the right of the yard and a circular drive arcing up to the front door. Wrap-around porches and a porte-cochere increased its size and set it apart from any house he'd ever seen. From his youth, he remembered Governor Carr's home on the other side of Old Sparta. This house might be equal in its stateliness, its grandeur. In town, he'd heard that these Cromwells were the third generation to live in this house. Dismounting, he wondered if the inside matched the splendor of the outside.

The door opened and a tall, lean woman stepped toward him.

"Welcome, Mister Collins," Maggie Edmundson spoke to the young man. "Mister Elijah and Miss Sarah are waiting for you in the parlor."

Michael would spend the day with the family, a test for each side, but he had concerns. Would he and Miss Caroline be congenial? Could he sway her parents' confidence to trust him with their daughter?

Sarah eyed him directly after they settled down.

"We would like our daughter to pursue advanced academics. She's very bright and needs the challenge of a tutor. The headmaster at Warrenton Academy felt she was actually bored."

"I understand. She simply needs a sparring partner who can stay a few steps ahead of her. I'd like that task."

He relished the idea of challenging a quick mind. The University allowed no females as of yet, but he knew about pressures being applied for drastic changes in the education of women. From all he'd heard from her parents, he thought Caroline represented this element.

The young man felt exhilarated about the prospects for this first possible tutelage. Recommendations from them would surely provide his schedule with all the work he needed. Even the empty apartment above Mrs. DeBerry's tearoom suited him for room and board. Everything seemed to be falling into place. Then he heard the sharp sound of shoe heels coming down the stairs.

With a quick knock, Caroline opened the parlor door and totally disarmed the confident young teacher. With her blonde curls, pursed mouth, and creamy skin, she struck him dumbfounded.

"Caroline, come meet Michael Collins," Elijah spoke to his daughter. The young man could only look into the azure eyes and limply shake her petite hand. His first words came only after he'd decided that he could talk without stuttering. Perspiration popped out on the back of his neck as his breath quickened.

If I could just rip away my bow tie and collar studs, I could breathe, he thought. Somehow, he had to make it through the next few minutes.

However, conditions worsened. He fell quiet during lunch with the horror that the family might find him dull and boring. What could he do? To the smitten tutor's relief, Will Cromwell joined the family and rescued the conversation. Periodically,

Chapter 4

though, Michael would glance furtively across the table at his new student. Once or twice, for a fraction of a second, their eyes met.

At least he's not a stodgy old man, Caroline thought. *Maybe I will survive this new plan of Mother's.*

Luncheon ended.

"Collins, let's go back to the parlor and discuss the possibilities of an agreement," Elijah Cromwell said.

"Uh-yes, yes sir. M-Miss Caroline, it has been a true pleasure," he stuttered.

Caroline shrugged, smiled, and bounded up the stairs to put on her riding habit. She planned to spend the rest of the afternoon exploring.

* * *

A new approach to the lower 40 brought Caroline into the grassy area opposite her usual path. She'd roamed afoot and picked an armful of wildflowers. Nellie trailed behind. Suddenly, she jerked upright, dropping her bouquet. There, sitting on the fallen log in the grassy area was the boy with the crooked smile. He lounged in the bright sun with his back to her as he gazed at the willow and the creek. He was bent over with arms resting on his thighs and a straw sticking in his mouth. She inched slowly toward him. Suddenly, he wheeled around with the startled look as if he'd been caught in an indiscretion. He'd smelled her perfume.

Hap watched her walk around the fallen log and situate herself on the trunk only a few feet away. His face flushed as he looked back down at the dropped straw. He waited. He could do nothing, frozen in wonderment.

She waited, too, for him to say something or do something.

What is wrong with this fellow?

She was used to men and boys fawning over her. She could not understand this silence. Wasn't a young man supposed to make the first move to get acquainted? She turned toward him, but all she saw was the side of his head staring down at the ground. Then he looked up and out toward the creek, as he fidgeted with the straw.

Is he going to run? she wondered. Instead, he dropped down on the log.

Anger rose up inside her. Here she'd exposed herself to this urchin from Station House Road. She'd violated all decorum for a proper young woman of society. After all, she was Elijah Cromwell's daughter, Coeffield King's granddaughter. She had a position and a station to uphold. Suddenly her condescending thoughts disgusted her, but she was angry.

With great propriety, Caroline stood, and, when she did, Hap shot up from his seat, his fingers looped in his back pockets. She stepped quickly, closing the small gap between them, looked him squarely in the eye, and slapped his face. Next, she placed her two small hands on his chest and shoved him as hard as she could. Her energy startled him. The young man toppled backwards over the fallen tree, arms flailing helplessly.

Looking down at him, she mimicked his crooked smile, dusted off her hands, and retorted, "There!" She strutted off toward Nellie.

Hap lay with his legs hooked over the tree trunk, his body resting on his elbows, his mouth agape.

Why in God's name did she do that? She could have broken my legs. Dang, she just went plum crazy.

But even with all that she'd done, he still hadn't uttered the first word, only whistling sounds and grunts when his body hit the ground. Fortunately, the heavy grass cushioned his fall, but her actions cut through any mask he'd had. If she were still here, he knew that he'd probably have shaken some sense into this spoiled young girl.

Willie had taught him many things about life, hunting, fishing, and love, but acquainting him with young ladies from the

Chapter 4

moneyed society was not a part of her teaching.

Caroline Cromwell, be wary of our next meeting, he thought, fuming with each stride back home.

Chapter 5
THE PROJECT

*C*aroline rode with abandon. Never once did she look back at the lower 40 and the chaos she'd created.

"Oh God, I've been so foolish. Please don't let him be hurt," she said through gritted teeth. She whipped her pony with her crop. "Now, I'm hurting you, Nellie," she cried out.

The main house loomed in the distance. She could see Maggie standing in the yard. Dashing past her, Caroline left her pony with the stable hand and fled inside, Maggie's eyes following her every step.

"I'll think about him later," she mumbled, spanking her clothes to rid the dust.

Right now she had other matters at hand, one being a new tutor. She lightly tapped on the parlor door.

"Come in, darling," her mother called out.

She sat with her parents in the parlor to discuss Michael Collins. She knew the answer to her own question, but she sat quietly as they talked about her future.

"Caroline, we've decided to hire Mister Collins as your tutor," Sarah said. "In a few weeks he'll work with you on a project, just to prepare you two for the fall session."

"That's just fine, Mother. I'll look forward to it. May I be excused?"

"Of course, darling. I-I'm glad you're so agreeable."

Caroline closed the door, but the sound of her heels on the staircase was not as quick as they'd heard earlier in the day.

Sarah looked at her husband. "Something's going on. She's never been that agreeable with me in her entire life."

Chapter 5

Elijah shrugged his shoulders, laughed, and hugged his wife. "Who can understand youth?"

* * *

Michael's mind raced as he rode back to his rooms at Mrs. DeBerry's. He would guide and discipline the Cromwell daughter in a project, perhaps in botany, one that would take them to the outdoors, into the warm sunshine and perhaps with picnics.

My God, I have gone absolutely daft. I am planning a tête-à-tête with a pupil. An uneasy feeling engulfed him.

For weeks the young teacher followed his leads for pupils and set up an appealing fall schedule. All his students lived in town and would come for morning sessions at Mrs. DeBerry's tearoom. Caroline Cromwell was the exception. The Cromwells agreed that every Friday he would come to Shiloh to meet with their daughter.

* * *

On his first Friday at Shiloh, Michael looked at the young woman. "I promise you, Miss Caroline, that you will see nature and science with new eyes. Collecting leaves and insects tells much about our own lives."

"Insects?" Her nose twitched.

He laughed. "Just you wait and see."

Thus began a close relationship between tutor and pupil, with the pupil failing to realize that she was an object of scrutiny.

After a few Fridays of study at Shiloh, Michael planned their final leaf gathering in Tarboro at the Episcopal church. He discussed it with Sarah Cromwell.

"Mrs. Cromwell, I am so impressed with the arboretum at Calvary."

"The plantings are outstanding, are they not? About forty years ago, the Reverend Cheshire decided as his own project to plant foreign and domestic trees. I'm amazed that most have adapted and thrived."

"It is a wonderful opportunity. I'd like to have Caroline's last leaf collection to come from the church grounds. I've contacted the rector."

"By all means, Mister Collins."

"Your daughter and I will lunch on the Town Common, with your permission, after our visit to Calvary. Please feel free to join us," he insisted, knowing full well that the lady of the house had been nursing a summer cold and had no use at the moment for anything but her chaise lounge.

She graciously declined and sent the two off in his buggy, for he had insisted upon coming to Shiloh and taking her into Tarboro. He was pleased with himself.

More time with my pupil, he thought.

The weather was pleasant for early June, adding to the momentum of Michael's spirited conversation. Caroline had never seen her teacher so animated. He made her laugh, to his delight. As they approached Station House Road, a lone rider came to the juncture just as Michael's buggy passed by.

It was Hap.

As Hap tipped his hat and smiled, Caroline's insides stirred. Quickly turning toward her teacher, she gushed with conversation and her own laughter, taking both aback. For her teacher, her attention was the first personal feeling she'd ever shown him. For the lone rider, her indifference was the second affront that she'd shown him.

Hap nudged his horse toward Shiloh and rode the distance to the Medusa Tree. He tied Willie's old horse to a lower limb, swung up on it, and began to tread toward the huge trunk of the tree. He'd been coming here to find peace, since the lower 40 no longer satisfied him. Yet, how could anybody find rest in a hanging tree?

At least no one will ever bother me here, he laughed.

* * *

In town, the Calvary churchyard proved the ultimate botany

Chapter 5

lesson. With her "new eyes," Caroline rushed enthusiastically about the arboretum, marveling at Reverend Cheshire's profuse plantings in the churchyard. She read each label and clipped her choices.

Her tutor sat on a garden bench and watched his protégé with amusement. Over and over, she returned to him, flushed with the morning air and excitement with her selections.

"We'll go to the Town Common now," he told her. "Come."

They moved toward his buggy.

"Mister Collins, thank you for giving me this day. Warrenton Academy could never do what you have done for me."

What she did not know is that a man enamored does not always interpret *thank you's* in the way they are intended.

"Next week we'll begin the creepy-crawly project," he said, as they munched on sandwiches and teacakes on the Town Common.

She giggled and shuddered. He liked it when he made her laugh and especially when she was enthusiastic about something he'd said, whether thought-provoking or casual.

* * *

When Monday morning dawned, Michael prepared for their new task. With a butterfly net and several small containers nestled beside him, he pushed toward Shiloh.

As he approached Station House Road, Hap Tyson coincidentally appeared in the distance, pulled rein, and watched Michael fly by toward Shiloh without as much as a glimpse his way. Hap had not been back to the lower 40 since his chance meeting with Caroline. But why shouldn't he go? She would be having her lessons with that new teacher. He turned and galloped back up the road. Whether she would come after her lessons with Collins, he could not guess, but if she did, he'd be waiting.

* * *

The few miles to Cromwell Hall flew by as Michael hurried his horse. When he rounded the last bend, he glimpsed the family cemetery. The stone angels peered out at him as he slowed his approach to the main house.

I wonder what Cromwell you all will watch over next? he mused, marveling over the majestic white marble figures. *It's got to be Georgia marble.*

Anyone in Edgecombe County wanting a fine monument could purchase one from the Georgia monument dealers, for the state ranked high in the quarry production of this natural resource, and stonecutters could fashion and polish a prime product out of this prime material. Elijah Cromwell had set angel statuary for his beloved mother and father, as his ancestors had done for three generations.

Pulling into the circular drive, the teacher handed his reins to the smiling stable hand. "Miss Cah'line waits for you on the side porch, Mister Michael."

The eager young teacher gathered his equipment and scurried up the steps to find his pupil. She was sitting in a swing letting the gentle breeze toss her curls, totally disarming Michael Collins again. How could he carry on a lesson with such beauty at his side? God knows he would try.

"We'll use the net for butterflies," he informed her, while twirling it around in his fingers, as he sat across from the swing. "But if we see any other creature to capture in its web, we'll do it." Picking up the box beside him, he continued, "This box will be perfect for keeping both the butterflies you catch during the day and the moths you get at night."

"That's easy enough. I'll put a lantern in the garden and watch for them. My only concern is bruising the moths' wings."

"Don't worry. The net should take care of everything."

She caught his gradual smile. "Oh no, now you're going to tell me about the creepy-crawlies, right?"

"Absolutely, but for them we need to find a fallen tree," he

Chapter 5

said, standing and directing her to his buggy. "Your father says we should ride down to the lower 40 to search for one. Fallen trees and old rotten stumps hide the best insect collections in the world."

Caroline blinked twice at the mention of the lower 40. She'd not ridden Nellie that way since she'd confronted Hap. She looked away. How could she decline when her father had suggested the location? He held her hand, as long as he dared, and helped her into the buggy. The steel-rimmed wheels turned slowly, pulling them closer and closer to the lower 40.

"Here we are, Miss Caroline. We'll look here first," he said as he reined his horse.

This cannot be happening, Caroline thought to herself, but she could not hint that something was wrong. They entered the haven, walking straight toward the decomposing fallen tree. She looked askance, not for insects, but for Hap. How relieved she was to find the grassy area empty.

"Well, what do we do, sir?" she asked with anticipation.

"Come this way, young lady, and I will show you the colony of all colonies of creepy-crawlies," he said, as he carefully removed a pocketknife and pulled bark from the end of the trunk half buried in the ground. The rotten bark peeled easily, revealing maggots, roaches, and a beetle or two. Caroline squealed and made such a face that Michael roared with laughter.

"Really now. You cannot expect me to touch those things," she said, her voice rising an octave. "They must be dirty, and they are disgusting."

"No, you will not have to touch them. Watch how I take this stick and scrape them into the containers. After we seal them, they will die and begin to solidify and become just right for mounting. Without a laboratory, they will last just long enough for your project. On to the creepy-crawlies."

Hap Tyson peeked from around a big oak. Fortunately, he'd

been slower getting to the secret haven, or they would have found him lounging on the fallen tree. He laughed to himself when he saw Caroline's face as she scraped the insects into the containers. Still, pangs of jealousy gnawed at him as he watched the scene and realized how different their lives were and how that breach would grow. Once more, he froze, compelled to witness the enjoyment of others, without their knowledge he existed. He did not count on this revelation.

Damn you, Caroline Cromwell, and all your gentlemen.

Blinded by anger, he stumbled away.

"What was that?" Caroline swung around in the direction of the creek. Was it Hap or an animal scurrying through the brush? She turned away knowing that she would come back tomorrow, no matter what.

The lesson ended.

Chapter 6
THE MEETING

*D*awn broke none too early for the young mistress of Cromwell Hall, as she'd awakened every hour on the hour.

Saturday and no project today! she thought, as she stretched in the deep feather mattress.

The early morning was cool, dry, and perfect for a ride on Nellie, but how could she be gone all day waiting for Hap at the grove? She could not let another day pass without their actually meeting and talking. Her sixteenth birthday was approaching, and she thought she'd heard her parents discussing a trip. She just could not go on vacation without explaining her behavior to the boy with the crooked smile.

At that moment on Station House Road, Hap rolled out of his bed, his feet hitting the floor hard. Holding his head, he mumbled, "I gotta see her. I gotta. I'll stay the whole dang day if I have to," he vowed, reaching for his clothes.

He knew that Saturday was not a day she would spend with her tutor, and he was willing to wait for hours. Divine intervention seemed the only way he would see her.

"Please, let this be the day," he pleaded, rolling his eyes upward.

Hap arrived at the grove just after daybreak and settled himself out in the open, drowsing periodically, until pounding hooves interrupted his slumber. Scrambling to his feet, he dove for big willow.

I am such a stooge!

Caroline flew into the clearing, expecting to see him on the fallen tree as before, but he was not there. She dismounted, allowing Nellie the freedom to roam and graze.

Why would he be here? she scolded herself. *I half killed him the last time.* Then she started laughing, recalling the way he'd sat on the log, the way he'd stood, and the way he'd fallen. She mimicked his actions and fell gently over the tree onto her backside. She rolled and laughed until she realized that the boy with the crooked smile was standing over her. He was not laughing.

"Wh-where did you come from? H-how did you...? Nobody was here."

And then it was his time to laugh. He took great pleasure in seeing her at his feet, flustered for probably the first time in her pampered life, and he'd caused it all. He could not stop, as if he'd stored years of laughter and needed to make up for lost time. Then he realized that she was laughing, too. How delightful that this emotion could become the means of forgiveness for each of them. He composed himself somewhat and extended his hand to help her. His dwarfed hers. The touch startled both, but he recovered quickly, and the strength of his arm lifted her effortless.

How in the world did I ever push him to the ground? she wondered.

As he towered over her, she remained totally unafraid. He helped her step over the fallen tree, and then they sat, not quite as far apart as they had before.

"I saw you with your teacher when you were gathering the creepy-crawlies," he said, imitating her reaction with a screwed-up face.

"Wh-creepy-crawlies? You were here that day?"

Forgetting her position, she leaned backward in laughter and almost fell off the trunk again, except Hap's quick reaction and strong arm stopped her. This time he hesitated before releasing her hand. They were quiet.

She broke the silence. "Do you know who I am?"

Chapter 6

He nodded, "You are Miss Caroline Cromwell, the young mistress of this plantation, Shiloh."

"Yes, and who might you be?" she asked, knowing full well.

That tantalizing smile crossed his face. "Hap Tyson, the meanest scoundrel in all of Edgecombe County. I live on Station House Road."

He lifted his head a little higher, waiting for the shock effect. None came.

"I know," she said casually, "and you were raised by Weird Willie."

His eyes widened with surprise.

"But why do you have that reputation?"

Hap shrugged.

"Listen, I done my share, but no one should blame Willie Pridgen for my behavior. She's a good woman." Anger rose in his voice. "Some of the scamps in town and even on the road call her a witch." His own words stung. "Well, they're wrong. Folks just don't understand us." Hap surprised her with his own question. "Are you back from that school for good? I know you got this teacher."

"How did you know about Warrenton?"

"Remember the day you came into Carver's Mercantile to buy fabric? You and your mother talked about it then. By the way, you almost took my nose off with that door."

"Well, I have just about decapitated you and broken your back. What in the world is next?"

Hap looked at her, shrugged again and grinned, but did not answer.

"My parents feel that I've done all I can do at Warrenton, but they want me to continue some studies. So, there you go. I have a tutor."

She shrugged this time and paused briefly. "However, I think we have something in common."

"What's that?"

"Oh, I feel a little misunderstood as well."

He nodded, and she smiled at him. She continued with a little more steam.

"My mother smothers me as if she were plumping up a pillow while I'm still sleeping on it. Maybe that's why I ride Nellie as much as I do, just to breathe and feel free."

Her feelings were his.

Hap looked skyward.

"The sun's not quite overhead, but I've been up a while. I'm hungry. Are you?"

"I am, but I have no food."

"Share mine."

He got up and strode to the willow.
"You know about the willow? About this hiding place?" she asked, as she, too, bounded off the fallen tree and quickly followed him to the thick greenery. "I cannot believe that we've both sat in here."

He looked down at her, pulled back the foliage and invited her into the inner sanctum. She curtsied and strode regally into the willow's shade and turned to look up into his face. The crooked smile was still there, and in an instant her fingers flew to his face and traced his mouth. Her eyes sparkled as he flushed deeply, taken aback as if she had again slapped his face.

"I'm sorry. Let's eat, Master Tyson. Your friend is famished," she announced and waltzed through the willow's branches.

"I'm sorry. Let's eat," he said. To himself, he murmured, "I'll never figger you out, Caroline Cromwell of Cromwell Hall."

Shaking his head, he followed her back to the fallen tree with his meager lunch, a couple of slabs of smoked ham, bread, and a peach. Caroline never considered that she was not having sandwiches and teacakes from Maggie's hand at Shiloh. She ate ravenously and felt the happiest she'd been in a long time. It was

Chapter 6

as if he had freed something inside of her, a sense of jubilation, yet peace. Her parents' friends would find her behavior scandalous, but never once did she consider the difference in their stations, not even their gender differences, not even their being unchaperoned. She simply saw a friend whose openness and honesty grabbed her heart. Never once did she sense fear, only joy. At least now she could get through the rest of the summer knowing that they had resolved their shaky beginning.

"I'd better get back home. Mother is always so curious. Thank you for coming and relieving me about our last meeting. Nellie! Oh, good gosh! I never tied Nellie!"

They ventured out into the open, calling for her pony, forgetting anonymity. Comfort and happiness consumed them, not reason and good sense.

At that same time, George Edmundson galloped down the road toward the lower 40.

Chapter 7
Confinement

Caroline's extended absence had disturbed Sarah Cromwell. "Go find her, George. Don't stop until you do."

George had searched all the main trails, but now he reached the lower 40.

"Oh, my God," he muttered, as he spied Nellie grazing in the distance. He pulled up and dismounted, seeing the blood oozing on the pony's back leg. He looked around. "Lord, where's that missy?"

Grabbing Nellie's reins, George mounted his horse and led the limping pony toward the lower 40. Squinting into the distance, he spied two small figures.

"Uh-oh. Who's that with her?" In less than a minute, he knew. "Oh, no, it's that fellow from Station House Road. What's she doing with him? He's on Shiloh land. He ain't supposed to be here," George mumbled, but he realized she didn't seem afraid of the young man. "How can that be?"

When Caroline saw George with her pony, she waved excitedly, but when she turned around, she realized that her companion had disappeared. She darted toward George.

"You found her. Oh, Nellie," she hollered as she reached the thicket.

"Was that who I think it was, Miss Caroline?" he asked suspiciously.

"What? Oh, you saw my new friend. George, please don't tell my mother. She wouldn't approve, but I like him. He–He–." Floundering for the right word, she finally stuttered, "He j-just understands me. I know we have different backgrounds, but we

Chapter 7

have so much in common, too. George, I am telling you this because I need your help. Please!" she pleaded, her eyes beginning to brim with tears.

He felt trapped. How could he keep her secret and betray the mistress of the house? "Miss Caroline, we're gonna talk to Maggie. She has the sense to figger these things out. Now, I'm going to put you up on my horse, and I'll lead Nellie. She's come up a mite lame."

The two slowly made their way back to the main house, each dreading the scene ahead. When Sarah saw them coming, she ran the length of the yard, stopping to raise her arm to her forehead.

My independent daughter. You're a vulnerable little chickadee and don't even know it.

And Sarah was right, for each step of the way Caroline mustered defiance and sat taller in George's saddle.

"Darling, I'm so relieved. You worried us. George, where was she?"

"Mother, I can answer for myself, thank you," Caroline quickly responded as she looked down from the back of the roan. The sparring had begun.

What in the world will Maggie say when she finds out what I've seen? George thought, as the two mistresses of Shiloh entered the main house, talking heatedly.

Inside, the parlor echoed their words as Elijah looked perplexed.

"Confinement!" Caroline raised her voice a little too high.

"Caroline, lower your voice with your mother," her father demanded.

"I'm sorry, but two weeks' confinement to the house and grounds?" Her mother's punishment rang in her ears. Sarah might as well have confined Caroline to a stockade for two weeks. The punishment was more for contrariness in their conversation than for her daughter's refusal to shorten her outings.

"May I be excused?" Caroline asked, with a sarcastic tone in her voice.

"You may," Elijah agreed, turning to his wife with a shrug as their daughter softly closed the door. "At least she didn't slam it."

Sarah smiled faintly, shaking her head.

* * *

Pushing Hap out of her thoughts was not easy, but for the next few days, Caroline embraced the task of capturing the huge moths of the night. She marveled at the sizes of these night creatures. Her lantern lured a large brown Prometheus with interesting gashes in its wings, but her prize was a giant luna.

* * *

"Mister Collins, they look like butterflies. How are they really different?" she asked during one of their final summer sessions.

"Moths do resemble butterflies, but most are nocturnal. Of course, our butterflies come out during the day. We, humans, either love a moth or hate it."

"Pardon me?"

"Well, one particular moth proves quite useful, while many are destructive. I find that quite fascinating. The useful one, at one stage of its life, spins a silk cocoon. Man takes the silk thread and makes beautiful fabric."

"Fabric?"

"Yes, legend notes that a Chinese empress accidentally dropped a cocoon in her hot tea and much to her surprise the gum holding the cocoon together unraveled into one continuous thread. Thus, the silk industry was born."

On and on, he droned, concluding with, "Silk is called the 'queen' and actually is the strongest of all natural fibers."

"You mean the silk in my mother's blouses came from a cocoon spun by a moth? How unusual, but you're right. It's fascinating."

She smothered a giggle as she imagined her mother with a

Chapter 7

bunch of cocoons all over her.

"Now, the destructive moth can devastate a garden or farm crop. Your father prays every year so that this infestation never happens at Shiloh."

"I see. Now, what do you think of my luna moth?"

"She's beautiful," he said, looking straight at her, as she pushed the moth around with a stylus, totally preoccupied with her prize. He continued, "Luna means moon, certainly an appropriate name for this night creature. No other has this pale green color and the distinctive long tails on its hind wings."

He took the stylus from her and lifted its wing to show her the long, ragged tails. Caroline peered up at him, as he said, "This female gives off a perfume that the male with his two large feelers on his head can smell miles away. You were very fortunate to capture her for your collection," he complimented her.

She looked back at the luna moth, entranced by all he said. Closing his eyes above her head, he inhaled her perfume, as she continued to stare at her prize.

The lesson and final summer project ended.

Chapter 8
THE BIRTHDAY

In mid-July, Caroline's 16th birthday celebration was quite a spectacle. She'd insisted on a huge picnic on the Town Common with every youth in Tarboro between the ages of sixteen and eighteen as guests. *Everybody*, she demanded. *No select group. Everybody.* Sarah could not imagine what had come over her daughter.

"Elijah, I've got no clue what she will come up with next. Maybe this gesture is *noble*? Is that the word I need? *All* the young people of Tarboro? That's her request. Strange, but noble?"

"Noble, nothing," mumbled George, as he overheard their conversation. "She jes' wants to see that young man in public."

He was right.

A picnic. A dance on the grounds. Surely the Virginia Reel and other folk dances would put her in Hap's arms without raising anyone's suspicion, but could he dance? No matter. She would teach him the next time she saw him.

While looking for Nellie that day, they'd mentioned meeting, weather permitting, but her confinement altered those plans. Rain delayed their rendezvous even longer, but she assumed that the next clear day must be their time. She was right.

* * *

"Dance? No, at least not the way you do. Willie's taught me the Virginia Reel, but no, I never learned anything else. Of course, all the school kids know that one."

"We'll practice. We don't need music. We can make our own," she insisted as she led him into the clearing and curtsied quite

Chapter 8

low.

Hap managed an awkward bow, but when she started humming and half singing, he lost no time proving to her that he could dance. They stepped and swung each other to the imaginary music.

"Don't ask me first off, but wait a few songs," she instructed him after their session was over. *Tomorrow cannot come fast enough,* she thought.

"I want to give you a present, Miss Caroline."

Hap suddenly became serious. He pulled a small item wrapped in tissue from his pocket and thrust it toward her. Her azure eyes grew big with excitement.

"Oh, it's nothing compared to what your momma and daddy will give you, but I give it to you with great admiration, and thank you," he gulped, looking down and frowning, "for allowing me to be your friend."

"Yes, we are friends, are we not? I like that. Well, this friend thanks you for this special gift that I have to open now or I will burst."

With that, she tore back the tissue and uncovered the daintiest chain she'd ever seen. Strung on it was the most delicate lavaliere, in the shape of a dogwood blossom. She gasped at its beauty. "Oh, Hap! Please. Will you help me with the clasp?"

"I saw it in Miz Carver's jewelry case. It just seemed to suit you," he said as he tried with his big hands to open and close the catch. He struggled, and she loved feeling his frustration as he muttered and mumbled with determination to get the chain around her neck. Her perfume was not helping either.

What'd you do, girl, bathe in the stuff? His eyes began to water, as the necklace was finally in place.

She turned ever so slowly to give him the first full view of his gift. He could not take his eyes off her face. She was radiant.

How could God have put together such a divine creature? he marveled. The crooked smile froze on his face.

"Well?"

"It-it's perfect," he finally whispered.

"Thank you, Hap. This is my first gift," she smiled, taking his hand and squeezing it gently. And this time, it was she who finally whispered, "I have to go," and turned toward Nellie.

He followed her and helped her mount, leaving his hands on her waist as long as he dared.

She turned in the saddle and looked down at him. *Hap Tyson, you are becoming more than just a friend, much more,* she thought, but she said, "I look forward to seeing you tomorrow."

* * *

Not one cloud streaked the sky the next day as the wagons rolled out of Shiloh. At the Town Common, workers placed tables and tents around the green. Local musicians tuned their instruments, and snippets of melodies filled the air. Young men and women poured onto the green to greet Caroline, thanking her for their invitation. Most she did not know, but one she knew quite well. Hap Tyson stood before her and shook her hand, showing only a hint of a smile as he caught a glimpse of the little lavaliere around her neck. Quite deliberately, her fingers ran around the edge of the chain, finally resting on the lavaliere itself. She hardly looked at him as the next person spoke to her and captured her attention, but her actions demonstrated her feelings. His spirits soared.

The music resounded down the green. "Grab a partner, gents, and gather round," the caller hollered. Many young men flocked to the honoree for the first dance.

She's just like the queen bee in a hive, Hap thought. A twinge of jealousy welled inside as he watched, but they had their secret.

Just at that moment, Josie Whichard sidled up to him and hinted for a dance. He obliged grudgingly, but his height gave him full view of the maiden of honor, as they edged closer toward

Chapter 8

each other.

"Change your partner," the band leader called out, but before Hap could reach Caroline, someone else swooped her away. Another young lady grabbed him, and her two hundred pounds on his toe got his immediate attention. Grimacing, he swore under his breath with each crippling twirl.

"Grab your partners and do-si-do," the caller's voice rang out.

The Virginia Reel! Maybe now, he hoped.

Everyone knew this dance and loved the spins and swings of the lively rhythm. Closer and closer, she came to him in the sets. His head spun with excitement, and finally he held her in his arms, even if only briefly. She was weightless. He forced himself not to swing her off the ground as he had done once at the lower 40. Both their foreheads beaded with perspiration.

The music stopped with his arms around her. She laughed, whipped out her silk handkerchief filled with perfume, and mopped his brow quickly. In two seconds, she was gone.

"Gather round everybody. It's time for food," Captain Cromwell announced. The crowds buzzed, but then they quieted as the father blessed his daughter and the meal. "We're glad you all came to share this special day," he said, his arm around his daughter's shoulder. "Now, enjoy."

The crowd nudged Hap forward. He drifted closer and studied the moneyed young gentry, vying for Caroline's attention, their charm dripping with each word. A strange feeling pricked his soul, actually angering him. He realized that he would never be a part of her world, but only a fleeting memory in their secret haven. Did she lure him into this situation on purpose? Was she toying with him? His heart pounded as he realized that, in this town at least, he would never be anything to Caroline Cromwell other than an urchin on Station House Road, an object of pity.

God, what a boob I am! He began to feel ill as he turned to leave the Commons, practically running over Josie Whichard. He looked down at her, then over his shoulder at Caroline. When he turned again, the crooked grin covered his face, but this time his eye also had a wicked gleam.

"Miz Whichard, could I escort you down to the soda fountain? I think this party is over." She cooed a delighted acceptance as he escorted her toward Main Street.

Caroline's eyes scanned the crowd. Where was he? She'd risked much when she mopped his brow, but she'd done it to several of the young men so as not to arouse attention. She knew he'd seen her finger the lavaliere, and when he held her in his arms for the Virginia Reel, she thought he was going to forget and swing her off the ground as he had done during their practice. Where was he?

Suddenly, his shock of hair caught her eye. He appeared to be leaving the Commons. *But why?* When she spied Josie on Hap's arm, she felt faint. Why was he doing this? She'd done everything she knew to show him recognition without divulging any secrets. Tears stung her eyes. She had done all of this for him…and for her. She'd deal with Hap Tyson tomorrow. Dabbing her eyes, she called for the next dance, only to have Michael Collins suddenly appear, bow, and ask for a spin on the green.

Chapter 9
CONFRONTATION

Sarah and Elijah stared at their daughter at breakfast.

"Are you all right, darling?" her mother asked.

"What?"

"Are you all right?"

"Of course."

"Well, I've never seen you twist your napkin like that before. You seem so preoccupied with something."

Will snickered, expecting the sparring to begin.

"I was just wondering about vacation," Caroline said, glaring at her brother. She turned to her parents and asked them a number of quick questions. "Where are we going? The Outer Banks? When do we leave? How long will we be gone? Are we going anywhere else?"

"Whoa, young lady, one question at a time," Elijah said. "Your mother and I are thinking next week would be a wonderful way to end the summer before school begins for both of you. How does that sound?" Elijah Cromwell paused. Both siblings looked at each other and nodded. Their father continued. "We'll take the train down to Morehead as we did a few summers ago. The rest will do us all good with no one to disturb us for days," he said.

Caroline thought that this would be like going to the moon for a year to relax, but she had no other recourse than to enter into the plans just for those reasons. Since her birthday and separation from Hap, she'd moped around listlessly, not understanding why he'd left her and what that snippy girl meant to him. He'd not come to the lower 40 for days, which puzzled her even more. She pushed her food around her plate.

"Elijah, what did Willie want when she came by yesterday?" Sarah asked, taking a sip of coffee. "You never said."

Elijah sighed before he spoke. "Advice."

"Not about that boy I hope?" Sarah asked. He nodded at his wife. "Not again," she said.

"*Again*. Sarah, you know I feel so responsible for Willie. We're all she's got. Her parents are dead, as you know. Look how we helped her when they died. She thinks that we saved her life. Remember she had no other family in Tarboro. Shiloh was her home for years before Grandfather freed her folks long before the war. Shoot, she and I grew up together. I'm probably the only friend she's got. You know all this. Please just understand. I have honestly tried to help her in any way I could since she came back to Tarboro, but this boy is something else. I swear he walks under a black cloud."

Elijah paused and looked at his daughter. "Caroline, didn't he come to your party?"

Caroline froze over her food and tried to stay casual as she asked with a barely audible voice, "What did he do?"

"Oh, just a prank. It seems he dipped Miss Morris's cat's tail in some lamp oil and lit it. The poor cat ran down Main Street, screaming and scaring downtown half to death."

"No, he didn't," Sarah said, disapprovingly.

"Oh yes. Finally, it rolled around in the damp grass on the Town Common to put out the flames."

"That's disgusting," Sarah said, shaking her head.

"Sarah, remember when he ran away from Willie after the first few months he came to live with her?"

She nodded.

"That boy's worried poor Willie half to death ever since. It seems it's his second nature to live on the edge," he scoffed, taking his last sip of coffee. "Wendell Tyson ought to come get him and take him back to Pitt County."

"What's his name? I forget." Sarah asked.

"Hap Tyson."

Chapter 9

Her father had barely replied when Caroline slammed her glass on the table, looked him in the eye, and said, "You have always taught us not to judge. You do not even know this Hap, Hap Tyson." She pointed a finger at him and asked, "How can you say these things without firsthand knowledge?"

After a shocked silence, she mumbled, "Oh, excuse me," and threw her rumpled lace napkin down on the table. Abruptly pushing her chair from the table, she left in a huff with both parents' mouths open in surprise. Will muffled another laugh, shaking his head as he'd done countless times at these outbursts. Caroline had been acting strangely since her birthday. Now, they had to go away on vacation with her openly hostile. Vacations are supposed to be happy and peaceful, thought Sarah, and she sighed, watching through the parlor door as her daughter trailed upstairs to her room.

* * *

No, she would not go to the lower 40, Caroline determined later that morning, as she took Nellie for a ride. But how could she stand not seeing him before leaving on vacation? Crestfallen, she reached the outskirts of the grove, her curiosity piqued as the thought of not seeing him became almost unbearable. Was he there? Arching her back, she stood in her saddle and strained to see through the trees. She succumbed to the temptation and galloped Nellie with her crop flying. Much to her relief–and chagrin–he was there all right, but he was not on the fallen log. He stood on the edge of the clearing, looking from behind one of the trees. Now, she would get answers.

"Hap Tyson, come out from behind that tree," she said sternly as she marched toward him. He sidled slowly from behind the big oak, keeping his face turned sidewise. "Look at me," she said softly. As he turned, a gash over his left eye jumped out at her. She stepped back. "What happened to you?"

"Just a fight, Caroline," he sneered, "and probably not my last, but do you really want to know what's happened to me?"

"What?" she whispered.

"You!"

"Me? What do you mean?"

"You! That's what has happened." His voice rose. "You came into my life and messed me up. What with all your finery and perfume, you made me feel I was your equal. But that ain't never gonna happen. You've ruined me."

He wagged a finger at her, then turned to avoid her eyes. "I was gitten along just fine 'til you wove your spell in my head and spun fairy tales around my heart so's I can't even breathe." Beating his chest, he turned back to face her and threw his hands upward. "Where's all this going? You tell me? Nowhere! My God, nowhere! I could die."

He seemed so angry that she thought he might shake her. Then, she realized that he was not really angry at her, just at the wide gulf between who they were. She could have been in his shoes, and he in hers, and it would all be the same. She began to cry, knowing that he was telling the truth. She was living a fairy tale, pretending that it was real. She, too, felt incensed—at her world, at her parents, at everybody who would say that this young man could not openly be her friend.

Tears flowed down both faces as they stood inches apart. He suddenly grabbed her shoulders and pulled her closer and kissed her roughly on the mouth. The roughness ended quickly, and the sweetness of that kiss lingered until once more his roughness prevailed. Brusquely, he pushed her from him, each breathless. Their tears mingled. Hap slowly shook his head, knowing that the kiss probably had ended their time in that secret haven forever. He charged the tree line and screamed to the treetops, his cry reflecting his loss. Reality kept pushing them apart.

Hap dashed into the woods leading back to Station House Road. He wheeled around to look at her once more, and then, Hap Tyson disappeared.

Chapter 10
VACATION '80

*A*s the Cromwells were leaving for Morehead, Michael Collins arrived at the station with a special box for his student.

"There's a small book inside that I think you'll enjoy on your journey. It's poems about the sea." He paused, then spoke softly as he clasped her hand in farewell. "I look forward to your return."

Peeking from behind Carver's store, Hap had a clear view of the coach and the Cromwells. Her parents' blindness to the tutor's affection for their daughter astounded him. Maybe they did see and wished something to happen between them. He pulled back behind the building and banged his head against the wall.

"Forget her," he muttered, over and over again. "Forget her! Forget her!"

* * *

The trip was long but pleasant enough as the Cromwells traveled the plank roads to New Bern and then boarded a train, arriving in Morehead after a two-day journey.

"Our hotel is brand new," Elijah said, motioning to the large building outside as the train cars screeched to a halt.

The Atlantic Hotel, a rambling, three-story structure, towered before them. Its huge cupola and double-storied porches fascinated them all.

"Father, it's beautiful and big," Caroline said, peering out the train car's window. "No. I don't believe it. We're getting out at the front door?"

They stood under the covered railroad platform, waiting for

their luggage.

"I've never seen a boardwalk like this, Elijah. It does go right up to the front door," Sarah remarked. "Why, if it were raining, we'd never get a drop on our heads."

"Service, my dear, service," her husband answered.

"Thank you, darling," she said, squeezing his hand.

"With the way Morehead is growing it will have more people than Beaufort in no time," Elijah said. "And, this hotel will become North Carolina's summer capital for sure."

"Now I understand why we're not staying at Macon House," Sarah smiled. "I know the hurricane was bad, but why didn't the owners rebuild the Atlantic Hotel at the same location in Beaufort?"

"Remember, my dear, the train stops here. We would be taking boats over, and on the mainland, the hotel is protected better from any harsh storms."

"Somebody could get lost in a second," Will said, awestruck as he gazed at the huge building. "I'm almost dizzy."

"I'd say it is perfection," Caroline said, oohing one more time.

On the back of the hotel, two wings extended with a large pier and bathhouses connected to the main building. The hotel was all elegance and charm, and as they explored the immense ballroom and dining halls, they all agreed that the most unusual luxury was the covered railroad stop with the boardwalk right up to the hotel's entrance.

* * *

Gong. Gong. Gong. Gong. Gong. Gong. One eye popped open as Caroline heard the faint chiming of a grandfather clock in the lobby of the hotel. Elijah had reserved a suite with a water view on the backside of the hotel, yet convenient to the center of activity. She raised her head, but six o'clock was too early for a bath.

She flopped down, rolling over, hugging her feather pillow,

Chapter 10

and imagined herself at the lower 40, facing Hap Tyson. She could still feel his hands roughly grasping her shoulders. Her own hand drifted slowly to her mouth as she remembered his crushing her own, but she also remembered the sweetness. She had probably lost him forever, but no one, no one, could take away his kiss. Even in her own immaturity, she thought that she would never experience that kind of passion again. Feeling the refreshing southwest breeze from the early August morning, she shuddered as she lay under her sheets. Vacation was here.

* * *

"No one is to bother her," Elijah instructed his family. "Let Caroline find us."

Even Sarah agreed, and his plan worked, as he watched with curiosity and pride as his daughter began to enter into vacation and all the scheduled activities. The Bakers, who owned the hotel, shared their philosophy with all their guests: We have it all, but there's no pressure. Just suit yourself. You are on vacation.

On their first day, Caroline and Will boarded a sharpie, a small sailboat the hotel provided to taxi their guests across the sound to the barrier island of Bogue. For a while, she wandered down the beach in the opposite direction from Will and scampered up a dune, placing her hands on her hips as she surveyed the beach.

"I'm like these sea oats, holding my own against the world," she shouted. Raising her arms skyward, Caroline felt the ocean breezes blowing softly through her hair and billowing her clothing.

"What delicious freedom! And no one—no one—to tell me what to do!"

Around and around she twirled. Nothing else mattered; nothing else counted. Just the moment. She felt a new sense of freedom, even as she returned to the hotel and her family.

Back at the hotel, the Cromwells sat down for dinner and were delighted with the seafood served with light puffs of fried cornmeal, spices, and a dab of sugar.

"Mother, you will have to get this recipe for Maggie," Caroline insisted.

Sarah smiled at her daughter, but she frowned at the thought of telling the best cook she knew how to prepare such dishes.

A Raleigh family, assigned to an adjoining table, became their favorite dinner companions. Coincidentally, the eldest son, Litchfield, was a rising junior at the university, a possible help for Will as a lowly incoming freshman.

The Bagleys retained large property holdings in Wake County. The more vibrant the capital city became, the more lucrative the real estate business grew. Jacob Bagley intended to make his mark in this profession and expected his son Litch to follow in his footsteps after graduation.

How could anyone refuse to purchase from these two dynamos? Elijah thought, smiling as one started a sentence and the other finished it.

"Well, Jacob, Mister Baker told me an interesting story that you might enjoy, you being in real estate," Elijah spoke to the gregarious gentleman.

"How so, sir?"

"He said a few years ago a Mr. Oaksmith had a vision for the east end of Bogue Banks, a new resort by the sea."

"Oh?"

"Sadly, he never saw his dream happen, so Mister Baker is hearing some rumbling about folks picking up this idea. Who knows? Interesting, isn't it?"

"Hmmm." Elijah could almost see the man's mind clicking.

This family's structure appeared planned and content, he surmised from the table chatter. It seemed that Rosemund Bagley had even selected a young woman as her son's intended. However, she was not aware that her boy had spied Caroline

Chapter 10

alone on the dunes on Bogue Bank and vowed to pursue her or to die trying. He was lovestruck. Elijah thought he had seen Litch cutting his eyes at his daughter. *Well, that's interesting, too.* He smiled.

During the following evening meal, the intrigued young man could not take his eyes off the Cromwell daughter. Not once during the entire meal did Caroline utter a word or cast a glance his way. None of the young ladies in Raleigh would have treated him with such aloofness. Nevertheless, he was fascinated. And Will seemed a nice enough chap. Maybe through him, he could get Caroline to warm up to him. Thus, began the maneuvers of a third lovelorn creature, captivated by the Dresden doll.

* * *

"Why, Miss Caroline, Litch Bagley at your service. May I ride with you this morning on the dunes?"

He'd startled her, as he came out of the darkness of the stables the next morning and stepped into the sunlight only a few feet from her.

"Of-of course," she smiled faintly and stammered. What else could she say?

"Wonderful. I notice that you like the gray mare. Is Nellie the same color?"

"How did you know about Nellie?"

She eyed him with a frown.

"Ahhh, secret powers," he laughed and steered her down the middle of the big barn to where the ponies were feeding.

The stable attendant had seen her and had already begun to gather a bridle and saddle.

"Thank you, sir," Litch said, as they both stood and watched the man lead the pony out of the stall and girdle her for the ride.

"You'll need the biggest pony we got for your long legs, sir," the attendant grinned as he looked up at the tall young man.

"You're right," Litch Bagley laughed back.

It was her turn to stare at Litch with curiosity as he bantered with the stable attendant. His face was slightly ruddy with high cheekbones and an aquiline nose. His full head of hair moved slightly when he did, but always seemed to fall neatly in place. He was immaculate.

The attendant walked the two ponies out of the barn.

"Miss Caroline," Litch said, extending his hand to help her.

She smirked and rolled her eyes, then swung up into the saddle and sped off.

A gull squawked above Litch's head, as he grappled with his own reins and threw his leg over his pony's back. Caroline turned back once to watch the oversized man on the undersized beast. Laughing, she cut through the dunes and galloped toward Fort Macon, sand spraying from the galloping hooves. Suddenly, she pulled up to wait for the trailing rider.

Litch reined his animal, grinning at her with as much enthusiasm as a shark after menhaden. He was smitten and wondered how many hearts she'd stomped on before his.

"Caroline Cromwell, I don't mince words, and I'm serious. I wish to come to Shiloh as a guest at your home. Would you...would you receive me?"

She stared at him, never changing her expression.

"You can do as you like, Litch Bagley. Will would love having you come."

His heart sank.

With that, she turned and walked the gray pony, allowing Litch to ride beside her in silence. The gulls soared overhead and cried out as one began diving for the fish below. Both stopped and watched the feast, the sun streaming overhead. Caroline untied her bonnet from her waist and retied it over her hair.

"No more serious talk, Mister Bagley. We're on vacation to have fun. Let's do just that."

Looking deeply in his eyes, she dazzled him with her smile.

Chapter 10

Half rearing on the gray pony, she sprang forward at a gallop, leaving the young man with his mouth half-opened. She never heard his heavenward yell, for the wind blew the sound down the beach away from her ears.

Chapter II

TALES OF THE SEA

Sarah leaned over and whispered to Elijah. "Our daughter is an enigma."

"Hush, dear, don't break the spell," he said, as the touring carriage creaked across the newly opened Beaufort bridge.

Caroline had persuaded them to ride over for lunch and tour the old village, especially the house claimed to be that of Blackbeard the Pirate. They were not aware that this day trip was a ploy to avoid Litch Bagley.

"Vacations mean family. Right?" Elijah gently nudged his wife.

"Hmmm. I'm just not sure about this," she replied, knowing her daughter all too well.

* * *

During the first weekend of the Cromwells' vacation, the Bakers planned campfire stories told by Captain Marshall Pigott. The guests spread blankets on the hotel grounds to listen to his tales of the sea. Weather permitting, the staff would serve a buffet on the verandah under the stars.

Will and Caroline shared a blanket and peered in disbelief at the old man. His gray locks hung to his shoulders with a scruffy cap scarcely covering all the wild sprigs. Deep crevices streaked his leathery face, and his voice sounded raspy as he introduced himself.

Litch Bagley hung back and watched Caroline.

"I fished these waters all my life," Pigott said. "Only once did I stray from Carteret County."

He nodded his head toward the eastern sky.

Chapter 11

"I worked over there on Ocracoke Island at the first official beacon along the North Carolina coast. That was back in '23. That lighthouse has warned the ships ever since, except when the Rebs hid the lenses from the Yanks. I stayed three years in the service, just long enough to find myself an Ocracoke gal. I married her, I did."

He paused, looking around with a twinkle in his eye.

"Well, ladies and gents, back then, the government used lightships off the coast to keep the boats off our shoals. The ships were anchored with cables to the ocean floor, but many times the stormy seas would break the moorings and cast the ships adrift or wreck them on the shoals. Then, it would just be the lighthouse and the surfmen. And I was one of the surfmen."

The younger children's eyes grew larger, trying to picture the angry seas. A small voice called out from the crowd. "Did you ever almost drown, Cap'n?"

"Aye, son. I have."

"Tell us," urged the boy.

Pigott chewed on his unlit pipe a moment.

"It was a September night during the hurricane season of 1830. The clouds had been banking all day long. From early morning, the islanders scurried to get their day's work done before the storm broke. Even the animals knew we were in for a big blow. The wind whipped and howled something fierce. Cap'n Gaskill called together everybody on duty to remind them of their responsibility.

"I was on the night shift that partic'lar evenin'. Each one of us looked at t'other for encouragement and silently prayed no ship would pass close. Aye, how wrong we were."

The old man seemed lost in his past as he gazed into the fire, shifting his weight to ease a hidden pain. He shook his head with the sadness of a heavy burden, then continued.

"As I stood in the lighthouse, lookin' out into the blackness, I could feel the power of the air currents round the tower. Our light flickered from the drafts. I could taste the danger, but I knew to focus on the sea. How close to being a hurricane this storm was I could not tell, but I soon saw the dreaded, as lightning flashed on the horizon. A wee flicker appeared betwixt the swells, and I knew it was a boat. 'Stay away!' I screamed. 'Stay off them shoals! Good God, stay off them shoals!' Course nobody aboard could hear me as that lone boat lurched closer and closer. Then I saw the warning lights on board, blinking for help. I returned the signal, hoping they could see that rescue was on the way. But I was afraid the ocean might claim another trophy for the deep."

The captain's chin rested on his chest. The group waited expectantly in silence. He took a deep breath. "Ya see, the U.S. Life Saving Services these days has better equipment now than we had back then. Today, the cap'n's words would be, 'Man the beach cart forward!'"

He paused briefly, then asked. "And do ya know what's in the cart, lads and lassies? Do ya?"

Many shook their heads.

"They got the Lyle gun, they do."

The crowd murmured.

"Aye, the gun that can shoot an anchor six hunnert feet and hook over the side of the vessel. They got the breeches buoy and now even the box that could be hauled in with pulleys from the Lyle gun shot. All we had back then were some cork floats tied to ropes that we would throw out to the survivors in the water. We'd get as close as we could, trying to save 'em while keepin' ourselves from wrecking on the shoals.

"Well, suh, that night I scrambled down the lighthouse steps, thinking there might be another wrecked boat to rot below the churning waters. As I opened the door, the wind flung the frame so fiercely that it almost sprung off the hinges. I clawed to save it. The rain poured in, blinding me as I stumbled up the stone

CHAPTER 11

walkway to the keeper's house.

"Cap'n Gaskill opened his door before I even knocked, as if he'd watched everythin' that was happenin'. His strong arm yanked me into the house just like I was a rag doll. His eyes pierced mine with the fear of God in them. 'Get ahold, Pigott, we have lives to save, our own as well as those in the vessel. We need no fright amongst us, man. The good Lord is with us always, no matter what. You got that, Pigott?' I'll never forget his words. He reminded me of a greater captain and His power.

"As fast as we could muster, Cap'n Gaskill and our crew headed out in two boats. We rowed until we thought our arms would fall from their sockets. The winds had begun to die down somewhat, but those swells were monsters and tossed us like the Devil himself was in control. But lemme tell you that mighty ocean soon learned the strength of the true Bankers. It was a miracle. We saved well-nigh all the crew of that ship. It was as if our prayers had allowed us to take dominion over the elements, as the Good Book says that we can. Later, it was a mighty happy crew that sipped brew to take the chill from our bones. Whatever was on the boat was lost, though, and to this day, treasures still fill those sunken hulls. But there be no bones from any crew members a-restin' down there with the fishes, thanks to us."

With that closing word, Captain Pigott looked around those seated around the campfire. The deep creases of his face smoothed with his toothy grin. He lifted his Jew's harp and began to play melodies from the soul of a sailor and ended with lively tunes that had the children dancing around the fire.

A thunderhead rumbled in the distance.

"Friends, it looks as if the skies will push our buffet inside," Mr. Baker said. "Let's give Captain Pigott a round of applause."

The old man bowed, waving his hand in gratitude.

"What brave men," Will said, as they folded their blankets and walked back to the hotel, lost in thought about what the old surfman had told them.

More than once, they turned to look across the sound. On the other side of the dunes, the waves had already begun to rise up and barrel over to rearrange the sandy shore.

"Can you imagine those surfmen battling such forces of nature? What year did he say?" Caroline asked, kicking sand as they trudged along.

"1830," Will answered. "Fifty years ago."

Only one person did not think of the Captain's tale as he shadowed the Cromwells back inside the hotel.

Chapter 12

SATURDAY NIGHT WINGDING

A storm did blow up, and that Saturday proved a day of recovery. The storm had passed, leaving debris on the shore and prized shells for the collectors. The sharpies once more ran their course to Bogue. Locals and the hotel guests combed the shores, but it was Caroline who discovered the best prize, a perfectly formed giant conch. Cleaning it carefully, she displayed it in the hotel lobby.

"No guest has ever found a better one. I promise," Mr. Baker assured her.

* * *

That night the hotel buzzed with excitement. The Bakers had prepared for the Saturday night dance, even inviting some local young people and musicians. Everybody seemed set and eager to participate, but one.

"Caroline, what do you mean that you're not coming down to the festivities?" her mother asked. "Everybody will be there, even some people from Morehead and Beaufort."

Sarah Cromwell knew nothing of her daughter's attempts to avoid Litch Bagley, but eventually, her father's convincing words stirred her to prepare for the evening. She never once imagined the surprise awaiting her.

Instead of having to ignore him deliberately, Caroline discovered that Litch paid absolutely no attention to her, but he did to her mother. He twirled Sarah until she was breathless.

"Please," she begged. "Punch and a chair."

Caroline watched from the sidelines in dismay. Finally, a shy young local boy asked her to dance, but he proved that he needed lessons. More than once he begged her pardon for his missteps.

Dumping his plan of aversion, Litch tapped on the young man's shoulder.

"May I cut in?"

"Oh, thank you, sir," the local boy sputtered, but he quickly added, "Oh, I mean it was my pleasure, miss." Backing away with great relief, he mopped his brow with each step.

Caroline was in a quandary. She wanted to appear uninterested, but she couldn't hide her own gratitude. The two broke into laughter as they watched the bumbler disappear into the crowd. Litch loved to see her laugh and he would be quite content the rest of his life to see that smile stay on her face. What made him think that he could dare stay away from her this night?

A lively tune ended, and slow lilting sounds of a waltz floated from the piano across the ballroom. Litch's heart pounded. With her small hand in his, he guided her to the middle of the dance floor and turned to hold her tiny waist. He looked deeply into her eyes, but Caroline looked away as they glided across the floor to the music.

Who are you thinking about? he wondered, irritated that it was not he.

Hap filled her thoughts and their times at the lower 40, but here she was dancing with someone who'd declared more than just a friendly interest in her. She looked up at the tall handsome young man.

You must be crazy, she thought. *You don't even know me. You're brash...and self-centered...and handsome.*

Her dazzling smile melted his heart, a cruel result, for she had no intention of their association going any further than this vacation.

Chapter 13
Recovery and Discovery

Sunday morning the hotel guests learned that Mr. Baker was a lay minister and knew the Bible. Laughing, he assured them that the sermon would not be on Noah and the Ark or any other similar theme after Friday's stormy night.

Walking over to a basket of shells, he held up a pristine white sand dollar.

"This season is definitely not Christmas and not Easter, but in this very special shell we can see many symbols that refer to the birth and to the resurrection of the Christ, celebrated during those seasons. I'll ask the shell queen to help me with this lesson. Caroline Cromwell, here, take it." Holding out the shell, he motioned her to join him. "Turn it over and tell us what you see."

A bit reluctant, Caroline approached Mr. Baker, took the shell, then turned it over and studied it. "A poinsettia, the Christmas flower."

"Now, what do you see on its top side? Think on the crucifixion and the resurrection."

"I see five lines extending from the center of the shell, two longer than the other three," she said, looking up at Mr. Baker, as she fingered the delicate shell. "I'd guess this imprint must mean the body of Christ, hanging on the cross?"

"Good," Mr. Baker said. "What about the holes?"

"One, two... I count five on the outer edge." Then squinting she added, "And some really little ones in the center."

"Think crucifixion."

"You mean His wounds?"

Again, she looked up. Mr. Baker nodded.

"Hmm, from the nails and the thorns?" she continued.

"I'd say so," Mr. Baker spoke quietly.

"I suppose the ones in the center could be from the centurion's spear piercing his side."

"You suppose exactly right."

Caroline smiled and returned the shell to Mr. Baker.

"The next time any of you see a broken sand dollar on the shore, break it along the lines of the Savior's arms and legs and you will see the secret inside, the dove of the Holy Spirit."

The children grinned, thinking about an excursion to Fort Macon in just a few days.

* * *

Mid-week, the sharpies bulged with the hotel guests and picnic baskets. The weather was quite favorable to make the trip across the sound to Bogue Banks. Litch and Caroline had only seen each other from afar the last two days, but the Bagleys planned to leave before week's end and Litch was determined to snatch as much time with her as he could.

The ferried carriages rolled toward Fort Macon. The families gathered, as the military attaché greeted them.

"Welcome to Fort Macon, one of the South's main coastal stands against the Union during the War. You're free to wander through the fort with your families. Soldiers on duty can tell you about it as you go through, but I must inform you that there's an unbelievable surprise for you over on the beach."

The hotel guests buzzed as they made their way toward the outdoor quarters set up for them by the Bakers. Umbrellas and blankets nestled in the sand, but to everyone's shock, there was an unexpected intruder, big, black, and wet.

During the storm, a sperm whale had become disoriented and beached itself close to the fort. The tides had moved it somewhat, but the struggling mammal seemed parked for the duration of its life. Disbelief and curiosity drew the guests closer to see the

Chapter 13

doomed creature.

"Mr. Baker, what kind is it?" a child asked, pulling on his coattails.

"A sperm whale with lots of teeth. Look at its head. Do you know why it's so big?"

"No," several children chorused.

"It has a large chamber for oil. The candles we use at the hotel are made from whale oil," he told them, "as well as the oil in our lamps."

"What will happen to it?"

Mr. Baker turned and pointed to some men standing on the dunes.

"The whalers we still have in this area will take care of it after we leave. The fort needs the area cleared as soon as possible. Meanwhile, you'll have to share the beach with this uninvited guest."

"Can you believe it?" Litch murmured. He'd sidled up close to Caroline.

"Oh! You startled me," she said, jerking her head to the side.

"Sorry," he spoke softly, never taking his eyes off the whale. "Let's change and meet back here. I want to touch it."

"Touch the whale?"

"Yes. Aren't you curious to know how it feels? C'mon. We may never have another chance."

Each went into a changing tent, and a short while later, Litch stood waiting and held out his hand to her, as she came out of the ladies' tent. He pulled her forward toward the hulk. Its blowhole opened for maybe one last spray. The two froze. They were looking at death, this effort a last cry for help.

"Nobody can do anything for this poor fellow," Litch said. "I suppose the whalers will cut up the carcass and remove it piece by piece."

"It's so sad," Caroline said.

They dropped hands and leaned over to touch the stranded creature. Its leathery skin shocked both.

"Oh, my gosh," she said. "I thought it would feel slick. I mean with that wet, glossy look, who would have thought gritty and leathery?"

Both turned from the whale and looked up the beach.

"Shall we walk?" he asked.

"Yes, let's. It feels funny not riding the ponies, doesn't it?"

"Oh yes, but this way you can't run away from me," he said, grinning.

She looked up and said with resignation, "Litch."

Suddenly, he broke away from her and dashed toward the surf. She could hear him yell as he dove under the first big swell. How she would love to be as free to swim just as he was doing, but her mother had said, "... only up to your knees, dear."

She had purchased the new princess-cut swimsuit, a one-piece blouse and trouser combination, but she determined that all the fabric would sink her if she did venture any farther. Her ruffled cap barely hid her curls from the sun.

She wandered casually, looking for any shells that might have eluded the beachcombers. An object among some seaweed caught her eye, washed up from the storm—a round object, covered with gunk. She swiftly reached down and picked it up.

"Hey, what'd ya find?" Litch caught up with her after tumbling in the rolling surf.

"A coin, I think. Maybe it's part of a treasure from one of the wrecks off Diamond Shoals Captain Pigott told us about."

She smiled and turned it over and over in her hand. Small sections gleamed in the sunlight, barely indicating the pure gold that it actually was. "I'm sure Mr. Collins will find a way for me to clean my coin of all its years on the ocean's floor."

"Who's Mr. Collins?"

"My tutor. I can't wait to show him all my treasures from the

Chapter 13

sea."

A bell rang in the distance.

"Lunch time. I need to gain a few more pounds," he said, patting his sleek mid-section.

"You do not," she laughed.

Once more she took his hand, but she focused her attention on the coin as they moved toward the feast on the beach.

Sarah Cromwell tilted her head and smiled as the young couple walked up.

* * *

And then the Bagleys were gone.

"I'll not think about Litch. I'll not," Caroline mumbled, although she could not help but feel a void the last few days of vacation. "At least I've bonded with my family in all of this."

Even the patriarch and matriarch marveled into the wee hours of their last night as the curtains gently rippled in the Atlantic breezes.

"I hope these new ties last," Sarah murmured, as she lay in Elijah's arms. She peered up in her husband's face. "What do you think of Litch Bagley?"

"Well, I don't know. We've only known him for a week you know."

"I think he's perfect for our daughter."

"What?" He raised up on his elbow.

"I've got this feeling he's the one."

"What one?"

"The one who can tame our headstrong daughter. That one. He asked me if he could visit Shiloh."

"You didn't tell me." Elijah sounded irritated.

"Forgive me, darling. I just had to be sure."

"Sure? Sure of what? What do you mean, woman?"

"I've been watching him watching her."

"Oh, you have?"

"He's smitten."

"And Caroline?"

"She'll come around."

"How do you know?" he asked.

"I just do. He better come to Shiloh soon. Maybe the first holiday. He and Will can travel together."

"You've figured it all out, haven't you?" He kissed her forehead.

"Uh-huh," she mumbled, drifting off to sleep with the decision made that Litchfield Jacob Bagley was a definite prospect for Caroline King Cromwell.

Chapter 14
The Return

Caroline's excitement enraptured Michael Collins. They sat in the gardens behind Cromwell Hall. The last roses of summer tipped the bushes, perfuming the air.

"Our trip—it was wonderful."

He hesitated releasing her hand. It was his first visit to Shiloh after the Cromwells' return. He loved her slight tan, knowing that most women protected their skin with layers of clothing, parasols, and porches. Caroline embraced the out-of-doors; her enthusiasm was infectious. As she talked, he envisioned every detail, from the hotel to the whale on the beach, but as she continued, he made a disturbing observation: *Who is Litch Bagley?*

"Mister Collins. Mister. Col-lins. Hello? Forgive me. I've been prattling on and have completely bored you. You-you have a peculiar look on your face. Is anything the matter?"

Startled, he recovered, assuring her that he was fine.

"Let me see your treasures."

She glowed as she removed the conch from a small valise.

"I won the prize for the largest shell found during our stay," she boasted. "Captain Pigott told me all about the critter, as he called it, that lived in this shell. Did you know that these shells have been used as horns?"

Still a bit distracted, he nodded mechanically and answered quietly, "Yes, Triton, a sea demigod and son of Poseidon and Amphitrite in Greek mythology, had a lower body of a fish. He used a conch as his horn."

"Mister Collins, you really don't look well. Can Maggie bring you some water or something?"

"Who is Litch Bagley?" he asked softly.

Caroline blanched.

"I-I beg your pardon," she stammered. "Litch Bagley? Why would you ask about him? I d-don't understand."

"You've mentioned him countless times as you described your vacation. I just wondered," he said with a faint smile.

"I did?" she replied. "Goodness, I did not even realize that I had. Litch and his family were on vacation at the same time. He and my brother will be at the university together this fall. They became friends, and we just seemed to end up doing things together," she answered, her mind racing to change the subject.

"Oh, Mister Collins, look what else I found on the beach. A coin. It remained on the ocean floor as part of a treasure and washed up on the beach just in time for me to rescue it from another day unclaimed."

She held up the grime-covered gold coin in triumph and knew that his intellectual curiosity would overcome his bizarre behavior.

"Now, I have a task for you, *mon professeur*. How does one get the deposits off of this gold coin?"

He took the coin from her, flipping it over and over in his hand, a hand that wanted only to reach out and touch her slightly tanned face and crush her curls between his fingers. However, his interest was piqued by her quest to clean the coin, and he looked up at her, shaking his head.

"I don't know," he said sheepishly.

Rarely had he been asked a question of which he had absolutely no knowledge, but Caroline Cromwell had done it. How humbling, but challenging. Yes, he would find out for her the answer to this problem, and anything else in the world that she wanted to know. However, one realization was plain to him: If she never saw him in any light other than as her tutor, at least he had that advantage over any man. He had her mind, but, God in heaven, he wanted all of her.

Chapter 15

Rufus Knight

By the time the Cromwells returned from vacation, Hap Tyson had visited the jail more than once. If he was going to have a bad reputation, he wanted to deserve it. The first charge was public drunkenness the night Caroline left Tarboro. Jeb MacMillan thought it peculiar that if Hap were as mean as everybody claimed, he also was the easiest criminal to catch and the most pleasant.

And here he was again.

"Need anything, son, before I lock the jail down?" Deputy MacMillan asked his prisoner.

"Oh, no, sir, I'm fine. I'll be asleep in no time. See you in the morning."

Shaking his head, MacMillan turned to walk out. The young man hardly smelled of booze, but he had to arrest him when he'd refused to move from the middle of Main Street, where he stopped the flow of traffic. Senseless, as the deputy saw it, but all the other times were, too. He made the call to bring him in. The young man appeared hell-bent on going to jail.

"Oh, deputy? Can somebody go tell Willie?"

"Huh?"

"She's always concerned when I don't come home."

"Don't worry, son. I'll ride on over to Station House Road and tell her."

"Thanks," Hap said in between yawns.

The deputy shrugged. The boy seemed more concerned about his mother than he did about himself. MacMillan knew that the sheriff would approve his arrest. He'd done his duty.

Hap smiled as the deputy closed the door. Jeb MacMillian had to be the tallest, skinniest man in Tarboro. His hawk nose and sunken cheeks made him look like a starving man. Only a smile or a plug of tobacco plumped his face. But the smile told the story. He was a gentle man. It was hard for Hap to think of him being the law to haul in criminals, but, heck, Tarboro didn't have that many. He'd been the most frequent occupant in the jail lately.

The young man settled down on his cot in the holding cell, propping his feet up with his hat cocked over his eyes. Why he thought of Rufus Knight he could not say, but he did. Maybe because he was another gentle spirit in Hap's life.

* * *

His relationship with the doctor at Penny Hill had begun when he was only four years old. It was the time Wendell Tyson brought his boy down the Tarboro highway to live with Willie Pridgen. They had stopped at Dr. Knight's office when Hap complained of a stomach ache.

Hearing the story of the boy's new life, Dr. Knight had peered over his glasses at Wendell. He never said a word, but Wendell could hear the ominous question in his head: *How would you like to be put in a strange place, even if it was with Willie?*

Wendell squirmed under the close scrutiny of the giant of a fellow, but Rufus Knight had softened, pulling the little tyke up on his ample knee.

"Just think of it this way, Hap. You're going on a new adventure. You'll be in a brand, new place with your Willie. She's waiting for you, just you, to be her boy. I think you're a fortunate young man. Does your tummy feel any better?"

He'd jostled him around, rubbing the youngster's belly.

"Yes sir, a little bit. Can we come see you sometime? Willie and me?"

"Oh, yes, and when I'm in Tarboro, I'll come down Station

Chapter 15

House Road for a visit. Would you like that?"

"Yes, sir!" Hap's crooked smile covered his face.

* * *

The town quieted outside the jail, the only sound from the occasional barking by a dog in the distance. Hap drifted and dreamed Willie's words of worry. He'd heard them a million times.

For many months, life had progressed smoothly for Willie and her new charge, but the first time she'd shown firmness with Hap, some time ago, she'd sent him to his room for punishment. Little fellow that he was, he did not hesitate a second to climb out the bedroom window and march down Station House Road. He'd turned toward Shiloh, but had gone only a short distance when he spotted the kindly old doctor in his buggy. Rufus Knight was making his way to deliver Amos Britt's fourth child. He had no time to spare, but he hoisted Hap into his buggy and took him along. The Britts' house sat at the end of a lane not too far from Station House Road.

As they rode, the physician asked the youngster, "Son, where were you going this bright, early morning?"

"Willie was mean to me, sir, so I was coming to live with you."

"Me?" His eyebrows shot upward, before he stifled a chortle. "Why, Hap? Why would you do that? I got no wife to look after either one of us. You got Willie all to yourself, just you and you alone. Didn't I tell you how fortunate you are?"

"Oh, you got nobody to take care of you? Maybe Willie and me can do that. Yes, I know she would. Please, can we? I promise I'll be very good."

Smothering his laughter, the old gentleman spoke as seriously as he could, "Hap, I have to travel around and doctor my patients, and you'll have to go to school one day. You can learn many things with me, but, listen, son, you can learn many more in school. You have to decide what you want to be when you grow up."

"Can I be a doctor like you, sir?"

"Hmm, maybe, but first you have to live with Willie, mind her, and go to school. Promise? Cross your heart, now, so I know you really mean it."

Hap followed his instructions in fast order as he had with Willie.

"Ahh, that's just fine, my little friend," he said, patting Hap's hand and hoping Willie was not in too much of a dither. He'd do his best to get him back before too long. His eyes rolled heavenward.

Please let this be a quick one, he prayed.

By mid-morning a frantic Willie had ridden to Shiloh. She stood in the kitchen, watching Elijah sip a last cup of coffee. Willie had grown up on Shiloh and felt free to ask Elijah's advice about Hap or anything. The elder Cromwell had freed her parents, but, along with other former slaves, they had remained to work the fields on the plantation. Now, with no family left, Willie felt those who lived at Shiloh were as much her family as any. In fact, she considered Elijah her oldest and dearest friend.

"We had a tiff. That scamp went right out his window and scooted. Maggie said there was no way he could've gotten past Shiloh. She's been sweeping and cleaning the porches all morning. He couldn't have walked this far anyway. Oh, Captain, what am I going to do? He's only four."

"Shush, Willie. I'm sure he's fine. Let me get my horse saddled and we'll head out. Just give me a minute," he'd said over his shoulder as he headed to the back door. "Meet me out front."

Elijah's assurance was comforting, but she still was worried. Would everything be fine? The child had to be between Shiloh and the bridge. She'd just missed him.

Willie sneaked looks at Elijah as they rode. If the situation were not so troubling, she could have enjoyed herself with her old

CHAPTER 15

friend, but she felt helpless knowing that Hap could be anywhere. He'd been gone for hours.

The sweat had begun to stand on her brow and drip down her face.

"Here, mop your face. It's a hot one," he offered, handing her his handkerchief.

Suddenly, they looked in the distance and spied Dr. Knight standing up in his carriage, waving at them. A small passenger at his side waved, too.

"Willie, Willie, I helped deliver a baby," Hap hollered.

Willie could not hear a word, but when she got close enough, she'd jumped from her horse, grabbed Hap and clung to him as if he were truly her own flesh and blood. His face beamed.

She really loves me. Maybe she forgot how I disobeyed her, he hoped.

Not for long, for she let out a stream of angry words that brought tears to his eyes. She put him down in front of her with her hands placed squarely on his slight shoulders.

"Thomas Rolland Tyson, you cannot run away like this ever again. You scared your Willie, and Mister Elijah, too."

Hap's head remained down; his jaw tensed; his mouth quivered.

"Talk it out with me. Whatever it is, we can figure it all out. You do not have to...run...from me. I love you, Hap. I do."

She dropped to her knees and tilted his head up to her. Slowly, she hugged him again. He'd been confused, but he began to understand. She did love him and wanted to care for him, but he would have to mind her for his own safety and her peace of mind.

Hap looked up at the kindly doctor.

"Thank you again, Dr. Knight. I liked helping you deliver Mrs. Britt's baby. That was fun."

"What? Did I hear right?"

Willie gawked at the doctor as she stood.

"Hap Tyson helped deliver a *baby*!"

"I'll say he did. He sneaked into the delivery room just in time."

"Willie, Willie, I saw life begin and I squealed almost as loud as the baby."

Everybody had laughed, even the new mother who'd whispered fondly to the doctor, "Rufus, you may have a new assistant in that boy."

Chapter 16
The Decision

*R*ufus Knight sat in his office at Penny Hill and thought hard about Hap. In frustration, he remembered from years earlier the independent little four-year-old who'd marched down the road, looking for him. The rumors about the boy puzzled him. If true, what had happened to Hap to make him go on these wild streaks? He wanted to kick himself for not having reached out more, but he was one of only three doctors in the county, and his workload was so heavy. The past was done. What could he do now?

"Please come, boy. Just come," he murmured to himself. He had no more thought it when he looked up and saw the strapping young man standing in the doorway of his office. The remaining streaks of light sinking into the Tar River across the road darkened his figure. Rufus walked slowly to the door and grasped Hap's hand.

"You got my letter?" he asked, and Hap nodded. "I'm so glad you came, son. Come, come, sit down here and tell me what's going on. I've been so worried."

Hap looked at the door.

"Any more patients?"

"No, no. I'm free. Just tell me everything."

Hap looked into that gentle, old face and said, "I love someone I can't have, Rufus."

"And who is this young lady?"

"Caroline Cromwell."

"Oh..." Rufus winced.

"You see what I mean? I'm a poor mutt from Station House

Road. You think Captain Elijah Cromwell would let me come calling on his daughter? Me—the meanest scoundrel in all of Edgecombe County? Huh? Do you?"

"Well, son, I can say this. You aimed mighty high."

"She fancies me, Rufus. I know she does. We've been secretly meeting on Shiloh."

"Whoa. You've been sneaking over onto the Captain's land to see his daughter?"

"Yes."

"Oh my, this is serious."

"Rufus, I've decided to break it off. Our lives are just too different."

"I understand. Go on."

"Well, we met, as we have many times, in this grassy place down on the lower 40. I just told her that she'd messed up my head and that we were never going anywhere. Damn, Rufus, we both cried and I grabbed her and kissed her." Hap looked down and scuffed the floor with his boot. "Then I ran."

He shrugged.

Not once in his early married life did the doctor's dear wife bear a child, but if Rufus could choose, there was no question in his head or heart that he would have chosen this young man who stood before him. He loved him without even understanding why. He thought maybe just the capacity to love or the need for love is a combination that cannot resist either way when marked by the Divine. The doctor stood and drew Hap to him and bear-hugged him.

He pushed him away at arm's length, stared him in the eye, and declared, "We will find a solution, Hap. Just give me some time to think these things through," he told the troubled young man. "But you have to remember that you are not alone," he said, squeezing the boy's arms. "Go now."

Hap moved toward the door, but he turned back toward his

CHAPTER 16

friend as he stood on the porch and said, "Wendell Tyson may have sired me, but you are as much a father to me as I have ever had."

With those words, he swung up in the saddle, waved, and headed back the few miles to where Willie would be waiting. Now he would tell her. Willie deserved to know everything.

* * *

On Station House Road, Willie paced until she thought her shoe soles would wear through.

"I gotta go see a friend, Willie, about something personal. I'll be back soon," he had said.

His comment disturbed her. Where did he go? What friend? And, how long was soon? An hour? Two? Or three? *God, help me with this boy... no, this young man. Give me the wisdom he needs to hear.* She heard hooves on the road. At the screen door, she paused to watch her adopted son ride toward her, ready to disclose either heartbreak or good news.

Pushing the door open, she forced a feeble smile. He dismounted, propping his foot on the lower step.

"We have to talk."

His face was troubled and serious. Her heart sank.

He climbed the rest of the steps and held the door open for her. Walking straight to her rocking chair, she tapped her foot ever so slightly and waited to hear her son speak.

"I'm in love with Caroline Cromwell," he declared as if he'd just told her the price of lumber in Wilson. He shared everything that he'd told Rufus Knight and reassured her that he'd relayed his story to the good doctor first, only because Rufus had asked him.

"Willie, I'm so sorry for all the misery I've caused you. I know you've suffered."

He paused briefly. She continued to stare.

"Remember when you talked to me about pain pushing me

toward a new path?"

She nodded.

"Well, it's time. I—I've just got to make new choices for myself." He fidgeted with his shirt sleeve. "I need to say goodbye to Caroline. Maybe I can get a fresh start in Pitt County. Pap's still there."

Hap watched her as she rocked, staring emptily at him. *Lord, what is she thinking?* he wondered. *She appears so far off.*

Actually, her mind was just a few miles away...at Shiloh. How strange that her life and that of her son had become intertwined with two impossible dreams involving the same family, in the same household. She knew that she had loved Elijah Cromwell, her old friend, all her life, despite the vast differences in who they were. She knew the torment that she'd suffered all these years, and she certainly hoped that Hap could escape that same heart-wrenching agony of never being able to fulfill his deepest desire. However, the consequence of his words hit her squarely in the face. Hap would be leaving not only Caroline, but her. Her head jerked back in the rocker and her eyes widened with disbelief and then with anguish. She screamed "No," over and over, until he knelt and awkwardly put his arms around her.

Willie's most devastating thought was the loss of one more person she loved. She'd already given away her only child. *How can I survive any more losses like that? How can I? How?* She began to sniffle and tears brimmed her eyes.

"I-I-I can't lose you," she said softly.

"You won't, Willie. I'm your son."

Remorse engulfed him. All he could do was hold her and rock the chair to soothe her hurt.

An hour slipped by; Willie and Hap were each lost in their own thoughts. Willie stirred and seemed to wake up. She ran her fingers through his shock of hair. By then he was seated at her feet with his head resting on her knees. He lifted his head to smile

Chapter 16

faintly at her. The bonding between them seemed greater than ever before. This truth would be the balm that would continue to heal.

"I have to see her," he declared. "I have to tell her goodbye."

"Yes, you do, son."

Chapter 17
The Reunion

Caroline studied the piece of mail with curiosity. She had no idea whose hand had scrawled her name. Shrugging, she tucked the letter into her pocket and would open it later, in private.

Michael Collins waited anxiously to begin the lesson, but during a break, she fingered the note. Tapping it on her thumbnail, she turned it over and broke the seal. Her eyes flew to the signature. She gasped.

Michael whirled, totally unnerved to see a smile that he wanted only for himself. He stared at the note she was holding. Something from Litch Bagley? His heart pounded.

Rejuvenated by this unexpected message, Caroline streaked through the rest of her studies. Her tutor had never seen such eagerness and response to all of his challenges.

"Miss Caroline, I must plead to stop. I have a headache. The throbbing just won't quit," he told her as he touched his temple. "I think I must call it a day."

"Of course, Mister Collins. Please do take care of yourself." She slammed her books shut, stood, and seemed ready for him to leave.

Taken aback by her curtness, he gathered his books and excused himself. *What was in the note, and who was it from?* he wondered. He rode dejectedly from the house to the edge of the small grove that contained the family cemetery, but he reined abruptly at the stir behind Cromwell Hall. To his surprise, he saw Caroline race to the stables, and in minutes Nellie kicked up dust as she rode into the fields, heading toward the lower 40.

Chapter 17

Remembering the day they found the creepy-crawlies, he wondered if she was going to the grassy area. How many times had she raved about that haven for thought or escape from her mother? *I wonder...*

As Caroline urged Nellie down the trail, Hap's scrawled note burned in her mind. His wanting her to come to the lower 40 must be important. It took nerve for him to write her at Shiloh. Not once did she think any pain or agony would come out of their meeting. She could only think of their last encounter and the passionate kiss, not the fact that he'd dismissed their relationship. Surely, he'd changed his mind. She knew that he had a plan.

At that same moment, George Edmundson spied Caroline streaking toward the lower 40. *Oh, for God's sakes. Where is that child going?* Out of curiosity, he slipped down the opposite side of the planted fields to circle around the backside of the grassy place. Why he did this would puzzle him the rest of his life.

* * *

Hap waited for her, just as he had countless times before. He sat on the fallen log, bent over with his elbows resting on his knees. He reached down to pull a long shoot of grass and chew on the end of it, hoping that this simple act could bring him the wisdom needed to get through the situation. Hearing Nellie's hooves, he strained to glimpse Caroline. His palms were wet, as was his brow. Wiping both with his handkerchief, he stood up, his chest heaving, and waited.

Riding full speed into the haven, Caroline reined Nellie hard enough that she reared. Not even waiting for help, she dismounted, marched over to him, and gave him a command. His mouth dropped open.

"Sit down on that log, Hap Tyson. Now," she said in a shrill voice.

Stupefied, he did as he was told, and as quickly as one could move, she stood before him, pulled back his head and kissed him with the passion he'd displayed earlier. The roughness turned to sweetness, just as before, only with it came her turn to give him the sensation of both. His arms gently enfolded her, and as he drew her down into his lap, his lips never parted from hers.

Finally, she pulled her head back and laid it on his chest and nestled in his arms. He could say nothing. Once more she'd totally disarmed him. All he could do was rock slowly. Love overtook the pain in his chest, as he savored that moment.

"I've missed you, Hap," she whispered against his chest.

Reality jolted him back to his task, but could he not wait until another time and not ruin the sweetness he'd just shared with her? *God, help me. I just can't do it now. I can't!* Hap released her, and they sat side by side on the log. He listened to her experiences of vacation. As she assured him how much he would have loved doing all that she had done on the Outer Banks, she was unaware that she was sealing his decision. They were indeed from two different worlds, with no hope of ever going beyond these few stolen moments in the lower 40. He smiled at her and loved her through every word she spoke. She held his hand and periodically squeezed it for encouragement. *Who is Litch Bagley?* he wondered. *She's mentioned him over and over. Maybe he'd suit her better?*

They stood. He towered over her and marveled how such a small person could be filled with such strength and determination. He knew he would do anything, anything for her. She slipped her arms around his waist and buried her face in his chest once more. Her golden hair rested under his chin. He bent his head and buried his face in her curls and breathed in her perfume. Placing his hands on her shoulders, he timidly pushed her away and stepped backwards. He put his hands in his back pockets and stared down at the ground.

"I love you, Hap Tyson," she said softly.

Chapter 17

He wanted to swing her up in the air in joy, but he could not. He turned his head sideways and looked at her with his crooked smile.

"That's the best gift a man could ever receive," he whispered. "I, I'll see you sometime," he stammered. "Not soon, but sometime."

Backing up as he stumbled over these words, he turned to run toward the creek and through the woods, the way back to Station House Road and Willie's house. He hadn't said that he loved her, but in the last moments, before he went out of sight, he turned to see her still standing by the log, looking and waiting for him to say what he could not say, looking and waiting for her to hear and know. Then he shouted to her.

"I love you, too, Caroline Cromwell!"

He waved and disappeared.

She jumped up and down excitedly and returned each of his waves. Her face was flushed with happiness as she mounted Nellie and rode toward the plantation house.

At that same instant, Michael Collins stumbled away from his spying and retched behind a shrub. He never knew he had so little control over his emotions. He could not learn everything in a book, not the feelings of the heart anyway. He had no idea who this young man was with whom Caroline showed such familiarity.

The young tutor thought his rival was Litch Bagley, who by now was up at the University in Chapel Hill with Will Cromwell. Michael Collins thought he had in his favor the fact that Litch was out of sight, but this strange young man was definitely not out of sight. He'd seen her kiss this boy with the passion of someone in love, as much in love as he was with her. He retched again. Somehow, he had to get back to his quarters without anyone seeing him. How could he face Caroline while knowing about her secret meeting and her declaration of love for this other young man? He needed time to recover and think.

From another vantage point, George Edmundson shook his head in disbelief. He'd seen them before, but he had assumed their meeting was by accident or was just a lark. Things had gotten even worse than he'd ever imagined. She was in love with this scoundrel. He could not imagine how this could happen, what with all the privileges and opportunities she had. Although he'd been hiding, he was close enough to hear her words: "I love you, Hap Tyson." His face screwed up in the realization that this was serious. Heaven help this family.

Chapter 18
THE VOYAGE

It was so easy. The words whirled in Michael Collins' head. He had convinced Caroline's parents and even the invincible Coeffield King, her grandfather, the most noted judicator in all of down east, that a European excursion was the perfect way to extend her education. Yes, extending her education in Europe was the key move. With a silver tongue, the tutor had weaved a magnificent, fantastical excursion that no one, not even Coeffield King, could deny his granddaughter. And, he, Michael Collins, had pulled off the coup. He had never been happier or more confident. He would have the young mistress of Cromwell Hall all to himself. On this trip, he would surely erase any doubt that Caroline Cromwell would be his wife upon their return. Of this he was certain. No more Litch Bagley or Hap Tyson! The man was jubilant. Thanks to Elijah, Miss Penelope Cromwell, a great aunt, would accompany Caroline. With no family obligations to tie her down, the plump old maid appeared the perfect choice. Eager to return to Europe, she accepted the invitation without hesitation, not to mention that she adored her nephew's only daughter. The Cromwells knew it was a good choice.

During summer visits, Michael had taught Caroline basic elements of conversation and phrases that she would likely use when they ventured across the English Channel to France. As the time for departure drew nearer, Caroline looked into her bedroom mirror daily and repeated the phrases. "Comment vous-appellez-vous, Monsieur? Moi? Je m'appelle, Caroline."

The greater concern, however, were two yawning trunks on the floor.

"Could I possibly wear *all* of these clothes?"

Maggie shook her head and folded another blouse.

Caroline appeared ready to embrace the voyage with vigor and to absorb everything she could to share with her beloved grandfather, as well as with her parents and her brother.

* * *

Boarding the ship in the New York harbor invigorated each voyager. Michael had sailed across once; Miss Penny, three times; Caroline, never. Each had a sense of excitement; each had a different agenda.

"Miss Caroline, I can't wait for you to see all these famous places. You can read about them in books, but it's not like seeing them in person."

"And, Caroline, dear, crossing the ocean will be such an adventure," Miss Penny added. "You'll see dolphins and whales and even sea turtles in the water."

"Just think of all I'll be able to tell Coffie and the family when we get back."

The threesome leaned over the railing, waving at the crowds below on the dock as their ship moved slowly from the harbor.

"I can't believe we're really going to be out on the Atlantic Ocean," Caroline said. "It will seem so different from the ocean we see when we are at the beach."

"Yes, my dear, and you will see plenty of it for the next ten days," Miss Penny said.

"Why don't we sit in these deck chairs for a while?" Michael suggested.

"No way, Mister Collins, I have to explore this entire ship," Caroline spoke out. "Aunt Penny, will you come?"

"No, dear, I'm going to do what Mister Collins suggested. I'll be right here when you get back."

She smiled as she watched the two young people walk away. What a nice young man, she thought, and then she busied herself

Chapter 18

with meeting the couple who had sat down beside her.

Caroline's initial excitement wore off, however, as she felt the deep vibrations of the ship's engines and gentle surges of the water. They had not gone very far from the pier; although the New York skyline was no longer in view.

"Mister Collins, I don't feel well," Caroline said, holding on to the back of a lounge chair. They had been strolling and watching for sea creatures for over an hour. The swells had increased, making it more difficult to walk without assistance. Michael had relished giving her his arm, but the more they walked, the more he noticed the pallor of her face.

"Miss Caroline, shall we sit? Maybe some refreshment," he said, looking around for a steward.

"No, Mister Collins, I am going to be sick and right now."

Her eyes grew bigger as her head swayed. Volunteering his handkerchief, he watched her make an ungraceful dash to the side of the ship.

"Throw the handkerchief overboard. I have plenty packed up," he shouted.

They both stared as the bit of fabric fluttered in the breeze and disappeared into the water.

Her stateroom became home for the next few days.

* * *

With Caroline fighting off seasickness, the forlorn young tutor learned volumes about Miss Penny, but the anticipation of *terra firma* kept his spirits high. Unable to bear her absence any longer, Michael slipped away and knocked lightly on her door. He had not seen her topside for two days. Hearing a slight stir inside, he watched the door crack open. Even in her state of disarray, she choked the breath from him. How he could keep his balance and his sanity around her, he did not know.

"How do you feel today, Miss Caroline? Maybe a stroll up on deck to get some air?"

"Wait a moment. I don't feel quite as terrible, but I've got to try it."

Not thinking to fasten the door, she went to her bureau and dragged out clothes with abandon. Finally making a selection, the young woman disappeared behind her dressing screen, shed her clothes, and haphazardly threw them over the screen and onto the floor, startling the young man standing in the doorway. He could not even turn away. She mesmerized him. Coming from behind the screen, she marched to the door with resolve.

"Well, here goes."

To their surprise, her discomfort was nearly over. No longer did her brain tell her that she was going in different directions at the same time. No longer did her eyes tell her that she was standing still. The slight rise and fall of the ship did not seem to affect her anymore. She did not know what changed, nor did she care. She was no longer seasick.

On the tenth day, the ship docked in Liverpool where a coach drove them toward London. Castles and cottages dotted both sides of the roadway.

At noon, they stopped at the Sow's Ear Inn for lunch.

"Where are you off to, missy?" the owner asked, as he directed them into the quaint dining room with its heavy oak tables and chairs. Clusters of daisies nestled in the center of each table.

"London, sir."

"Ah, of course, to see the Tower and Buckingham Palace, I'll wager," he said, to which she shrugged.

"What's Yorkshire pudding, Aunt Penny?" Caroline asked as she looked at the menu.

"It's a type of bread, darling. Usually, they use the drippings from a roast to give it flavor. I'm sure they'll serve us some."

"I like mutton," Michael said.

"And, it's the specialty of the house. May I bring three servings?" the owner asked, looking at each of his visitors. Three

Chapter 18

heads nodded.

"May I suggest our trifle for dessert?"

"Trifle? That doesn't sound very good," Caroline said.

"Ah, but you've not had my wife's. She soaks sponge cake in Madeira wine and layers it with custard, jam, and fruits. For her final touch, she crowns it with huge dollops of whipped cream."

"My heavens, I'll never be able to get up from the table," Miss Penny said, as she sat back in her chair, fanning herself with her lace glove.

* * *

London seemed both formal and exciting, with many people on the sidewalks, the air filled with loud shouts and a dazzling variety of activities to view. But to all three visitors, their hotel was absolutely perfect, an oasis of calm and gentility, tucked away on a quiet side street.

Michael knocked on the ladies' door at 4 o'clock that afternoon, suggesting that they take an afternoon tea.

"Tea? Gracious, I have not recovered from lunch," Miss Penny said. "You two run along and have your tea and crumpets. I need rest before supper."

More than once during their London visit, Miss Penny remained in her room or in the hotel lobby and allowed the young people time to explore the city on their own, but two places Miss Penny insisted they see together, London Bridge and the Kensington Gardens.

"In all my travels, I've never seen any more breathtaking gardens than these with their formal avenues and, my favorite, a sunken Dutch garden."

"Will we see tulips?" Caroline asked.

"No, darling, they're not in bloom now, but they'll have something blooming. I promise. By the way, the gardens were cultivated for Queen Caroline over 150 years ago. How about that, dear?"

"Queen Caroline?" she said, turning toward Michael with a smile and raised eyebrows.

Michael was grateful when Miss Penny gave him opportunities to endear himself to Caroline. His feelings were strong enough that he knew he would have to share his affection and soon, or die.

Maybe in France? His mind whirled.

Chapter 19
La Belle France

"Tell me more about France, Mister Collins," Caroline spoke, as they stood on the deck of the small boat, sailing them across the English Channel.

"Well, did you know this country is the shape of a hexagon?" he asked.

"A six-sided country?"

"You've seen Texas on a map and how big it seems compared to the other states. France is smaller than Texas, but almost four times bigger than North Carolina. And the mountains, the countryside, the castles... It'll take your breath away."

As he continued to describe the country, her excitement increased. With each word, he moved closer until his last statement was almost whispered in her ear. Not even realizing his gradual advances, she bounded from her seat and twirled around toward him.

"Oh, Mister Collins, the family and especially my grandfather will love hearing all these experiences. They will be ever so grateful for your idea of this trip. How can we ever thank you?"

Michael grinned broadly but said nothing.

The little channel boat landed in Le Havre, and the three visitors took a coach to Paris, the city that invariably captured the hearts of all who dared to embrace her charm and beauty.

Ah...la belle France. Michael's own excitement intensified.

"Aunt Penny, can you believe we're in Paris?" Caroline turned to her great aunt in delight as their coach stopped in front of their hotel, a small three-story building, covered in fretwork, just a few blocks away from the Place de la Concorde, a focal point of the inner city. As they dined that night at their hotel, Michael plotted their course for the next two weeks with ideas that left his companions breathless. Once more, he hoped that Miss Penny's ample girth might limit her ability to join in many of the excursions. He was right.

"My goodness, Mister Collins, you and Caroline will have to excuse me today," she would say. "My rheumatism is kicking up. You young people go right on with your plans and I will have dinner with you two tonight. Please. Please. Don't worry about me. I'll be just fine."

With as much concern as he could muster, Michael would hold Miss Penny's hand and assure her that they could rest and retire at the hotel, just as she was. More than once, however, she would hustle them off on their outings.

"Tosh, tosh," Miss Penny would respond. "You cannot miss out on such wonderful experiences. Remember, Caroline, your family will want to hear all about it."

Of course, Michael knew she would insist that they go ahead with his plans.

At the supper table one evening, Michael proposed a trip to Versailles.

"Miss Caroline, it's time. I've saved the best for last. We've seen the Notre Dame–"

"Yes, with its spires and gallery of kings."

"Uh, yes. And the Louvre–"

"Yes, with Mona Lisa's wonderful smile."

"Uh, yes. And Les Invalides–"

"With Napoleon's tomb."

"Now, does this mean that you are going to recall every shop you saw on the Champs Elysees?" he laughed.

"Non, mon professeur," she laughed back.

"Well, I will not name the other sites, or you will never hear

Chapter 19

my plan for us tomorrow. We are going to take that train ride I promised you to the most beautiful of all palaces. Louis XIV spent a fortune there, but unfortunately all at the expense of his people. It's a miracle that it's been saved. The art's incredible. The sculpture's incredible. The gardens? Breathtaking." He turned toward Miss Penny. "Now, Miss Penny–"

She had already raised her hand in decline. "You'll have to take this trip without me, I'm afraid. My, my, you've had such an ambitious agenda."

Once more he grinned like a Cheshire cat.

Chapter 20
THE PALACE

"Versailles," Caroline murmured. The French word rolled off her tongue, as she and Michael ate breakfast their last full day in Paris. "Yes, I want to see the beauty and splendor of it all, especially the Hall of Mirrors."

"We'll leave this morning at 10 o'clock," Michael said. "The concierge says the train ride's only twelve miles, so it should take us less than an hour. We'll lunch early and tour the palace."

Pushing a lock of hair from his forehead, he continued, "Then, on to the gardens. I'd say the return trip will have us back at our hotel by 6 o'clock." His voice dropped. "I'm sorry Miss Penny won't be with us to enjoy the palace, but she's visited it before." He wrinkled his nose. "We'll have much to fill her ear."

The train ride through the countryside from Paris to Versailles was picturesque and friendly. People waved from their farms and yards as the train chugged along making its way toward one of the wonders of the civilized world.

"Are you sure, Mister Collins?" She stared at him wide-eyed. "This palace started a war?"

"Absolutely. It was ridiculously expensive, and Louis XIV made it the seat of power and waged war on Spain within those very walls. Just a few years ago, it was headquarters for the German army during the Franco-Prussian War."

"Incredible that something so beautiful could be part of something so terrible."

Michael smiled. Somewhere on those grounds he would find a place, a perfect spot for refreshment, and then he would reveal his heart. He could wait no longer.

Chapter 20

* * *

Versailles exceeded all of Caroline's expectations. The Hall of Mirrors was her favorite, just as most felt who entered the palace. She and Michael clasped hands as the guide took them and others through the palace. To Caroline, clasped hands meant clasped spirits, but to Michael, it meant intimacy. He hardly saw the splendor of the palace for the splendor on the eager face of his pupil. *I have so much more to teach you,* he thought.

After the tour ended, their open carriage meandered through the gardens.

"Sir," Michael called to the driver, "pull over to that bench and pond, *s'il vous plaît*. We'd like to rest and enjoy some refreshment."

Wine and cheese nestled in a woven basket.

"Mister Collins, today has been incredible," Caroline said. "What a lovely spot to end our tour."

He helped her down from the carriage and watched her walk to a bench. Meanwhile, he pressed a coin in the driver's hand. The man winked and laughed as he clucked his horse to move away. Michael could make out *l'amour* through the driver's giggles. *Oh, yes, l'amour.* He turned to see Caroline waiting.

"Caroline, I've never seen you more beautiful." He dropped the *Miss,* as he sat down beside her. "Please, may I offer you some cheese with a little glass of this wine?"

She nodded, but she refused the wine.

"But we must celebrate such a wonderful day. Here, just a small glass," he coaxed, until she shyly accepted.

After one glass, she forgot herself, and a second glass generated laughter and an extra sparkle to her eye.

"Please forgive me, sir. I am not accustomed to wine."

Yes, I want you mellow and receptive to what I'm about to say.

"I have something to tell you. The time seems perfect, as well as the place."

He slipped his arm slowly around her shoulders and moved himself closer. Tipping her head back, she blinked to focus as he spoke to her.

"My dear, Caroline, we have had this wonderful excursion and seen the loveliest of sights of this entire world."

He picked her hand up and pressed it to his lips. He looked into her startled eyes.

"You must know how I feel about you. I find myself hopelessly bewitched by you," he said through a smile, playing with her fingers. "Upon our return, I wish to ask your father for your hand in marriage. I want you–" he breathed heavily, "–for my wife."

Before he could let her think through his words, he pulled her closer and kissed her firmly. She strained against him. Thinking only of returned passion, his arm slipped lower to her waist to gather her even closer. Then he felt her teeth sink into his lower lip, jolting him back to reality.

"What are you doing?" he cried out, grabbing his handkerchief. "You've drawn blood!"

Jumping to her feet, she glared at him as she found *her* tongue.

"You cannot be serious, Mister Collins. You are my teacher. My friend. My family's friend. I-I'm–why I'm flabbergasted." She shook her finger at him and continued, "And I'm embarrassed. What have I done to make you think that you could take these liberties? What? Sir? Please tell me what!"

As tears of anger stung her eyes, she paced before him and hurled more words at him, words that he would not forget.

"Ugh! How could you–how could you ruin this wonderful excursion?" she screamed, stamping her foot. "Tell me–did you plan this tactic from the first?"

Mortified, Michael cowered before her. How had this situation gotten so out of hand? His head spun. Surely, she must

Chapter 20

have known something of his feelings, unless he had totally misread her. He was older and should have been much wiser. Obviously, she still yearned for Hap Tyson, but he thought a different continent, a different atmosphere. And now she thought him repugnant and unconscionable. Damnation! He'd ruined everything. He'd been such a fool.

"I-I am so sorry," he muttered in despair. "I thought you knew how I felt. I've been foolish. Please, Caroline, forgive me. Please."

He gathered up his belongings.

The trip back to Paris proved extremely awkward. Both sat stiffly in silence, in seats opposite one another, lost in their own thoughts about their *situation*. He was correct–they arrived at the hotel at 6 o'clock, but Caroline had no intention of spending the evening with Michael Collins or Miss Penny. She begged off with a headache after such a tiring day, while he spent the dinner hour with Miss Penny, spinning visions of the palace's splendor.

"But, son, how did you hurt your lip? It's so puffy and purple."

"Oh, I'm fine, Miss Penny. I just cut it on a chipped wine glass," he assured her, shuddering at the untruths one had to tell to save face.

Chapter 21
DECLARATIONS

The staccato tapping on Michael's stateroom door jolted him upright in bed. They were at sea again, retracing their path westward across the Atlantic. Cracking his door, he gawked in surprise. Caroline stood there eyes cast down to the polished planks of the deck.

"Don't say a word," she said, raising her hand to him. "We must talk without Aunt Penny hearing any of our conversation. It's early, but I thought the decks might be relatively empty before our breakfast seating," she said as she finally looked up at him. "Meet me on the upper deck by the shuffleboards."

She turned on her heel and left him clutching his bedclothes as he peeked around his door.

Michael dressed quickly with one thought in mind: *Maybe she's going to forgive me.* He scrambled to the upper deck, only to see the lone figure, pushing the shuffleboard stick aimlessly across the marked boards.

"I'm here," he said weakly, hoping she could hear him above the sounds of the ocean. She turned toward him and motioned for them to sit in the chairs at the side. The wind swirled her unruly curls under a small scarf. It was moments before she spoke.

"Mister Collins, I am trying to comprehend your actions at Versailles, and I'm having a hard time. Maybe I'm too naive to go prancing across a continent with a man, even though adequately chaperoned, and not be aware of the man's secret intentions."

He nodded slightly as he looked toward the ocean and not at her.

Chapter 21

"I never dreamed you had these feelings for me, never, ever. Did I show such familiarity that would have given you any inkling that my feelings were the same as yours?"

He shook his head.

"No? Well, I hate to say it, Mister Collins, but they are not."

He winced.

"I find that what you did was a betrayal of friendship. You had no right to take advantage of me the way you did."

She folded her arms in front of her. The two young people were silent.

"However, I want you to know that I will say nothing of this to my parents or my grandfather. It is buried, Mister Collins, buried. The reason? I do not want anything to upset my parents or my grandfather, and if he found out about this, he would be truly upset with you. I'll tell them all that we had a charming excursion so I could extend my education and share everything I saw with them. Nothing more. Nothing less. Is that absolutely clear?"

His eyes closed.

"Very clear, Miss Caroline. Now, if you will, please excuse me? I don't think I'll make it to our breakfast seating. Express my regrets to Miss Penny," he barely whispered as he stumbled down the deck to the stairway. He hoped that he would not be too blinded by his emotion to clear the steps. Falling on his face was all he needed at this point. He'd lost her forever.

* * *

Upon her return, Caroline either stayed at Shiloh or at her grandfather's side. She declined trips to Mrs. DeBerry's with her mother and her friends. No way would she be in the same building with Michael upstairs in his room at Mrs. DeBerry's establishment. To Coffie's delight, his granddaughter shared entire days with him and even suggested that she move into his Tarboro house on the Town Common. She did not want him to have one lonely moment, not one. She loved him so, but she also could not stand the constant questions from her mother about the trip abroad and Michael Collins. Caroline would bite her tongue at the mention of his name. *If you only knew him and what happened.*

Chapter 22

A Happy Lot

*K*emp Battle was the president and administered a new beginning for the University of North Carolina. The school had shut down six years before because of financial difficulties. Since then, the Bagleys and others had been amazed how Battle pushed for state allocations and combed the countryside for donations from alumni and citizens. Battle was successful beyond most dreams, and North Carolina had a state university once again.

On this day early in the fall term, Litch Bagley lounged in his room in Old East, looking out his window, which picture-framed South Building. He knew he was fortunate to be at the university, even if he was the fourth generation who'd attended. And, if he ever had a son...

The knock at the door startled the young man. He jumped to answer it and found Will Cromwell standing on the threshold with the grin of a Cheshire cat. He pulled his friend forward, pumping his hand the whole way to the chair he offered.

"Tell me, what do you hear from home? I hope you've come to invite me to Shiloh for our holiday break," he said, smiling and thinking about the possibility of seeing Caroline again.

Will slowly pulled a letter from his breast pocket, held it between his thumb and forefinger, dangling it in front of Litch's nose. An impish grin spread across his face.

"What does it say, man?" Litch asked, eyeing the letter. "You're killing me."

"Well, my friend, Mother has worked out all the details of a Thanksgiving homecoming and insists that young Master Bagley accompany her son Will to Shiloh."

Litch leaped from his chair and slapped Will on the back.

"What great news! You and I are going to the Eagle Hotel for lunch, my treat."

They left his room and strolled arm in arm up Franklin Street.

Miss Hilliard's dining room was bustling as usual, and the two young men waited patiently on the porch. They romanticized about the upcoming vacation, complained about their studies, and talked about whatever came into their heads. They were a happy lot. Somehow the conversation touched on politics and one university scandal.

"Did you know former President Swain's daughter married a Union general? We heard about it up home from some former students here. In fact, Carson Thomas helped burn General Atkins and Mr. Swain in effigy. He even told my father that somebody had written on a blackboard in a classroom that the University had busted and gone to hell," Litch said.

"How did Miss Swain and the general fall in love? How did they even meet?" Will asked. "I mean, how did they find the time to be in each other's company long enough to get to know each other well enough?"

"The scuttlebutt is that the general paid a visit to Swain's house the April of Union occupation in '65, right before Appomattox. They met for the first time and it was love at first sight, or so we hear. I'm telling you the village tongues wagged. The two were married that August. Can you imagine, a romance between the North and South, and so soon? Maybe one of the few good things that came from that bloody mess. Well, man, tell me the plans for getting to Shiloh. Yee-ha!"

"Master Bagley, please," Miss Hilliard gave him a stern reprimand from the doorway as she stifled a giggle. She never could resist his charms, even if she was old enough to be his grandmother.

Chapter 22

"Why, Miss Hilliard, do I see a little grin creeping around that pretty mouth of yours? Yes, indeedy, it's there all right." Turning to Will, Litch asked, "Don't you see it, too, Master Cromwell?"

"Come along, boys, your table is waiting and so are those sweet potato biscuits."

Chapter 23
Homecoming

Thanksgiving break came with valises hastily packed, with train tickets hurriedly purchased. Traveling was not easy, but homecoming always made it worth the effort. Sarah Cromwell and Maggie had planned for weeks all the cooking and preparing of the house, from flowers in every room to student violinists for entertainment at the holiday feast. Mrs. Cromwell even worked her wiles on her high-strung daughter to keep the atmosphere between them pleasant enough.

However, Caroline paced Cromwell Hall with mixed emotions about Litch's impending visit, but what could she do without raising suspicions about Hap Tyson? Somehow, she would make it through. She'd not seen his distinctively crooked smile for weeks, but that seemed to be exactly what he wanted, not her.

I can wait, she thought.

Even Fate Edmundson was coming to help with the festivities. Sarah liked George and Maggie's adopted son and always admired his devotion toward Will over the years as they'd grown up together. One day he would take over when George slowed down. Sarah smiled as her plans jelled for this special day.

"They're coming up the drive, Miss Sarah," Maggie hollered as she looked through the lights to the right of the front door. She had cleaned those glass panes every day for a week now, and somehow there always was a fingerprint or a smudge. She, too, wanted perfection in the household, for Will Cromwell was the nicest young man and always treated her as respectfully as anybody had in her entire life. He was partly her child, as she saw it, watching him grow to manhood through all these years. When

Chapter 23

he had departed for the university, she had hidden her tears for Fate's loss as well as her own, but by this time, Fate was serious about his girlfriend, Shug Maples. To Maggie, it seemed that God had filled a gap left by Will's absence.

"Oh, he looks good, Miss Sarah," Maggie said over her shoulder as she pulled the heavy front door open with a big smile. She walked down the steps. "Welcome, Master Will. We're glad you're here."

"Maggie!" Will shouted from the carriage, "Hey, Litch, this lady is the best cook in Edgecombe County. I make a wager you'll gain at least five pounds this weekend."

He jumped down and nearly lifted her off the ground.

"Lord, can this be the child I put diapers on a few years back?"

Will's head popped backwards with laughter.

As he released Maggie, he spotted his mother, clinging to a porch column. Steeped with pride and joy for her son, she walked slowly down the steps where he met her at the bottom.

"Mother," he said quietly.

She tenderly put her arms around her firstborn, closed her eyes, and whispered, "Oh, son, I've missed you so. Yes, you will be in the mansion in Raleigh one day."

He always laughed at her comments about his being governor, but slowly, he began to see that she was serious. He shrugged at her, but secretly wondered if one day, he would not shrug at her suggestion.

Caroline watched from a second-floor window with a slight twinge of pain, but how could she be jealous of him? He *was* the nicest brother she could ever hope to have. In fact, Will was *wonderful*. All her life, he had given her surprises and loved her through many tough times and crises, especially with their mother.

She turned to face them all downstairs. Would this turn out to be disastrous or pleasant? She wondered which, as she came down the stairs to look into the eyes of Litch Bagley and her brother.

Litch drank in the sight of her. She was even more beautiful than he remembered. *God, keep my eyes in my head.* Rushing toward her, he reached for her hand at the bottom step and led her to the group under the entry hall's chandelier.

"Miss Sarah, I know where your daughter gets her beauty." He smiled, looking from one to the other.

"Litch Bagley, you would charm the spots off of a toad if you talked long enough," Sarah chided, but secretly, she relished every silvery word he spoke.

Caroline decided disaster, not pleasant, would be how the week would proceed. If he gushed over her like this every day, she would have to escape somehow to break this nonsense. She would find a way.

Laughing, Will whisked his sister away from Litch, whispering in her ear, "Oh, don't mind the fawning, dear one. You've got to get used to all this courtly talk. Why, soon the line of forlorn suitors will stretch from Tarboro to Shiloh." He squeezed her shoulder and winked.

She wanted to kick him in the shins, but how was he supposed to know that Hap Tyson laid claim to her heart? *How can life get so complicated*? she asked herself, as she grimaced teasingly at her brother's handsome face. She whispered back, "The girl who lands you, Will Cromwell, will get the best, I know that. Who will snare your heart, brother?"

He laughed and shook his head. "Hey, what are you two conspiring about?" Litch demanded as he hastened to catch up.

"Oh, nothing, friend, but it is time for us to see the grounds and land. Caroline, we'll meet you after we get settled and change clothes. Of course, Litch has to sample Maggie's delicacies, right, Sis?"

"Yes, I suppose," she sighed. Her eyebrows raised as her

Chapter 23

shoulders dropped.

"Suppose? After all I've heard? No, I demand a tasting."

* * *

"Maggie, if your sweets are indicative of the rest of your cooking, Master Will is absolutely correct in his evaluation of your skills." Litch tapped his midsection and announced, "Now, we must go exploring and work off some of this heavenly food."

"Pshaw, you two, go on. My head's gonna get too big for my Sunday hat. Git," she ordered as she took her broom and shooed them out the door.

"Where's Caroline, Will? She is coming with us, right?" he coaxed.

"Of course, Litch. Anything you wish, Litch," he teased back.

Caroline then appeared in her riding apparel. Soon the threesome was roaming the fields and timberland. Caroline and Will showed their visitor the creeks where fish were plentiful this time of year.

At every chance, Litch would wedge his mount in between the other two, forcing Will to drop back. As he trailed, Will hooted these brazen moves and thought to himself that Litch would mess up for sure if he kept up this kind of pressure. He knew his sister too well.

Chapter 24

Plans and Schemes

*M*eanwhile, Michael Collins brewed his own plans. He desperately needed Will's help to break this bonding between Hap and Caroline. But how? Honor in protecting Will's sibling? His family's name? Sarah's invitation for him to join a Cromwell family gathering had given him hope, and now he must devise a strategy, a scheme to make Caroline as miserable as she had made him on the European excursion. Oh yes, she must suffer.

The afternoon luncheon would arrive none too soon for the young tutor. He guessed that Will knew nothing about Caroline's encounters with Hap Tyson, but how could he speak with her brother about this delicate matter? He knew, for his own sake, that he had to disclose this secret as a way to improve his chances of breaking the bond between Caroline and Hap. The man grew desperate by the minute.

* * *

"You did what, Mother?" Caroline raised her voice a decibel the day before the family gathering.

"Surely, I told you, my dear. I thought it would be a wonderful gesture for us to thank Mister Collins for his suggesting and carrying through your excursion. Why are you troubled? I do not understand."

"W-well, Litch is here, a-and, oh never mind. That's fine."

But, the frown remained on her face. How she would get through this ordeal, she could not imagine, but one thing she knew, she would stick close to Litch Bagley.

As the door opened letting in the last guest for the luncheon,

Chapter 24

Caroline smiled through gritted teeth at her tutor in the entry of Cromwell Hall.

"Oh, Mister Collins, come meet Will's houseguest, Litch Bagley. They're both at the university. You will sit across from each other and have intellectual conversations."

The two men shook hands and exchanged pleasantries. She quickly took Litch's arm as he steered her toward the dining room. Michael did not know whether this young man also was smitten by Caroline, but as the luncheon began, Litch could have not been any more entertaining. He immediately began conversations that totally distracted the man from his worries. After the meal, the guests scattered, feigning overindulgence in Maggie's cooking. Michael found himself out in the side yard, sitting in garden chairs with Will and Litch. If he ever had a chance, now was the time.

"Have you heard anything lately about that scoundrel Hap Tyson?" Michael looked at Will. He broke a sweat, but gained courage by the moment. Will looked startled; Litch, puzzled.

"Who is this character? Hap who?" Litch asked.

"Sir, you know I've been away at school," Will replied. "Why would you mention him out of the blue? I find this rather odd."

"Just chit-chat. I see him around town some and just wondered when the last time the deputy jailed him for being drunk or caught him in a little lawbreaking." He wrinkled his nose as if the subject was disgusting. "I didn't know if your parents might have written you about any further mis-adventures he was involved in."

Will's memory was jogged enough to think of Willie Pridgen knocking on their door to ask his parents for advice on getting her son out of some scrap or other. He also remembered when his own sister defended Hap as they sat around the dining table. Strange how the presence of this n'er-do-well had arrived in his family's household...again. Strange, too, that Michael Collins, who had such close proximity to his sister, would bring Hap's presence to his own attention. Something weird was going on, and he intended to find out what.

"Didn't Hap Tyson attend Caroline's sixteenth birthday on the Commons that time and dance with her?" Michael asked. "I would not want such an unsavory character having anything to do with my sister."

Michael tried to weave the threads of doubt and suspicion as best he could without blurting out that he'd seen these two declaring their love for each other at the grassy haven right here on Shiloh.

"Mister Collins, I'm not sure what's going on. I know you wouldn't bring up this issue if you didn't have some notion behind it. What is it, sir? If my sister is in any danger or any trouble, I want to know."

Michael casually wiped his brow and then patted his palms dry with his handkerchief. He thought he had Will in the grip of anger and suspicion, as well as desire to protect his beloved sister.

"Well, if you must know, Master Cromwell, I think Caroline has encountered Hap Tyson on this plantation, right down there in that grassy area on the lower 40." He nodded toward the trail.

"How do you know this, sir?" Will practically choked on his words. His mind wanted to deny such a possibility, but he knew the independence of his sister. He also knew the compassion she had for those who had no privileges, and he especially knew the defiance she had exhibited in the past with their mother. If their mother had wanted her to marry Litch, or even Michael, Will knew his sister would fight to have the say-so for herself and not allow the decision to be maneuvered by anyone else, not even her mother. He felt rather embarrassed, because this contrived visit by Litch was one such maneuver in which he willingly had participated. He owed his sister an apology.

Looking up into Michael Collins' eyes, he recognized for the

Chapter 24

first time that this young man, and not just Litch, had feelings for his sister. How blind had he been? But he was certain that Michael Collins did not lie. If he said he saw Caroline with Hap Tyson, he did. If he'd heard of an encounter, then it had happened. He *was* her tutor.

"Thank you, Mister Collins. I'll speak to Caroline. This matter will be taken care of."

Looking toward the sky, Will spoke further to Michael.

"Dusk comes mighty fast. I suppose you and the rest of the guests need to be heading back to Tarboro. Thank you again, sir. I am sure I speak for Litch in that we have enjoyed your company. Right, Litch?"

"Right," Litch affirmed, stunned by the words spoken by Michael Collins. He was certain he detected in Michael a passion for Caroline and marked him as a rival for her affection. He felt immediate despair about the man who had Caroline's attention all during the week, and now another competitor, Hap Tyson, whoever he was. Litch could hardly contain himself until he and Will could be alone.

* * *

Will owed his friend an explanation for the bizarre conversation in the garden. As they sat in the plush, stuffed chairs in the guest bedroom, he tried his best to explain.

"Litch, I don't know where to begin, because without Caroline's explanation, I'm not even sure I understand what's going on."

"Who is this fellow Hap Tyson anyway?" Litch asked as they spoke in low tones.

"I really don't know, but he's always had the reputation of being a rogue, a mischief maker. He came to live with this woman on Station House Road as a child and just seems to have lived an unruly life ever since. Caroline had a birthday celebration on the Town Common last year and invited all the older young people to her party. Hap Tyson was there. He danced with her, but so did a lot of other fellows. I don't know...but all I do know is that Mister Collins would not lie. If he saw them together, they were. If he heard that they were together, they were. He's her tutor for God's sake."

"Listen, pal, you've got a situation here. If Caroline were my sister, I would make sure this scurrilous ingrate did not come within a country mile of her. I'm serious, Will. What are you going to do about him?"

"I'm not sure, but I do know that I have to talk to Caroline first."

"Why? Get hold of this guy now and set him straight."

"I—," Will stuttered.

"Look, buddy, we need action."

"We?" Will responded.

"Well, yeah. I hope I have an interest in this situation, Will. So, yeah. Let's find this character and give him the word."

"Litch, you are pushing me. I've never done anything like what you are suggesting."

"Listen, Will. Show some backbone! Don't you think the Captain would like to see his son belly up and give this jerk his comeuppance? And by the way, do you really, really trust this Collins fellow?" Litch's eyes narrowed as he leaned forward.

"Well, sure. He's Caroline's tutor."

"I know, but..."

Litch never finished his sentence. Both seemed to grasp the same fact about Michael Collins. He had more than an academic interest in Will's sister.

Chapter 25
FACE TO FACE

Caroline repelled the undue pressure from both Litch and her family. She could not believe how her mother and father assumed that Litch Bagley was her only serious suitor. They might have been playing the game in jest, but that made her furious that she could not breathe without Litch at her side. And, with this Mister Collins' issue, she would be forced to stay close by Litch to stave off any close encounter with her tutor. How could her parents be this heartless?

Days before, she had written to Hap and begged him to meet her at their secret place that very afternoon. The day seemed free from social obligations, with the young men staying in the house, reading novels from the Cromwell library and planning for the Christmas holidays. No one seemed to notice as she slipped from the main house and engaged Nellie for an afternoon ride.

Returning to his room, Will happened to see her leave through the open fields toward the lower 40. He suspected an escape from the family or a meeting with Hap Tyson. He winced at the thought. Whichever it was, now was the time to confront her. Litch had put the pressure on him about Hap Tyson, but when it came to Caroline, it was *I*, not *we*.

He quietly tiptoed down the stairs.

"Master Will?" Maggie called out from the kitchen.

He stopped, raising his finger to his mouth to shush her. He smiled and winked, as he gently closed the back door. In minutes, he was galloping toward his sister.

Up ahead Caroline found the grassy haven empty. She was disappointed and would just welcome Hap even more with this anguished waiting. Startled, she turned toward the main house. Surely, she could not be hearing the hoofbeats of another horse.

I will not hide. Absolutely not. Even Nellie stood in full view. But who would be coming down this far anyway, unless someone had seen her leave the main house?

Please, God, not Litch.

Her brother burst through the grove.

"Hello, little sister," Will said. He saw relief in her face as her hand flew to her chest.

"Oh, Will, it's you."

"I cannot believe this place."

He slid from his horse's back and tethered it to a nearby shrub. Putting his hands on his hips, he asked, "Why haven't you told me about this–this sanctuary? No wonder you come here." He walked toward her. "My word! These willow branches are fantastic."

Reaching out, he allowed the foliage to run through his fingers. Quickly, he ducked inside and poked his head out. "No raindrops can touch this head." She laughed at the silly expression on his face.

Finally, he quieted, slowly walking from the tree, and started one of the hardest conversations of his life.

"I saw you from my window and decided that we haven't had enough time together." He paused, "Why did you come alone, Caroline?"

"Oh, I don't know. Maybe the pressures from the family were getting a little too much for me."

She nervously looked over his shoulder across the creek toward the woods, thinking that Hap might stroll through at any minute.

My God, he's coming. She's looking for him now, he thought.

Faltering slightly, he reached for her small hand, putting it between his two, and spoke with as much compassion as he could,

Chapter 25

"Dear Caroline, I have to ask you a very private question. Consider your answer. Please. It's very important to me...and to our family."

He hesitated as he searched for the right words.

"Yes? What is it?"

"I hear that you've been seen with Hap Tyson on this very spot. Is it true?"

He felt her hand pulling away from his. "What about his reputation? People say he is the meanest scoundrel in Edgecombe County, which is most certainly not something we would want you to be associated with."

He waited. Her startled expression quickly turned to anger. *Oh God, it's worse than I thought. She's not denying it.*

"Will," she hissed.

"I'm sorry. Forget I asked." He raised his hands in denial and shook his head. "No, no," he murmured. "I'm not sorry. I care about you, Caroline, and I want the best for you. Can you honestly tell me Hap Tyson is the best for you? What opportunity can he offer you? A person like Litch can at least—"

He could not even finish before she screamed, covering her ears and wheeling around to lunge at him with both fists aimed at his chest.

"Will, how could you?"

"Wait, Caroline!" he barked as he caught her wrists.

At that instant, Hap entered the clearing after splashing across the creek. He saw Will holding Caroline's wrists. To him, her brother looked dangerously aggressive, but he did not know what was happening. By the time his long legs carried him over the creek and onto the grassy area, his own voice rang out.

"Hey!" he shouted.

Startled by the interruption, Will stood stunned, stunned by the sight of the angry young man flying through the air toward the two of them. Breaking Will's grip on his sister's wrists, Hap swung Caroline around behind him, crouching in a defensive stance. Will's hands shot up as a boxer's. Feeling the honor of his family at stake, *oh yes,* he would fight this scoundrel for his sister, face to face.

"Sir!" he hollered back, waggling his fists menacingly.

Regaining his senses, Hap put his palms up in front of him, shaking his head, and said, "Mister Will, no fight. We don't need to fight." He backed up.

But Will's pent-up instincts triggered, and no backing up or words could stop him. He swung wildly at first, missing Hap completely, but he quickly swung again and connected, sending Hap reeling with a perfect clip to the jaw. Caroline could do nothing but clasp her hands over her mouth in horror.

"Get up, you scoundrel!" Will growled.

Staring up at Will from the ground, Hap wiped the blood from the edge of his mouth and rose slowly, eyeing the young man standing over him. Once more, he put up both hands up and uttered, "I want no fight, man. Listen to me. Back off and talk. I got no quarrel with you." Never turning his head, Hap asked out of the side of his mouth, "Caroline, are you alright?"

She stood frozen, mute. Quickly, Hap glanced her way, allowing Will just a second to fling himself headlong into his midsection. Both tumbled, over and over as a single four-legged beast. Struggling to stand, each pulled the other upright, with Hap grabbing Will's wrists, as Will had done to Caroline. Will struggled helplessly, but then he kneed Hap's groin. The searing pain made Hap feel faint, but he was able to yell, provoking Caroline's hysterical screams.

"Stop! Stop! I can't stand it! Please, you've got to stop!" she shouted at them both.

As Will towered above Hap, he threatened more punches with clenched fists. Hap squatted in excruciating pain, trying to gain enough balance to stand. Swinging his arms, Hap raised up

Chapter 25

swiftly, never realizing his head would butt Will squarely under his chin. A well-placed boxer's punch could not have touched a more vulnerable point; Will staggered, with Hap never once using his fists.

Will lost consciousness while still on his feet and wobbled crazily with a dazed look on his face. As his eyes fluttered upward, he began to fall, neither pitching forward nor slumping down, as one probably would expect, but straight backward as a tree felled in the woods. His head and neck smacked squarely on the fallen log. Both Caroline and Hap heard the crack and saw his head jerk strangely to one side. Both winced in shock. Both tried to imagine the immense pain Will would have been feeling, but then, both realized Will Cromwell was not feeling anything. He was not breathing.

Chapter 26
WITNESS

*H*ap's chest heaved. Leaning over, his hands on his knees, he gasped for breath. His head swam from lack of oxygen. Every limb of his body ached with the pounding that Will had delivered.

Caroline had dropped to her knees, begging her brother to wake up, but he could not hear her and would not speak to her ever again. Will Cromwell was dead.

Suddenly, strong arms lifted Caroline to her feet. Looking up in a daze, she stared at George Edmundson.

"Miss Caroline! Miss Caroline!" He gently shook her. "I got to go get help. You stay here with Master Will. We'll get him to the doctor. Yessuh. Don't you fret none. Master Will will be all right, you hear?" he said, as he scrambled toward his horse. His face streamed with tears as he raced to the main house to tell the family.

* * *

Even though George was not that close, he had seen it all. He had followed them, hoping that he would find no trouble, but his doubts vanished when he saw the fight from start to finish. He had stood frozen back on the edge of the grove, afraid to interfere. Caroline's cries distressed George even more as he feared for her safety as well. And then the fall…

The wind and dust grated George's eyes, as he dug his heels in the sides of his horse.

"Oh, God in heaven, make Master Will be all right. He's just gotta be all right. Oh, please," George cried with each gallop to the house. "I can't be for sure if that boy hit Master Will. They

CHAPTER 26

sure were *rasling* mighty hard, but one thing is for sure, that scamp tried to stop him. But why did Master Will keep a-goin'? Why? Oh why?" he wailed to the air.

The closer George got to the house, the more he realized that another rider had been on that same road. Dust was settling before he stirred it up again. But who? Was someone else there?

At the back door of the main house, he dismounted on the run, meeting Maggie with a wild look on his face. "Maggie! Maggie!"

Her face dropped; her jaw clenched. "What's wrong, George?" she demanded. "Tell me what's wrong!"

"It's Master Will. He's down at the lower 40 out cold. He ain't moving, Maggie. He's hurt real bad."

Hearing the commotion, Sarah and Elijah rushed to the back of the house.

"It's Master Will, Captain." George crushed his hat as he sobbed.

Sarah crumpled. Elijah struggled to hold her, while talking to George.

"What happened?"

"They was fighting, and-"

"Who was fighting?"

"Will and Hap Tyson."

"What in God's name was he doing there? Where's Caroline?"

"Cap'n, she's with Master Will."

Elijah jerked around. "Maggie, stay with Sarah. George, get the wagon, get Fate, and anybody else you see to come help," Captain Cromwell barked his orders like a military man with a mission.

"Yessuh, Capt'n," George said, looking straight over the Captain's shoulder at Litch Bagley. *Was it you? Did you see, too?*

George turned to run for the barn, calling for his son.

"Fate? Fate?"

He entered the barn and saw his son at the other end. Slowly, he walked toward him.

"There's been an accident. It's Will, son. You gotta come help me." He grimaced. "I have to tell you it's bad, Fate. It's real bad."

"What happened?" Fate asked, plunging the pitchfork into a pile of hay. He walked to his father, his eyes widening with each stride.

"He-he may be dead." George winced at his own words.

This father had no time to be delicate with his son, no time to love him through bad news, no time to rock his boy to soothe the pain. George felt nauseated as he watched his son absorb the news that his best friend, his lifelong friend, might be dead.

Fate fell to his knees and sobbed openly, repeatedly throwing his head back and screaming, "No, not Will! Lord, not Will!" He fell forward, beating and scratching the dirt floor. "Oh noooo... Noooo," he howled.

"Fate, Fate. Stop, son. Will needs you. You gotta help me. I can't do this by myself."

Totally numbed, Fate lay still.

"Son?"

He twitched. Slowly he got up from the dust of the barn. With his tear-streaked face, he stood before his father and nodded. He wiped the wetness with his sleeve as best he could and dusted his clothes.

"You can weep later, son. We all will. Master Will needs us now."

Chapter 27
THE BLACK CLOUD

Hap Tyson felt as if that black cloud was sweeping over his head once again, the same cloud that seemed to have followed him his entire life, but this time he was genuinely afraid for his life. Will Cromwell was dead. By accident, not by intent, but nobody in all of Edgecombe County would believe him, the boy whom everyone blamed for everything that went wrong. He was in deep trouble. He looked at Caroline and rolled over, retching as privately as he could. Caroline's tear-stained face was buried in Will's hair.

Hap had not wanted to come that day, but her note sounded desperate and forlorn. He had thought today might be the time he could muster enough courage to let her go freely out of his life. Now, their fragile bond weakened because of tragic circumstances that both would relive the rest of their lives. A life had ended because of them.

The sound of horses' hooves pounded their way.

"Go before they come," she begged. "I'll tell them it was a terrible accident. You have to go. Please!"

Hap lost all sense of judgment. He knew he shouldn't leave her, but he feebly hoisted himself up and looked down at her. Both were resigned to the fact, despite this shared calamity, their growing friendship likely was broken, over. These new circumstances forced their feelings into the background. Hap struggled to the creek, turning to look at her once more. She was lost to him forever. Sobbing uncontrollably, he left their haven.

* * *.

Moments later, Fate burst into the grassy area. He jumped

from his horse and ran toward his friend, lying motionless in the clearing. When he got close, he tiptoed as if not to disturb him. Dropping to his knees, he looked into Caroline's face. Could they not just wake Will up from this sleep? But he knew better. Will Cromwell was dead.

Fate reached out and touched Will's face gently and sobbed once more. Maggie had always told him that weeping begins the process of healing. She also used to tell him that any wound "had to hurt real bad before it would feel any better."

Surely, he would feel this pain as long as he breathed.

The other riders halted the wagon at the woods edge, both silent the entire way, but no longer. George leaped down and knelt down by his son as he looked at the Captain's boy. He turned slowly to look at Elijah Cromwell, disbelief frozen on his face. How would they all endure?

The Captain's eyes darted around the haven as he walked, as if he were looking for answers and perspective on the scene before him. Elijah could not understand how such a thing could happen? He dropped down beside his son, his mouth gaping.

"Will? Will?" His voice rose. "Will, you get up, boy."

With no response, he reached over and gently shook his dead son. "Will."

"Father, Will's gone."

"No, not my son. He can't be. He-he-just–can't..."

Elijah's body shook. They'd all been happy just hours ago. Now, tragedy.

"George?" His voice cracked as he called to his friend.

"Yessuh, Cap'n."

"You and Fate help me pick up my boy and lay him in the wagon. Maggie gave me blankets."

He paused and then looked at Caroline sternly, "Where's that scoundrel, Hap Tyson? Where is he, Caroline?"

"He's not here, Poppa," she whispered. "It was an accident. I

Chapter 27

saw the whole thing."

"Fate, you go find that boy. He won't get away with this. He has to answer to Captain Elijah Cromwell, Willie or no Willie," he spoke in a fierce monotone. Fate did not have to ask what to do next, as Elijah nodded toward the creek. George's son leaped forward, spurred on by the Captain's words.

Chapter 28

PURSUIT

*H*ap's legs cramped, hardly able to bear the bulk of his body, but he knew that he must keep going. The sound of breaking tree limbs echoed behind. He would have to change direction and avoid Station House Road and Willie's shanty. Anyone would think to go there. Now, he needed a good friend, and he thought of Rufus Knight. He would go to Penny Hill. He was in deep trouble.

Branches and briars tore at his flesh as he stumbled through the underbrush. He had to cross the road without being seen and make his way to the doctor's office. God, he was exhausted, but knowing that somebody followed with fresh legs pumped his adrenaline. Who could it be? Not Elijah. He would be with his son. Not George. He was too old. In his mind, it had to be Fate. The sound of the snapping limbs suddenly faded, as his pursuer went crashing through the woods toward Willie's house. *Whoever it is, God protect her from his fury.*

Hap wished he could have explained to Willie about the horrible accident. He would have explained that he had not put one fist onto Will's body. *But why did he keep coming at me? Why?*

* * *

Fate, Will's best friend, went through the last tree line bordering Station House Road. He clung to a big oak and leaned briefly against the trunk to catch his breath before approaching Willie's house. His mind raced. Would Hap be inside with a rifle aimed where he stood at the woods' edge? He peered around the huge trunk, and to his amazement he saw Willie in her flower

Chapter 28

garden, singing at the top of her lungs. There was no way she could have heard him come through the undergrowth, but where was Hap? Fate could not leave Willie without asking.

Walking slowly around the tree, he crossed the road and moved toward this mother, who was so accustomed to hearing bad news about her boy. Now, he would bring her more bad news, maybe the worst she'd ever heard about Hap.

Willie felt his presence and slowly turned.

He was surprised by her expression. It was warm. Instantly, he felt uncomfortable, but then she gasped when she saw his torn flesh and drenched body.

"Fate," she whispered, "what has happened to you, son? Come in and let me wash your cuts."

"Miss Willie, I need to-"

"Fate, you're hurt. Now, shush. Let me help you."

He followed her into the cottage.

"Miss Willie, I can't stay. I-"

"Sit," she said, pointing to the chair as she rummaged for cloths.

She bathed and nursed his wounds with great care. He was confused by her tenderness. How could he avoid causing her pain? He was bringing her the worst possible news about her son.

Dropping his head, he winced as she cleaned his cuts. He'd been wild and careless as he'd run through the woods. Feeling stupid, he now realized the magnitude of his injuries, but his wounds were superfluous compared to Will's. Almost helpless, he looked up at Willie who had unconsciously reached out and touched his head. He had to ask the inevitable question.

"Where's Hap, Miss Willie?"

Her hand recoiled.

"Why do you ask such a thing?"

"He's done something terrible...again, Miss Willie," he stammered as he saw a frown cover her face and a shiver race through her body.

"What, Fate? You can tell me."

"He done killed Mistuh Will Cromwell, my best friend."

A little yelp was all Willie could muster as she fainted dead away. Fate scrambled from his chair and caught her as she grasped for the edge of the table. Now, it was his turn to nurse her; he picked her up and put her on the bed in the corner of the room.

"Miss Willie, you all right? Can I get you anything?" he asked when her eyes fluttered.

She could not look at him, shaking her head to his question and biting her knuckle to hold back her screams. As she thought of her beloved Elijah, a scream forced its way out, throwing years of pain to the corners of her house. She only screamed once, but a dazed look covered her face as she lay on her bed, shuddering. She closed her eyes.

My poor Elijah. You've lost your son, and now so have I. I can't even be there to comfort you. Oh, Hap, what happened? Where are you, son? God go with you now, for I am useless to you.

Quietly, Fate stood up, feeling stiff from his run through the woods. He realized that Willie could not help him at all. He wouldn't disturb her again. Somehow, he would figure out Hap's route. He gazed down Station House Road and knew someone in trouble would never go to the middle of Tarboro to hide from his crime. It had to be Bethel or Greenville. Only a few hours of light remained. He would have to move fast.

Chapter 29

THE RACE

For the first time, Hap Tyson tasted real fear. In the past, he felt nearly invincible in all his mischievous acts. The county sheriff and the deputy often said that if he were so bad, why was he always so easy to catch? Hap confessed to them his wrongdoings, but he stoutly denied all false accusations. The sheriff and the deputy had been around him so often that they had no problem believing him. They knew that the townspeople had to have a scapegoat for all their local ills, and Hap's living with Willie Pridgen made him an easy choice.

Hap could see the road through the last thicket of undergrowth. As best he could tell, no one had seen him. Now, the big test would be to get across the road and past Shiloh and remain unseen. The family graveyard would be a perfect place to reach, far enough from the main house and yet close enough to find a good hiding place behind the tall markers before running across the road. Yes, the angel markers would do just fine to provide cover.

He rubbed the sweat from his brow on the sleeve of his shirt, the part that the briars had not torn. The mansion rose in full view. His next moves would be the riskiest. Moving forward as stealthily as he could, he reached the graveyard. He leaned on the tallest monument and breathed heavily; he let his back slide down the cool Georgia marble. Hap tilted his head skyward and looked up into the face of a stone angel atop the tombstone, a statuary frozen in time. Yes, a frozen angel. Here he was, being protected by a community of frozen angels. Wouldn't the folks in Tarboro find that amusing, the meanest scoundrel in Edgecombe County, hanging onto the coattails of a bunch of angels?

Hap could rest no longer, but before he got up he looked around and wondered where Will Cromwell would be laid to rest. Shaking his head as if to clear his sorrow, he focused on only one thing, and that was his escape to Doctor Knight's office in Penny Hill. Adrenaline and fear empowered him to dash to the other side of the road to find shelter from the eyes of Cromwell Hall.

Chapter 30

THE GUEST

In all of Litch Bagley's twenty years, he had never faced the death of a close relative. Both sets of grandparents were still alive, as were all of his aunts, uncles and cousins. Now he was witnessing the most traumatic situation a family could possibly face, the loss of a child. *My God, I've lost a good friend. Maybe my future brother-in-law.* He bemoaned his own plight, for he'd even seen the end of the fatal scuffle.

Realizing that Will and Caroline were not in the house, Litch had gone to the barn.

"Both'em gone riding, suh," the stable boy said. "Can I saddle the roan for you?"

"Yes," Litch answered, guessing that the two had ridden to the lower 40.

He had come up to the sounds of Caroline's cries, only to see Hap Tyson and Will Cromwell tussling. In the next instance, he saw Will standing over Tyson, who raised up and chin-butted his friend, knocking him out on his feet. Will Cromwell fell, hitting his neck on the fallen log. He'd actually seen his friend die. Staggering backwards, Litch somehow pulled himself up on the roan and galloped as fast as he could back to the house, stunned at what he had seen and realized what this tragedy would do to this family. He thought of his own family and shuddered as he rode.

Leaving the roan tied up outside the barn, Litch slipped around to go in the front door of Cromwell Hall, praying no one would see him. The library door stood ajar, his chance to hopefully be alone and process what was about to explode and change life at Shiloh forever.

Noise from the back of the house brought Litch out of the library, only to see Elijah carrying Sarah up to their bedroom. The Captain rushed down the steps just as Litch got to the bottom, only to see a father's face in such agony that Litch could only gasp.

"Oh, Litch, there's been an accident. It's Will. Please stay by Sarah's room. Help her any way you can until I get back." The grip on Litch's arm spoke volumes of the tragedy waiting for the Captain on the lower 40.

"I promise, sir. I am so sorry," he managed to whisper.

* * *

Litch had sat outside Sarah's bedroom ever since Elijah had placed her on her bed. He felt helpless that he could do nothing for this woman. Retreating to his bedroom, Litch found a nap impossible. In frustration, he jumped from his chair and looked out the window just as Hap Tyson slipped into the woods across from Shiloh. His head jerked forward; his eyes squinted. Had he really seen someone disappearing into the underbrush, or was he just hoping that it was that Tyson fellow? Rubbing his eyes, the young man strained at the heavily wooded area across the road, but he saw nothing. He stared a while without seeing so much as a single tree branch stir in front of him. *Probably my imagination*, he thought as he turned to walk into the central hallway to again sit outside Sarah's door.

A quick glimpse out the hall window made him freeze. This time he was certain that he saw something–a distant figure darting from tree to tree, moving deeper and deeper into the woods. He turned quickly as his name floated out through Sarah's bedroom door.

"Litch?" she said faintly. Maggie pushed the door open and motioned to him. He looked in at the two women.

"Come sit with me, Litch. I need you to give me comfort. My

Chapter 30

son's dead. Help me, help me," the distraught mother pleaded to her young guest.

He was beside himself. He had information about the culprit, but he certainly couldn't tell this woman, delirious in her sorrow.

Litch held her outstretched hand as Maggie took a cloth to soothe Sarah's brow from the ache that surely pounded her forehead. In Litch's heart, he thanked her for giving him the opportunity to seek Caroline. They had never spoken on this issue, but they seemed to have had a silent understanding from the beginning. He truly hoped one day he could be part of this heritage. His thoughts began to choke him and he, too, wept as inconspicuously as he could. He was thankful that Sarah's eyes were closed. He grasped her hand more tightly and tried to imagine his becoming the son she no longer had.

Chapter 31
The Medusa Tree

Hap moved quickly, but he realized that his strength ebbed with every step. He needed to stop briefly before he went too much farther toward Penny Hill. His brain was too numb to function, but he thought of one place between Shiloh and Penny Hill that could possibly shield him from anyone looking for him. Of course, the Medusa Tree! His crooked smile spread; he felt a rush of possibility. He would hide in the tree until darkness became his protector. He felt better.

The Medusa Tree stood alone off the main road, and, yet, its proximity to the forest's edge was no more than fifty yards. Hap emerged from the tree line and moved as swiftly as he could. God, here he was asking the help from a tree that had taken the lives of many Edgecombe natives. First, the angel, and now, the executioner. Pulling himself up onto one of its sprawling limbs was not easy with all the aches in his body, but he knew the tree well from the many times he'd climbed it to hide from the world. Yes, he would find refuge in the Medusa Tree. He settled on the limb above the hole in the heart of the tree. A lightning bolt had done this damage years ago. This was the perfect place to rest until dark. In the night, he would go up the road to Penny Hill and help.

Hap dozed as he sat on the big limb above the yawning hole. Many of the tree's limbs snaked outward. He awoke with a start, cramps ripping through his body. He managed to stand, trying to stretch the cramp in his leg, but when he did, his usual good balance failed him.

"Oh. Ohhhhhhh. Oh nooooo," he cried out as he began to fall.

Chapter 31

His body twisted. His arms flailed out at a nearby limb, but he missed it, as his fingernails ripped through the bark. He plummeted straight down, with his right leg spearing its way into the hole in the bosom of the tree. His body slammed into the trunk. He found himself hanging upside down with his right leg jammed into the tree's vacant heart and his left leg sticking straight up in the air. The pain in his right knee was excruciating, as was the pain in his right foot. He was stuck with absolutely no room in the opening to move. As tall as he was, his head was dipping below the bottom branches of the tree.

How dumb! How stupid! he grimaced. Surely, he could pull himself up and grab a limb, but the more he tried, the more futile his attempts. Blood rushed to his head. He felt faint.

"Lord, I do not want to be a victim of this tree!" he railed out.

He raised his head to keep from losing consciousness, but the cramping in his leg forced his head to bang on the huge trunk. Upside down the world looked bizarre and hazy. His head throbbed unmercifully.

"What?..." He squinted and looked sideways as he heard a piercing noise, a squeal, the squeal of some wild animal. He gasped for breath, looking from left to right. A wild boar, he guessed. Oh Lord, he'd seen serious wounds caused by these animals, which sometimes left victims with missing limbs.

He jerked his head toward the shrill sounds. Panic forced a greater struggle to free his leg, but the more he twisted, the worse the pain, the more hopeless the escape. Even in the distance, the boar appeared huge to him with unusually long legs.

"The b-b-better to rear up the tr-tree to make a strike, uh, uh, uhhh," he garbled, continuing his struggle. He was in terrible danger.

The feral sow pounded the earth as she raced across the field toward the Medusa Tree, sensing danger for her piglets, hidden on the edge of the woods. The smell of Hap's blood filled her nostrils. The closer she came, the more feverish his shouts, the more frenzied his waves to anybody who might hear or see from the road or across the fields. Anybody! God, he would die here on the Medusa Tree! He could not hold his head up any longer. It was going down. All red-eyed and drooling, the boar readied herself to strike.

"Oh, God. *Oh, God*! Willieeeeeee...Caroli-i-i-ine..."

Chapter 32
The Slow Ride Home

The task of moving Will's body to the wagon had been a heart-wrenching experience for Elijah and George.

"Easy, now, George. Just a little farther."

"Yessuh, Cap'n."

The two men had wrapped Will's body with the blankets and cushioned his neck, so his head did not dangle. They had taken such pains that both were sure it had been an hour to get Will situated. It had not. When they had finished, the young man's body seemed pathetically lost on the planks of the big wagon.

"Caroline, take Nellie and—"

"No, Father, I won't leave Will. Don't even ask me."

"You don't need—"

"But, I do, Father."

Her father resigned himself and helped his stubborn daughter up on the wagon. Biting his lip, George tied Nellie and Elijah's stallion to the back of the wagon. What a God-awful ride for them all, he thought, looking at the Captain and his daughter.

"O-oh, Will. Oh, m-my son."

The father broke and wept openly, unashamedly, with loud sobs. He stroked Will's face, telling him all the things he wanted to, as if they were sitting together for one of their infrequent man-to-man talks.

"Your mother had such plans for you, Will." His voice broke with several gasping breaths. "Sh-she could—see you in—Raleigh." He sobbed again. "Even in the governor's mansion, b-b-but no more...nothing."

He touched his son's hair. His boy would never bring glory to

Edgecombe County. He sighed and rubbed his eyes with his handkerchief.

The wagon moved so slowly, for Elijah was intent on not disturbing Will's injured neck. Every time the horses started to speed up in the least, he would call to George.

"Keep it slow, George. I don't want to jostle him."

Leaving her father to touch and talk to his dead boy, Caroline moved to the end of the wagon to mourn in her own way. She had no idea about what was happening on the other side of Shiloh, but a cold chill covered her body. She felt the pall of death hovering.

She also felt guilty that she had let her own feelings somehow cause Will's death. Common sense told her that this was not true, but her emotions were overpowering. Right now, she could only mourn the loss of her brother and dismiss any thoughts of Hap and his plight. Looking over her shoulder at the main house, she dreaded facing her mother and the rest of Shiloh. The threesome rode in silence, except for an occasional sob or sigh from her father.

"George, pull right up to the back door."

"Yessir, Capt'n," George answered as they neared the back of the house.

"That's it, George. Go on inside and tell Maggie to prepare the downstairs guest bedroom for Will." Captain Cromwell had returned for duty, as he barked orders. "Caroline, you go find your mother. She'll need all of us, now. I'm fine. I-I'm fine." He nodded as if to convince himself. "George, I want you to ride to Dickens and tell him about our tragedy and that he will need to be here at sunrise to take Will to the funeral parlor. I'm sure Maggie will want to spend the night here. Of course, you may too, George. Maybe you can sleep a few…"

"Mistuh Elijah, you know old George will be right back here as soon as his hoss can bring him," he spoke out firmly. Elijah gripped his arm.

Chapter 32

"I know, George, your word is your bond." The Captain smiled, turning to look once more at the ashen face of his son.

George left Maggie in charge of preparations in the house, while he would make the preparations with Dickens. This day had been made up of many sad rides for him. *What's one more?* he thought, as he rode out of Shiloh and passed the graveyard where a fresh grave would be dug in another day.

Meanwhile, Elijah carried his son's body to the bed. Maggie stood, towels draped over her arm, a water basin in her hand, ready to clean Will's body and to dress him in night clothing, which seemed to her the easiest thing to do.

"Maggie, I'll–" Elijah began, but Maggie quickly stopped him.

"No sir, Mister Elijah. You leave this task to Maggie. It's my last gift to him, sir. I insist."

He smiled weakly back at her, nodding in agreement. She shooed them all out the door, turning to gaze at Will's face. Nature had begun to work its course.

"Now, Master Will. I'm just going to take your shirt and pants off just like I used to do when you were just a b-b-boy," her voice cracked, but she quickly began humming the half-remembered songs of his youth.

His nakedness never bothered her for an instant, for she had bathed him, changed him, dressed him all his young life. She would not have had it any other way. She smiled to herself when Elijah had suggested that he do the duties. She'd surprised herself as she had waved him off as if she were the mistress of Shiloh herself. *Sometimes one has to seize authority, and, Lord, this was one of those times*, she thought. And at this moment, she had the honor to care for Master Will, to make the very last effort she would ever make for him. She busied herself with her task.

Chapter 33
Overcome

*F*ate laughed as he fingered a scrap of cloth dangling from some scrubby undergrowth. Hap had plunged through the thickets just as carelessly as he had, both running with abandon. He looked down at his own shirt, shredded and bloody. Miss Willie had soothed his torn flesh, but new wounds had opened up.

Crazed with fury, Fate stormed through the opening to the graveyard. Hap's footprints in the dirt showed that he had rested on a marker's edge. How dare he sit on Will's grandmother's monument? His anger intensified, as he broke from the cemetery and raced down the road in front of Shiloh. He paused briefly looking for more prints, only to glance up at the opening door of the main house.

Litch Bagley rushed out.

"Fate, oh thank heavens!" As he ran down the steps, he waved his arm wildly toward Penny Hill. "He went off that way. Dammit, Fate, don't let him get away."

"No suh, he's as good as mine," Fate assured.

"Get a horse from the stables. You'll run him down in no time."

The stableman gladly relinquished his own mount as Fate grabbed the reins. As he swung up into the saddle, he glanced back toward the road to the lower 40 and noticed a dust cloud rising skyward. Soon they would all know for sure about the fate of young Master Will. In the upper yard behind Cromwell Hall, the remaining laborers who lived at Shiloh huddled and rocked from foot to foot. Some sang gospel songs, while others prayed

Chapter 33

out loud. All longed for good news, not the dreaded news they sensed. Fate reached the main road at a full gallop, as he felt the power of the animal under him respond to the urgency of the popping reins on its flank.

* * *

Fate would never have known that Hap Tyson was hiding in the Medusa Tree if he had not heard the shrill squeals of the charging wild boar. Turning his horse off the road, he galloped toward the tree at full speed and hit the sow just as she was about to snap at Hap's head. His screams of Willie's and Caroline's names filled the air, as Fate dodged branches and warded off the boar's attack with the bulk of his horse. The sow flipped, yet scrambled to her feet almost immediately. Stunned, she turned toward the woods with ears flopping, but periodically she stopped and looked back to see if her enemies were approaching. The woods swallowed her up, her distant snorts fading in the distance. All became quiet.

Fate remained perfectly still on his horse as he watched the wild swine make her way into the thickets beyond. He knew there was no danger from Hap; the young man was still unconscious.

Finally, he nudged his horse under the branches to look at his ill-fated enemy. Fate had saved his life for sure, but now his motive lay in the desire for justice in the courts. If he walked away right now, Hap would surely die within the hour, with all that blood rushing to his head. Fate was tempted, but visions of Maggie and George would not allow him to leave this helpless man to die. Facing that guilt would be unbearable, especially a death that he so easily could prevent.

Fate bent over from his saddle and caught one of Hap's arms, then the other, pushing his back between the trapped man's shoulder blades until he was in a fairly upright position.

"Hap! Hap! Hey, man, wake up!"

Hearing his name through a semiconscious fog, the injured

young man realized that he was still alive. He could not see who was behind him on horseback, but the strong wiry arms that hooked under his torso left no question in his mind. He arched his back and swiped at the limb above, and with his added strength and a boost from Fate's shoulder, he heaved the bulk of his weight upward, pulling the useless leg from captivity.

Grunting and grimacing, Hap refused to scream out of pride, but never in all his wildest dreams could he have imagined the intense pain shooting from his foot and leg. *Oh, God! Oh, my God! Just save it! Ohhhh!* His head kept dropping to his chest as he tried his best to keep from fainting again. He bit his lip hard enough to draw blood.

As Hap clung to the limb, Fate dismounted and climbed up to help his disabled enemy. Hap offered no resistance and no words, as the two men somehow shimmied down the final lowest limbs of the Medusa Tree. Pulling Hap over to the knurled trunk was no easy task for the smaller man, as he propped Hap up as best he could. He knew that the grotesque position of Hap's leg meant bad news if it could not get attention soon.

"Hello-o-o-! Hey!" A voice called out, and then a shrill whistle pierced the air. "Do you need help?" Rufus Knight stood in his buggy, cupping his hands to his mouth as his voice boomed from the road.

"Yeah!" Fate shouted back, waving him over to take a look. Hap could not believe it as he looked through swollen eyelids at one of the three people in the entire world who loved him. Then, he fainted away.

"Fate, my God, what has happened to the boy?" The doctor jumped down from his buggy and looked quickly at Hap's injuries. "Good Lord!" he exclaimed as he, too, noted the twist of Hap's leg. "We gotta get him to the hospital and fast." Turning to Fate, he quickly added, "Com'on, help me hoist him up. My buggy will hold him."

Chapter 33

"Yessuh" was all Fate could say, relieved that someone else was making the decisions and relieved that someone prevented him from making the biggest mistake of his life.

"Fate, you tell me everything as we ride," the doctor insisted. "Talk to me, son."

Both Fate and Doctor Knight struggled with Hap's body, which seemed much heavier than it really was. Grabbing some whiskey he had under his seat, Doctor Knight forced some down Hap's throat. He knew the boy needed to remain unconscious until they could get him on an examining table and figure out the problems and the answers.

As Rufus drove the buggy, Fate sidled up on his horse as close as he could to tell the man all he knew about what happened on the lower 40.

"Don't know it all, but I can tell you Will Cromwell might be dead."

"What did you say? Might be dead? How, for God's sakes?"

"He did it, suh," Fate said, nodding to the back of the buggy.

"Hap?"

"Yessuh."

"He was on Shiloh land?" the doctor asked.

"Down in the lower 40. They were fighting. I guess." His voice trailed. He turned away to smother a choke in his voice.

"How'd you two get way out here?"

Recovering somewhat, Fate explained his pursuit of Hap and the incident with the tree and the boar. The more he heard, the deeper the doctor's brow furrowed. Turning his head, Rufus Knight looked at Hap, shook his head, and clicked the reins to make the horse go faster. He didn't like the looks of that leg and foot.

Chapter 34
DEATH ON SHILOH

*C*aroline entered the house. She stared at the guest room door, trying to envision Maggie attending to her dead brother. She shuddered and walked slowly up the staircase to her mother's room, only to find Litch sitting by Sarah's side, holding her hand, and telling her wonderful stories about himself and Will at the university. She waited outside the doorway, listening and weeping, not wanting to break into the exchange between these two, who seemed to have found a lifelong tie, her son and his college friend. But interrupt them at this time? She must.

Wiping her tears, Caroline moved into the doorway and walked silently to her mother. Litch rose quickly, smiled feebly at her, and backed quietly to the door, only to bump squarely into Elijah. Embarrassed, he whispered his apology and continued to back away from the grieving mother, father, and daughter.

"O-oh, Sarah," Elijah said, his voice cracking, and collapsed at her bedside. Elijah cried opening his arms, and his wife, muffling her own cries, tugged at her husband's hair. Caroline hugged the two, bobbing from one to the other, crying her sorrow for them all.

"Miss Sarah, Mister Elijah, Miss Caroline," Maggie called softly from the doorway. "Master Will is prepared in the guest room. If you all want, you can view him now. I've done the best I could, with your approval. George says Mister Dickens will be here at sunrise. He's back, sir, just like he told you he would. Y'all can come pay your respects."

She disappeared just as quickly as she appeared, escaping the scrutiny of her employer, for she was crying as much as if she were

CHAPTER 34

in mourning for her own son.

Sarah reached out her hand and gathered her strength, not only for herself, but also for her husband and her daughter. After all, she was Coeffield King's flesh and blood, and she was supposed to be strong and staunch in the face of crisis. They would have to say goodbye to their one and only son, the bearer of their name, the last of the Cromwell men in Edgecombe County.

The three slowly entered the guest room with fear and trembling. Maggie pointed to the chair by the bed. Sarah sat. Elijah and Caroline stood close, leaning forward, smiles of pain crossing their faces.

"Will? You just look like you're napping," Sarah said. "Doesn't he, Elijah?"

She lovingly put her hand on her son's head. She did not touch his skin. She only wanted to remember her son, alive and warm.

"Oh my gosh, Father," she said, turning to speak to her husband. "Elijah, we must send word to Father." The bereaved man nodded.

Coeffield King would want to know this news immediately about his only grandson. Sarah could not imagine what her father would think or do once he knew the story of Will and Hap. She shuddered as she looked back at her son and thought that only a few hours ago their lives were the happiest she'd ever known. *God never promises us a life without troubles*, she thought, recalling Scripture, *but He also assures us that He will not give more than we can handle. God, help me handle this tragic turn. I don't think I can on my own.*

Sarah laid her hand on the edge of the bed, her fingertips slightly caressing the sleeve of Will's nightshirt. Elijah and Caroline sat on the loveseat and held each other to ease their sorrow. An hour passed. Then two.

Elijah stood up and tiptoed to the bed, "Sarah? Darling? We

all need to go. You need your strength for tomorrow."

"I can't leave him, Elijah, I can't."

"I know, sweetheart, but he needs both of us to be strong for him now. When Dickens brings him back, the people will come. We need our strength." She only nodded.

Elijah reached for her hand and steered her from the room. Caroline took her mother's chair and sat staring at the handsome face of her brother. She clasped her hand over her mouth and turned quickly to stare into the face of Maggie Edmundson, who had slipped into the room. Her head riveted back to her brother's, for she saw a dreadfully stern look on Maggie's face as their eyes locked

"Maggie, don't blame me," she begged.

"I ain't said a thing, Miss Caroline," she said with ice in her voice.

"It was a horrible accident," she countered. "George–" She never finished. *God in heaven, he must have seen it all.*

Never looking again at Maggie, she ran from the room and dragged herself up the stairs. Litch stood at the top, looking at her helplessly. He reached out and pulled her up the last few steps, holding her with arms that wanted to shut out her grief and pain.

She did not pull back from his help.

He lifted her and carried her into her room. He sat in the rocking chair by her bed and rocked her in his lap until he felt her breathing in even rhythm on his chest. Periodically, he would release her and gather her close to him again to reassure himself that she was real in his arms. For over an hour he rocked her.

Finally, she stirred, her hand still delicately placed on his chest. She raised her head slightly, looking up into his face, and smiled.

"I need sleep, Litch."

He got up with her still in his arms and placed her weakened

Chapter 34

body on the bed, her golden hair shining in the moonlight from the window.

"Would you go get my dressing gown in the wardrobe over there, Litch?" she asked in a whisper. Jumping toward the armoire, he opened the door and touched the softest cotton and lace gown he'd ever felt. He brought it to her bedside and, as he extended his hand to her, she sat up. "Turn around, Litch. Please?" she whispered again, as she threw the gown tent like over her head and undressed under the fullness of the gossamer fabric. Allowing her clothing to fall crumpled to the floor, she collapsed on the bed and fell into a troubled, but deep, slumber as her head hit the pillow. He knelt beside her and whispered.

"I love you, Caroline. I will do everything in my power to ease your pain."

His words fell on deaf ears, for sleep, as difficult as it was, overcame her.

Litch had glimpsed her undressing through the bureau mirror. He had seen only illusions as she wriggled from her garments, but was thrilled that she had allowed such intimacy to happen between them.

She's mine. God, thank you. She would never have allowed anything so personal to happen if something did not exist between us. Tyson is her past. I am her future. She's mine.

He pulled the rocker over to the bed and sat through the night by her side.

* * *

For kindred spirits, silence can communicate as much as a thousand words. Such was the night between husband and wife in the upper bedchambers of Cromwell Hall.

The master and mistress of the house lay in each other's arms and never shut their eyes the entire night, each lost in their own memories and the *what ifs* about their only son. Sensing a loss of heritage, Elijah grappled with his own selfishness of wanting his name carried on into future generations. On the other hand, Sarah wrestled with her ambitions for her blond Adonis, struck down by a ne'er-do-well. She knew Coeffield King would make Hap Tyson pay for stealing the life of her son. Oh yes, she knew her father. He would stop at nothing to punish this scoundrel for snuffing out the seed of his family.

Chapter 35
Touching the Enemy

Michael Collins could not sleep. In fact, he had not had peaceful sleep in a fortnight, ever since he became aware that Litch Bagley would arrive at Cromwell Hall. He felt guilty for planting the seeds of doubt about Hap Tyson, but a man pining with unrequited love often resorts to desperate means to save face or seek revenge. Countless evenings and early mornings, he'd risen in frustration to wander under the oaks of the Town Common. His quarters at Mrs. DeBerry's allowed him proximity to the huge bowling green at the town's core. He felt intimacy with every tree bordering the big plot of green now laced with autumn colors.

Michael slumped down on one of the town's memorial benches, commemorating the fallen sons of Tarboro in the war between the states. It felt dank. He shivered and wondered why he was so melancholy this night. In a lethargic stupor, the young teacher gazed down Main Street as if he were looking at the parted Red Sea. Could he expect an enemy charging forth to extract himself from this sleepy little village on the Tar? Shaking his head in an attempt to clear his vision, he swore he was seeing a stirring at the other end of Main. Someone was traveling rapidly across the bridge. Surely, he hallucinated; yet, the dust began to build as a carriage pushed its way forward. Where would a body be going at this hour? Just as Michael posed the question, the buggy swerved and headed toward the hospital on St. Andrew Street.

Michael jumped from his seat and ran toward this disturbance in an otherwise peaceful evening in Tarboro. He knew nothing, and yet he felt he would know everything soon. His mouth felt parched and dry as his feet hit the bricks of Main. Darting onto a dirt side street, he kicked up his own dust as he continued running. Then he saw what looked like Hap Tyson's head resting on the back of the buggy's seat. The closer he got the louder the moans from his rival. The buggy's horse and the rider's whinnied as he charged onto the scene, but they quieted when the rider turned to touch their noses and whisper to them.

"Wh-what happened?" Michael asked as he stared down at Hap's mangled leg.

Fate did not feel bound to answer the young man, but soon the doctor ran from the small building with an orderly, carrying a stretcher. Rufus Knight bent over Hap and ripped his pant leg as if it were paper.

"Give me the splints," he demanded of the orderly. "Fate, give him another shot of whiskey. Pour it down him even if he fights you. He'll need it and a bunch of prayers for this ordeal."

The leg was dislocated drastically. It would be a Divine miracle if he could pop it back into place without ligament damage, but he knew he would have to try. Preparing himself, the doctor looked up into the bulging eyes of Michael Collins. "Get yourself around here, man, and help hold this fellow. He'll be sailing up to old St. Pete if you and Fate, here, don't hold him down with all your might. He's a strong one."

Repelled by the idea of touching Hap, Michael recoiled at each word. "Uh" was all he could say.

"Look here, man, out of common decency, hold on and now!" the doctor bellowed.

Michael's hands shot out, one on Hap's shoulder, the other on his arm. He felt the hard sinewy muscles in Hap's arm and despised it for having held Caroline, whereas, he had not.

Fate followed suit. Both men looked up at the doctor as he rolled up his white shirtsleeves. Not once did he take his eyes off

Chapter 35

the mangled flesh. With his towering bulk, hulking over Hap, the doctor maneuvered the leg under his deft fingers.

Hap screamed only once, practically lifting all three men in his struggle before he passed out again. The rest was easy.

The orderly had waited patiently for the other three to move away from the buggy so he could perform his own duty. He was nowhere near the height of Hap, but his own bulk announced that he could pick this man up with no problem. He placed the wounded patient ever so gently onto the stretcher. With Fate handling the other end of it, the two men carried the *meanest scoundrel in Edgecombe County* into the little hospital.

Once more, the doctor performed his own miracles, binding and stitching the injured leg, all while praying over this young man, who he felt was like the son he'd never had. *Shoot, half the county's children I delivered*, he muttered to himself. *I feel like they're my own as well, but why do I covet this boy as mine?* Rufus Knight could only surmise that he felt his potential and the boy would probably never have a chance if he did not do something for him. He gazed down at the boy in troubled and painful sleep and realized his own tears dropped on the bed linens.

* * *

Michael stumbled away into the night and retched behind the hardware store. He leaned on the building and looked back at the little hospital in amazement, as he recounted the episode. He remained in the shadows and watched the doctor and Fate Edmundson come out of the building.

"You're going to the sheriff's office?" the doctor asked.

"Yessuh, I promised I would."

"If you have to, Fate. Do what you have to," he said, turning to go back to his patient.

Cleaning himself up with his handkerchief, Michael watched Fate walk to his horse and head to Main Street and Sheriff

Haydon's office. Racing down the alley beside Cobb's Hardware, he peeped around the corner just in time to see Fate enter the sheriff's door. He salivated to hear their conversation.

The darkness hid his slipping across the street unseen. Standing at the corner of the sheriff's office, Michael could hear muffled voices. The door opened. Fate and a deputy stepped onto the porch.

"Listen, Fate, he ain't going anywhere in that condition. The sheriff and me will take over in the morning. Tell the Captain we'll handle everything."

"The Captain thanks you, I'm sure."

The deputy nodded, leaving Fate standing alone.

The next moments confused Collins as he watched Fate. The young man staggered down the steps and clutched the horn on his saddle. His head crashed down on his arms and he cried with more emotion than Michael had ever seen a man display. What had happened to cause him to cry with such heartbreak? How could he sleep now with all of these unanswered questions? He had to find out. Yet, there was no way that he could rightfully disturb this insurmountable grief in front of him.

Fate finally pulled himself up in the saddle and headed toward the bridge and Shiloh.

My God, something's happened at Shiloh. Caroline!

No sooner had Fate reached the bridge than Michael stumbled up the steps and reached for the sheriff's door. The deputy looked up in surprise as he saw the second strange visitor that he'd had that night, but he was ready to talk to anybody after the solitude of a night shift. He told Michael Collins all he knew.

Chapter 36

DICKENS

*B*raswell Dickens had buried them all for the last twenty years. Having learned embalming from the war doctors, his father had opened a funeral parlor in Tarboro after the Civil War. But now it was just Dickens, as everyone called him, to see to the final arrangements. He supposed he'd prepared as many paupers as he had the wealthy. He showed no prejudice and adjusted his fees to accommodate those who had not. Dickens keenly felt his responsibility to usher his clients to their rewards in the best manner. Many a pauper received a little better than maybe the penny could buy, but Braswell Dickens believed in giving back to the community and the return had been good for him and his family.

Everybody knew old Dickens was on call at any hour no matter what the need. The rap on the door jarred him, but he rose from his bed without a qualm. George Edmundson was standing on his porch in front of him.

"Mister Dickens, there's been a terrible accident at Shiloh. The Captain needs you at dawn."

"What's happened, George?"

Dickens flinched at the news from Cromwell Hall, for he'd known this family for as long as he could remember. Only a few years older than Elijah, he'd had the task of laying to rest the elder Cromwell and his beloved wife in the family cemetery.

"Thank you, George, you tell the Captain I'll be there at dawn."

He closed the door with a silent nod and walked to his desk to prepare his papers. The elder Cromwell, like other Cromwells, had ordered the finest Georgia marble marker with exquisitely carved angels atop. No dollar had ever been spared. Dickens surmised the family would request another for Will. He'd snatch another wink if possible before he departed for Shiloh. He had promised he would be there by dawn and he would. *What a long and sad night for Elijah and Sarah*, he thought. *Old friend, I'll be there for you soon.*

Dickens returned to his bed and whispered the bad news to his wife. Sighing deeply, she reached out to hold her husband and to comfort him, as surely he would comfort the Cromwells come dawn. She knew the ride would be long and hard, for her husband had admired this family for years. Sometimes she wondered how he handled his job of burying the dead day in and day out. He never seemed to complain, but she knew the toll was there. She pulled him even closer never realizing that what she did was the mainstay of his existence in being a funeral director. She empathized ultimately and strengthened him with the warmth of her breath above his head as she prayerfully uplifted him to the Maker. Never had he not absorbed the peace she rendered. Never. The furrow of his brow softened as he began to doze.

* * *

Dickens had hardly tapped on the huge front door at Cromwell Hall when Maggie opened it wide and beckoned him forward into the huge entry hall of the mansion. Small in stature, he felt dwarfed by the aura of the spacious plantation house. Never had he entered without this feeling, but it only lasted a minute, for Elijah never wanted a guest to feel awkward and overpowered by its grandeur. Dickens' gaze went upward as he heard a faint footstep on the winding staircase, only to see his friend standing with the look of a dead man. The hairs on his neck and arms stood up. He, himself, would have a longer recovery from this tragedy.

Elijah reached out to shake his hand, but he fell into Dickens arms. The slight man had difficulty holding him up, but he managed.

Chapter 36

"Mister Elijah," Maggie spoke softly. "Come now, sir," she continued, taking his arm, and coaxing him toward the guest room. Dickens could hardly contain himself, but his professionalism took charge. He began his duties. Once the initial details had been covered, he signaled his people outside to come in and remove the body. This part might be the hardest for his friend, releasing the body of his only boy, but Captain Cromwell responded dutifully, if reluctantly.

Both men respected each other and understood their own ways of handling difficult situations. Just as he thought, Dickens received instructions to order the Georgia marble marker and the carved angel for Will's grave in the family cemetery.

Chapter 37
THE BLACK DRESS

*C*aroline stirred, slowly opening her eyes, thinking that they would never fully recover from all her crying. She glanced at the nearby chair and saw to her surprise that Litch had stayed by her side the entire night. She could not believe he had done that, but she was too exhausted, emotionally and physically, to be worried at a time like this about an apparent impropriety. In fact, she was grateful that he'd thought enough about her to comfort her. She had been awakened by Dickens' carriage and knew he'd come to take poor Will away. Quietly, she slipped out of bed and tiptoed to the front window.

The light from the dawning sun streaked across the sky, intertwined with wisps of clouds. Breezes through the open window whipped Caroline's gown as she stretched her arms upward. *God, he's yours again.* Her lips moved, as she bowed her head.

The eyes that watched from behind only saw the veiled beauty of the young girl. The breeze billowed her gown and sent its hem over his arm resting on the rocker. The young man could scarcely contain his emotions, but when she raised her arms, he focused more on her grief. Forcing his eyes shut, he pretended to doze as she turned and walked by him to the armoire to prepare herself for a most difficult day. He listened as she poured water from the pitcher on the washstand. Totally lost in his own dreams, Litch jumped when he felt the gentle prod of her hand. He grabbed her fingers and pressed them to his lips. This startled her.

She quickly pulled her hand away.

"Go now. I'll see you downstairs," she whispered.

Chapter 37

Standing slowly, he saw that she had dressed in black. He despised the color on her, but he knew the customary fashion to mourn the dead. How helpless he felt as he turned back at the door and looked at her. Smiling faintly, he slipped through the opening. The gossip mongers will prattle, he thought, when they hear the story of the lower 40. He would be by her side as much as he could. Yet, the holidays were over, and now he would have to return to the university to finish his studies, as remote a possibility as that seemed to him.

Chapter 38
BAD NEWS

Coeffield King always "got up with the chickens" as his father used to say. He relished the early hours, as he sipped coffee on his veranda. He and Jacksie had lived in several houses in Tarboro, but they favored this one above all, a two-story Georgian home on the Town Common. Little strands of ivy clung to its front walls, snaking up behind the biggest English boxwoods in Tarboro.

Now he slept alone in this house with only sweet memories of his late wife and the one daughter he adored. Sarah Cromwell had given him a fine grandson and a precocious granddaughter. Consumption had robbed him of celebrating his 25th wedding anniversary, but even with the loss of his beloved Jacksie, he felt blessed.

The old barrister's eyes opened right at five o'clock as they did every morning. Looking down, he realized his favorite book of Poe lay open against his chest. He picked it up and smiled at the volume that so fascinated his grandchildren. Every visit, they would rub the red velvet book, causing its once blood-red brilliance to fade a bit with each touch. He would read the scary stories and wistful poems dramatically, in his rich lawyer's voice, but they always seemed more interested in touching the unusual cover of the book.

"Where was I?" he murmured as he found his place. He dozed off and on, enjoying his lazy moments.

The knock on the front door startled him. Such an early caller couldn't be good, he lamented. Running his fingers through his thick gray hair, the elderly gentleman struggled up from his bed

Chapter 38

and stumbled, half-falling, to his robe and slippers. He grabbed his bedpost, then tottered out into the hallway. As he slowly swung open the heavy door, he saw Braswell Dickens' face. King's eyes fluttered. Taking a deep breath, he reared back, his six-foot frame as erect as his 68-year-old body allowed. God willing, he was ready for the news from Dickens. Or so he thought.

"Morning, Mister King. I regret calling on you so early, but it's Will," Dickens spoke softly.

Coeffield King grasped the door frame.

"Sir?" Dickens' arm shot out to help, but the old man lifted his hand and shook his head.

"What about Will? Tell me," he managed to utter.

"Your grandson's been in a terrible accident. It seems there was an altercation with a Mister Hap Tyson. Will fell and his head hit a fallen log at the lower 40. I'm so sorry, sir, but he did not survive. Miss Sarah wanted me to come as soon as I could. She knew you would be awake at this hour." He paused. "Forgive me, sir, for having to bear the sad news, but Miss Sarah wanted me to prepare you before they come to town this morning."

King nodded, as his eyes drifted to the dew-covered Town Common in front of his house. "Will," slipped from his mouth in the softest voice.

"She knew you would want some time alone before she comes. You have my deepest sympathy, sir. May I help you in any way?" The undertaker offered these words to one who never seemed in want of anything.

"No, no..." He seemed to look right through Dickens, but snapped from his daze and spoke with a choking voice. "I-I... am sure you have served our family well in its time of need." He pressed the back of his hand against his forehead. "Sarah's right. I do wish to be alone," he said softly. "Thank you for bringing this news, my good man."

Nodding slightly, he turned to close the massive door and fell heavily against it, then struggled to regain his balance. All he wanted at the moment was just to make it to his chair in the parlor. Just to look at the portrait of his beloved Jacksie over the mantle. Just to breathe again. He felt choked. Reaching feebly for the French-door opening of the parlor, he struggled to the grand piano that Jacksie used to play. Just a few more steps to the chair, he thought, a haven where he could sit and talk to his beloved. He looked at the portrait and thanked God that the artist had captured her features so lifelike, especially her deep blue eyes.

Collapsing into the armchair, the man's bulk melded into the soft crushed leather. His own father had found refuge in this old chair, and now it was his turn. His head rolled to the side.

"It should have been me joining you, my love, not Will. God in heaven, his life was just beginning. Now, gone... gone," he grimaced and choked on his words. His body shook. The last male heir in their immediate family had been struck down. "Jacksieeeee..." he screamed, then slumped.

* * *

Coeffield King was sixty-eight-years old, a widower for eighteen years. The old lawyer had outlived his wife and many of his contemporaries. Could it possibly be that his beloved Jacksie had been dead and buried at Calvary for eighteen years? No, his mind repeated every time the question arose. Another question always followed. Would he ever relinquish his law practice? No, his mind repeated again. Not a day passed when he did not think of his vow that night as he watched John Constable and Nate Jones dangle from ropes on the Medusa Tree.

His vow to be the best lawyer in Edgecombe County packed his agenda. Only conflicts of time and interests ever forced him to decline a case from the local citizenry. Just as Braswell Dickens had buried the wealthy and the poor, Coeffield King had represented the wealthy and the poor. He was the best civil,

Chapter 38

estate, and general law litigator in all of down east.

A man needs representation in this world, he always said. Jacksie had even cross-stitched those words into a sampler, which still hung on his office wall. As he grew older and reflected on his life and career, he could count only one time he had been wrong in considering a case. Despite that one time, Coeffield King was respected and revered in Edgecombe County and the entire eastern end of North Carolina. He had hopes that his one grandson would carry on this tradition and his reputation.

But now, his family would bury his one grandson, the only remaining male heir. He had always doted on his grandchildren. Why not? He was the only grandparent they had known. Elijah's parents died even before Jacksie. The Cromwells had been older parents in comparison to Sarah's, but tuberculosis and broken hearts show no preference to age or gender.

Now, Will would never know the love of a woman, as Coffie had with Jacksie Thrash. From his chair he looked up at the book shelves on either side of the mantle. Many of the volumes contained stories of struggling young lovers, as his pursuit of Jacksie Thrash was not an easy one. Why in this world would he think of such things in his despair over Will?

"You'll never know, Will. You will never know." He moaned. "Your grandmother was worth every last effort," he said, as he gazed up at her portrait, and then his eyes wandered around the room.

"Did I ever tell you this story, Will? Your grandmother and I were desperate to marry. Disputed land lay between Shiloh and Justice Thrash's farm. My father represented the Cromwells in the legal dispute, which lessened my chances to come calling on your grandmother." He got up and paced the parlor floor.

"Once in a while I'd see her around town," he said aloud, "but church at Calvary became agony. Even our rector could sense conflict between our fathers. Then one day, we went to the rector and begged him to marry us." Coeffield King stopped and smiled at the portrait, then continued to speak aloud. "'Stay here,' he told us. 'I have a plan.'"

The old man pulled out his handkerchief and blew his nose, before he continued. "Oh, Will, we were so scared as we huddled in the rector's tiny office, but he did it. He got our parents to sit in the sanctuary, and he gave them three choices. They could make peace and plan a wedding the likes of which Tarboro had never seen, or the rector could marry us without their permission. We were of age.

"But the rector's last choice got them. He told them that they could poison us like Romeo and Juliet and bury us side by side in a crypt right out in Calvary's churchyard. He told them they had until the bell in the tower tolled to decide.

"Oh, Will, those four folks didn't have a chance. They were stunned by the choices, and dumbfounded when they realized they had to talk serious business...and with each other. Did I ever tell you this story, Will?"

Even if he hadn't, he choked as he realized that he would never have the chance to tell him anything, ever again.

"The bell never tolled, Will. The bell never tolled."

He fell back into his chair and sobbed.

Chapter 39
ACCUSATION

Tarboro's small hospital had only a dozen rooms on one floor, financed privately and by some state funding that somehow found its way down east from the legislature in Raleigh. Grateful for the facility, the few doctors in the area used its surgical room whenever they could, even though for years they had used their offices, houses, even barns, in order to save a patient's life. Hap Tyson had returned from surgery and lay in one of these rooms. Rufus Knight had prayed every step of the way that he could save the boy's leg, and that every suture would knit perfectly, or at least prevent the leg from being useless.

Hap clutched his pillow and stared out the window at the backs of the main street stores, especially Carver's Mercantile where he had first encountered Caroline. So much had happened to both of them since that day in Carver's store. Hap's tear-stained face was contorted in grief. Life seemed hopeless.

The room's door was ajar as a silent figure slipped past the orderly on duty and entered.

"I reckon I was hoping you was dead," Fate spoke with menace in his voice. Hap rolled half way and showed his tear-stained face to the young man who had saved his life.

"Then, why didn't you let that old boar bite my head in two?" he asked hoarsely between cracked lips.

"I ain't figgered that out yet. Maybe 'cause of my upbringing. My folks always preached to save life, not destroy it. All I know is you done killed my best friend." Fate winced. "You done ruined life for so many folks, Hap Tyson. Why'd this have to happen?"

His eyes were slits as tears fell.

"It was an accident, Fate. I never touched Will. Caroline saw. She saw everything. Ask her."

"What is going on in here?" the night nurse hissed as she stuck her head through the door. "Young man, get out of this patient's room, and now."

Hustling him along the hall, she scolded him all the way out of the front door and then swung around to hurl her wrath at the orderly on duty at the desk.

Ask Caroline, Fate mused sarcastically, as he shuffled down the steps. She would say anything to save her boyfriend. He kicked at everything in sight as he trudged back to Elijah Cromwell's horse. He would return it tomorrow. Right now he needed his bed and the comfort of Maggie and George. Then he remembered they were at Shiloh, and his spirits sank, for he knew he would have to spend another restless night alone. Without Will, he could not imagine what life would be like. He needed comfort. And, now! His Shug was the answer. She had always seemed to be able to soothe his soul. Yes, he needed his girlfriend more than he ever had in his entire life. Will was gone!

Chapter 40
The Rector's Words

The rector at Calvary received the Cromwells, father, mother, daughter, at exactly eleven o'clock. He was a short, stout man with a fringe of gray hair encircling his shiny, bald head. His black coat pulled slightly over his rotund midsection. A lacy ascot fell above his shiny belt buckle. He invited them into his study.

Their meeting would be short, for there would be no conversation about burial, only the service. Will would be interred in the family graveyard with all the other Cromwells, but Sarah and Elijah had definite feelings about the service, about favorite scripture, about Will's favorite hymns. How could the rector refuse the wishes of these people, sitting before him in such grief? Even with the rubrics prescribed by the Episcopal funeral service, he would somehow integrate these final wishes for their son's service. He always felt helpless when faced with the loss of young life. No amount of divinity schooling could totally prepare someone for comforting the comfortless.

"I am so sorry for your loss," the rector broke the silence after they were seated. "Will was one of the finest young men I have ever had in my parish." The man had prayed for Divine guidance in his words. "Somewhere in my life, I've been repelled by the words people utter when they say that tragic situations must have been God's will. No, God does not will tragedy and hurt, as you are experiencing. God has put us in a natural world with natural consequences. What He does is give us our wills and our choices and equips us to deal with this natural world ruled by the Prince of the Air. God and His Son and His Spirit rule the Kingdom of

Heaven and allow us to live on this earth, His creation. But, still, it is a natural world with natural consequences."

He paused, hoping against hope that his words were received as intended.

"All of you know the scripture. Your God is a good God and He will see you through this tragedy." He paused, his hands clasping and unclasping. Elijah and Sarah Cromwell sat with heads bowed, listless and emotionally drained. Caroline seemed preoccupied, lost in thought.

"Thank you, sir," finally Elijah whispered.

Each head raised. The rector stood and walked around the front of his desk. "I am just thankful that I knew Will and that God lent him to all of us for his eighteen years. We'll treasure our moments, and the good ones will eventually overcome the painful ones. We are all here for the glory of God." Then, he fell silent, crossing his arms in wait. *Silentium est aureum...*

Examining the family closely, the rector thought he saw a flicker of relief in each face, as each stood. Perhaps his words had provided some small measure of comfort. Elijah held his wife's hand gently, his arm encasing the wisp of the girl who the minister guessed must somehow be at the center of this tragedy. All three extended their hands in gratitude. Healing seemed to have begun. The pain was still great, but the three Cromwells appeared ready to show the resolve they would need to get through the day and maybe the days to come.

Oh, God, I stand before you in all humility, for truly these were Your words, not mine, the rector said to himself.

Chapter 41
TROUBLE

At mid-morning, Willie woke Hap out of a troubled sleep in his hospital room. She tried to smile, but her frown would not go away.

"Hap, I've been so worried. The nurse said you could have lost your leg if Rufus Knight had not found you."

"Willie, I can't believe what happened. It's terrible... I-" he said, slowly reaching for her hand. She squeezed it briefly.

"What did happen, Hap? Tell me, son. Tell me everything. Don't you leave one thing out."

She released his hand and waggled her finger at him. How many times had she plucked him from one serious situation or another? Could she do it again?

"Caroline sent me a note, Willie. I just had to go. My plan was to never see her again. I had planned to tell her just that." He stopped, trying to pull his thoughts together. "But Will was there."

As Willie listened to Hap's explanation, she could not believe what she was hearing. Coeffield King's grandson was dead because of her son.

"Hap?"

He could read her face and knew the question she wanted to ask.

"Willie, I never hit him. I swear to you, I never struck him," he said with pleading eyes.

A cold fear filled her heart and gut. This lawyer, especially this lawyer and grandfather, wouldn't let such an incident go by as just an accident. She feared that Hap would be charged with something, and she suspected that Coeffield King would somehow bring his legal experience to bear on the situation. No amount of fanning could dry the perspiration on her forehead. She had to get away without showing Hap how worried she was.

"Hap, son, your Willie needs to go. I don't want you to tire yourself out. You've got to rest and get stronger." She smiled weakly at him, bending over to peck him on his cheek. "I'll be back real soon. Doctor Knight's the best. He's not going to let anything happen to you."

Running her fingers through his hair, she allowed her hand to trail down his face and ended up patting him on the shoulder. Her visit was over.

Willie Pridgen tasted fear as she left the hospital. She was the most scared she had ever been in her life. Even Wendell Tyson's drunken binges paled when she thought of Hap standing accused of Will Cromwell's death. Rubbing her arms, she tried to calm the goose flesh and the chill she felt.

"Lord, Almighty, what am I going to do? What are we going to do?" It seemed as if a heavy weight pressed against her chest. "Rufus Knight, you gotta have an answer, 'cause I don't."

Chapter 42
Retribution

Before entering her grandfather's house, Caroline swung around and glimpsed the small hospital in the distance through the wooded area behind the line of stores on Main Street. Somewhere within the confines of those walls lay Hap, broken in body and spirit. Before she could think another thought, however, Elijah hurried her up the steps and through the massive doorway.

"Oh, my Caroline," her grandfather whispered.

He enfolded her as he always did, his bulk dwarfing her. He looked down, tears falling onto his starched dress shirt.

Shaking her head, she wept, too, as she looked into his craggy face, aged by time and sadness. What was he thinking of her now after such a horrendous ordeal? Could he be blaming her for Will's death?

His eye caught Sarah's face. He released Caroline and rushed to hug his daughter. Both faces showed great pain. Slowly, he pointed to the parlor. They followed him and watched as he looked at the portrait above the mantle. He pivoted and seemed empowered, for his first words, after the family settled on the settees, with Jacksie peering down at them, shook them all.

"This scoundrel shall stand trial," the patriarch declared with a steely voice, standing in front of the mantlepiece. "We shall count on the courts to show that Edgecombe County has no need for the likes of one Mister Hap Tyson. His life is over as he knows it, and no one will prevent our family from gaining the satisfaction of his punishment," he sneered, one balled fist striking the other open palm. "His scurrilous behavior profanes human decency. We don't need him in our community. We shall demand and will receive retribution."

No one in the room misconstrued the old man's speech, a call for retaliation against *all* of Hap's bad deeds. It sounded as if Coeffield King rued the day that Hap Tyson first drew breath and would not be satisfied until he drew his last...and soon.

Caroline sat stunned, her mouth open slightly. Elijah stared at his father-in-law in disbelief, trying to comprehend the old man's message, but Sarah rose excitedly, feeling that vengeance was hers for the loss of her only son. Her eyes glittered, and for the first time, she smiled, as she walked to her father to rest her hands on his shoulders and to look deeply into his eyes. She embraced him, the one man she thought who would eradicate, or at least lessen, the great pain in her heart.

Lunch in the dining room proved relatively funereal, as the family ate the meal sent by Mrs. DeBerry, each not really tasting any of the food, each sitting in awkward silence. Finally, Sarah reached across the table to put her hand over Caroline's, but her daughter quickly drew away and looked at her father, sitting opposite her grandfather. Elijah shook his head slightly, as Coeffield King pushed his food around his plate.

Caroline bowed slightly to her grandfather as they were leaving, but she did not accept his parting hug. Elijah offered a tentative handshake. Only Sarah showed true affection for the old man standing in the doorway, kissing him on both cheeks, and only Sarah waved as their carriage pulled away.

Chapter 43
THE WRONG CHOICE

After his family left, Coeffield King collapsed in his chair by the fireplace. Jacksie Thrash peered down from her portrait with those azure eyes that she'd passed on to her granddaughter. The family had left him alone to consider his harsh declaration against Hap Tyson and his vow to seek retribution for Will's death. His wide emotional swing from depression to anger had exhausted him. He felt a disturbance in his soul as he sat clutching his head, eventually looking at Jacksie's portrait with a sense of guilt.

Over the years, he had made only one wrong choice in his practice. He did not want another on his record, as he remembered Jacksie's caution about removing himself from a case long ago when he sensed an injustice to a young widow in the county.

* * *

Many years ago, King had been hired by a wealthy landowner from nearby Rocky Mount to handle a title dispute. The case was routine in his mind, until his opponent, the young Widow Bowden, had walked through his office door and pleaded her case.

"Don't take my land, Mr. King. Don't take my home," she had begged. Whereas he now had shown no compassion toward Hap Tyson, he had felt compassion for the widow. He'd been taken by her fragile appearance and by the beauty of her face. And once he listened to the woman's plight–the loss of her husband, as well as her parents–he was not so sure whether real justice would be served if he took her land and her home. He knew the law was on his client's side, and yet, he also knew that his client would never miss the small parcel, much less the little cottage.

The young lawyer could not get to the Edgecombe County Courthouse fast enough. To his dismay, he found the deeds, documented on legal paper in total disagreement. How could titles be miswritten and misfiled? He had just assumed that the former owner never cared, or never realized the problem, and had allowed the widow's family to live as they had for many years. He also knew that the wealthy new owners felt no compassion. They had no ties. Today was today. The past was the past...to them. He knew what he had to do.

Now, many years later, he was faced with another question of compassion...for his granddaughter, of course, but also for Hap Tyson. But, how could he ignore his grandson's death? He looked up at Jacksie.

"Yes, I listened to the widow with both ears, as you said. I heard her plea, and I was moved by her plight." His head bent down as he remembered the day he rode out to her cottage and saw her rocking on the porch as if she'd been waiting for him. He remembered her calm voice.

"My father always said to hold on to the land, Mister King, and that's what I'm trying to do."

The land had seemed to give her solidarity. If he took it, she would be adrift with no way to rebuild her life. And now, a similar realization hit him: he had never listened to Caroline with both ears, much less Hap Tyson. Yet, he had listened to the widow, speaking of her husband's ill-advised ventures, which eventually left her penniless. He never questioned the moral issue at the heart of the widow's case. So, he had recused himself, much to the chagrin of his client, and, in secrecy, retained a young lawyer in the area to handle her case. With old letters from a family trunk, some legal documents, and even a painting by a traveling artist, the widow's representative convinced the court to favor the young widow. And this time the challenged property lines were drawn

Chapter 43

correctly and filed correctly. The Widow Bowden's home was saved.

Why would he do all of that and not give credence to his own granddaughter's feelings?

King raised his head from his arm and looked up at Jacksie's portrait. He had drifted into a slumber, but he shook his head, clearing his thoughts of the widow and Caroline. He needed to focus on Will.

"Jacksie, the boy took our grandson's life. I can't turn my back on my family's grief or my own."

He looked at the portrait of his wife and wished she could offer advice. As he examined the destitute, impoverished, deprived person in Hap Tyson, compassion kept pushing its way into his lawyer's brain. Would this play out according to the law, or according to justice?

He thought back again to other examples of justice based in retribution. With a drunken mob in control, John Constable and Nate Jones had no chance, as they became the first two men to swing from the Medusa Tree. Did they? Or the young Widow Bowden whose home and land were in dispute? Or, now even Hap Tyson? He slumped, but then raised himself up.

"This is good, Jacksie," he said, waving his finger in the air. "If I look at the other side as well, I can help the district attorney prepare the prosecution," he convinced himself. Somehow he had to dismiss whatever sympathy would be generated by Hap Tyson's miserable upbringing by remembering only one thing: his grandson, Will, lay dead in a casket. The fire in his belly gradually churned. Yes, he would champion the cause. He would be the force behind the law and justice. Hap Tyson would pay.

* * *

The hour of the funeral arrived.

"I am the resurrection and the life, saith the Lord: he that believeth in me, though he were dead, yet shall he live: and whosoever liveth and believeth in me, shall never die," said the rector as he led the casket and the family into the church.

Calvary Episcopal overflowed. Many mourners clustered at the arched entry to hear the words, celebrating Will's life. Frequent moans floated down the aisles of the sanctuary.

At the end of the service, the grieving family struggled to stand and follow the casket out the door. Well-wishers grasped their hands or patted their shoulders as they passed. One or two slipped through to hug Sarah or Elijah to lift their spirits, but sadness overwhelmed them all. Coeffield King and Elijah helped Sarah and Caroline climb into their carriage, as the other family members filled the carriages lining the street. It was time to carry Will to his final rest... The cemetery of angels waited.

Will Cromwell's funeral at first seemed like a hazy dream, but soon reality settled in. Each member of the family was consumed with grief, and they greeted friends and the public with as much composure as possible. The next several days were not easy for any of them—especially Caroline, who carried the guilt of Will's death in her heart.

* * *

After the funeral and burial in the Cromwell cemetery, Coeffield King embraced his newfound mission. He siphoned the town for the dregs on Hap Tyson. He quizzed anyone he could find to paint a cankered portrait of the young man. He did not know much about the boy, but he began to hear stories of mischief and vandalism, and even about Hap being jailed. He heard about Hap growing up on Station House Road, a disreputable part of town, and in the care of a woman called by locals as Weird Willie. The picture that was emerging could be manipulated easily enough to frighten anyone who would be called to sit on a jury, if there was one. Surely, this scoundrel had watched the Cromwells over his lifetime, and surely, he had grown envious of their wealth and privilege. Surely, this rascal had deliberately killed the one person

Chapter 43

barring him from having the fair Cromwell daughter. Back at his house, King's fist crashed onto his polished mahogany desk as he felt the first round of his investigation completed. He would have much to discuss with the district attorney.

* * *

The next step would be the hardest, bringing his granddaughter around. If she held any affection for this boy, any at all, she would make the effort to put him in the worst possible light all the more difficult. She might not agree with such a concerted push to punish Hap Tyson. Her grandfather knew her plight, yet he needed her to see and agree to his own side of whatever case would be brought against Hap Tyson. She had been silent since Will's death.

How could he break into her conscience to defend the family's name against this young man for whom she seemed to have such affinity? Lord knows why she seemed to favor Hap Tyson, he thought, when every fine young man in the county would die for her attention. Somehow, he would have to reach the recesses of her mind to recognize the importance of her family's honor.

Her mumbled words of "accident" and "Hap never lifted a hand" plagued him, but surely a prosecutor could lead her to the simple truth of the incident: Hap Tyson had killed Will Cromwell. They could do this. Had he not won hundreds of civil cases before, securing restitution for clients wronged by the actions of others and representing clients who were defendants in a variety of lawsuits. To his way of thinking, this was an open-and-shut case, even if he had never before been on the prosecuting side of a criminal matter. Why would this one elude him?

No. Never.

Chapter 44
THE CHARGE

When the sheriff served Hap papers bringing murder charges against him, Rufus Knight posted bail for his young friend and kept him at Penny Hill all the months before the trial. Willie agreed that Hap needed to get out of town. Reluctantly, she hugged him goodbye, but the doctor's reputation in the community and his promise to be Hap's guardian had persuaded the judge to grant bail instead of jailing the accused. Christmas and winter passed with Hap's knee healing as well as they could have hoped. Only a slight limp and stiffness remained. Doctor Knight said that with a miracle Hap could strengthen his knee and even lose all signs of hesitation in his walk before the trial date in the spring.

Hap and the doctor roamed the woods on the occasional warm days of early spring and lounged on the banks of the Tar across the road from the doctor's little brick office. Somehow in all their conversations, they avoided discussing the impending trial.

Sitting on the river bank one day, the doctor finally addressed the matter of the trial.

"Hap, when this nightmare is over, and it will be over, I want to send you to school. I got such faith in your ability. I even mentioned it to Willie before we came to Penny Hill."

Hap opened his mouth in surprise.

"Well, I never had a son, you see, and I suppose you come to being as close to one as I'll ever have." He sheepishly looked out over the swirling currents of the river as they sat on a log. "You would make me proud if you'd accept my offer." Hesitating, he

Chapter 44

faltered over his next words. "I've been in touch with your pappy, son. He wants to come to the trial if it's all right with you. Whatsay?"

Hap was speechless. He had not thought of his father in years. Willie had consumed his thinking and now Caroline. His father? His Pap?

"Doc, I haven't thought of him forever. My God, he wants to see me in court? No!" he shouted, jumping up and stuffing his hands in his pockets. Words tumbled out. "I just can't think about him right now. What do you think? Should I? My pappy! I-I dunno. It'd be so weird. Gee, Doc, he might come drunk. He just might puke all over everybody."

"Your pappy's changed, boy. He's put aside his jugging and worked real hard to make a decent living. You remember his land in Pitt County?"

"Sure, I do," Hap said, as he settled back down on the log.

"Well, that piece of earth has made him a pretty penny. Yessiree. A pretty penny. Your daddy has gotten into the tar pitch business. He didn't want to tell you until he'd proved himself. He's done well, Hap, very well indeed." He paused. "Your father wants to help with your education, too, if the trial goes your way, and it will, I'm sure of it."

Placing his hand on his shoulder, he continued, "By the way, I think I've found just the right man to defend you."

"Who?" Hap's eyes widened. He certainly knew of no one.

"Linc Connors from Greenville. He'll be here this afternoon."

* * *

Linc Connors could not wait. Doing well in a case of this magnitude would be a huge accomplishment in his career. He grinned at the prospect of engaging the district attorney in Tarboro, in a case involving Coeffield King, the greatest lawyer east of Raleigh. Linc's law practice spanned only a few years, but he had shown great promise as Greenville's bright young lawyer on the way up. He pulled rein on his horse as he jumped down in front of the doctor's office.

As Rufus and Hap came out from the back room, Linc studied their faces. The younger man looked as if the weight of the world rested on his shoulders, but the older one showed a bit of hopefulness. Neither knew that the man who'd ridden from Greenville to Penny Hill would accept any case involving the illustrious Coeffield King, no matter if the words came out of the young district attorney's mouth. Linc Connors hungered for a reputation.

"Okay, my friends," he said. "Let's get down to brass tacks. Hap, I have to hear it all. Every little thing. No matter how many times you two have gone over the details, it's my turn to hear it all. You must remember that considering what you went through, the mind will sometimes play tricks on us and hide things. I'm not saying that is the case here, Hap, but all threads must be woven properly. Does that make sense?"

"Of course."

Two hours passed and Linc Connors realized that the case teetered on a precipice. He had listened to Hap's emphatic words, but he could not be assured that the sister of the deceased would not declare that her brother was dead and by the hand of his client.

"Hap, let me ask you a few more questions. When you and Will were scuffling, are you sure that Caroline saw everything that happened between you two? Could she by chance have closed her eyes in horror, or could she have turned away in fright?"

"I just assumed she saw it all. She was so close."

But, then he declared again with presence of mind, "There is no way Caroline would let me be convicted of something that I didn't do. Mister Connors, I never even hit Will Cromwell with my fists. We tussled, of course, and he hit me, but I tried to stop him, not hurt him. You have to believe me."

Chapter 44

Linc tried not to frown at this naive young man, but how many cases had he heard a family member testify, proving that old proverb that *blood is thicker than water? Oh, those familial bonds will win every time over other relationships. Well, most of the time,* he thought, *but would it be true here?* He had no clue.

On the other hand, if Hap's declaration was true, then he would have to prove that what she saw was an accident. Just a freaky, horrendous accident. There was no plotting. No planning. Just a quick confrontation. A fall, a crack, and then deathly silence.

Linc rubbed his hands together.

"Now, Hap, did you actually see the other man? George Edmundson?"

"George? I don't know when he came up. All I know is that he was just there."

Well, the fact he was there...hmmm...might help, Linc thought. *Maybe George Edmundson had seen it all.* Linc would have to find cracks in the prosecution's case and break them wide open. This case was not going to be open and shut as he had hoped, but he would try his damnedest, King or no King. He mopped his brow and smiled, trying to project as positive an attitude as he could.

Chapter 45
The Trial

Tarboro was astir the day the trial began in early spring. Never had the downtown buzzed with such interest in a case before. St. Andrew Street was filled as the buggies and carriages pulled in from Shiloh, Penny Hill, and the surrounding area and halted as close to the courthouse as possible.

Spectators were streaming into the building long before the start of the trial. Fate ran up the courthouse steps. He had promised himself that he would not miss one moment of Hap Tyson's trial. The handrail flew through his hand as he leaped two, three steps at a time to the balcony. Perspiration stood out on his forehead as he searched quickly for an open chair.

Please, Lord, satisfy my soul with the verdict. Don't let my best friend die without him paying.

The distraught young man jerked around with anger at the gentle touch on his shoulder. Maggie Edmundson scowled at her son. She need not say a word; he knew what she was thinking.

* * *

When he was only five years old, Fate had seen deputies lead a convicted murderer from the courthouse to the jail. It was a rare moment in Tarboro, an event, something to see.

"Fate, the law's the law," Maggie had said, trying to comfort him, for he had never seen a shackled human being before.

"But, Momma, they're treating him like an animal. I don't understand," the child insisted. He had remembered her patience and her explanation that the lawmen had to chain the man, once he was found guilty.

"Son, if we did not have the law, all of us would be in a mess

Chapter 45

of trouble.

Somebody has to keep us straight. The law and the judge and the deputies all work together. We need 'em all. God has said that this is good to have government in the land. You'll know when you get as big as your daddy."

* * *

Now, here they were in the courthouse, mother and son challenging each other's thoughts.

Fate's stare broke as he read caution in Maggie's eyes. Her words from years ago stuck in his mind. His face relaxed and only until she saw this change in her son did she turn to find her own seat. Scanning the lower chamber, Fate sat forward on the front of his chair. He looked back and forth over the lower chamber, wanting to remember this scene in his brain forever.

Will, it's for you. The law will get him. He'll be in chains.

* * *

As he neared the courthouse with Dr. Knight and Linc Connors, Hap sensed the crowd's disfavor. He strained to find Willie among the throng, as the people pushed to get glimpses of the accused. He couldn't see her. Several carriages from Shiloh were tied at the rail, and he knew that very few spectators in the courtroom would be on his side. More than likely, no one. He yearned to see Caroline, if only a glimpse, before his trial started.

She will never let them convict me about something I didn't do. I just know it. Hap repeated this thought over and over, trying to convince himself of the fact. He turned and took a quick look at Coeffield King's office. How much pressure had the family put on Caroline, convincing her that he had thrown the fatal punch? Oh God, the jury could hang him on the Medusa Tree if they believed he had actually done that. *But, I didn't; I didn't. Caroline knows it. Doesn't she?*

Hap's confidence dipped, no matter how many times Linc Connors smiled and patted him on the back. Who was he to go up against the district attorney, backed by the Cromwells, Coeffield King, and the entire town of Tarboro? Nausea overcame him; he rushed to the latrine outside the courthouse. As he heaved, Hap realized it was he, not his father, who was throwing up at the trial.

When he returned to the front of the courthouse, he heard the words, "murderer," "scum," and "scoundrel" while he and his lawyer climbed the steps, approaching the heavy oaken doors. Before entering, Hap looked over his shoulder at the crowd that seemed even more menacing, but he quickly darted through the door. In the hallway outside the main courtroom, he spotted Caroline peeping out from under her bonnet, as she stood with her family. Their eyes met. Never in his life had he seen such sadness. Once more, he weakened.

When Caroline saw Hap, her head spun with memories of their being together on the lower 40. It amazed her how strong their friendship had become. Before the accident, she could have imagined the possibility of a life together, but now? Only impossibilities. Her heart's desire would have meant forsaking family, position, substance, everything for this young man. How could this be? She felt too young and inexperienced to have such deep seated feelings. Now, just as Hap walked past her, she felt faint. *Oh no, I've got to have air*. Moving quickly past her parents, she headed outside for the corner of the courthouse steps.

Hap noticed her walking to the front door. "Linc, do we have time to get some fresh air before we start?" he whispered.

"Sure," Linc said, turning to escort him out of the building. Making their way to the left of the front door, the two stood on the other side of the porch from the lone figure. Caroline turned slowly, feeling Hap's presence. Once more, their eyes met. Hap could see her lip quivering under the strain of her silence.

* * *

Coeffield King always timed his courthouse entry before a

Chapter 45

major case. With his office across the street, he knew the pulse of the court's procedure. This day as the old lawyer opened his office door and began walking across the street, friends and neighbors greeted him with encouraging smiles and handshakes. They liked their famous lawyer who had made the town of Tarboro so well known in eastern North Carolina. While moving as quickly as they allowed, he enjoyed the warmth of his people. Yes, they were his, and he noted the strong congeniality of small-town camaraderie. How many times had he mounted these steps to argue the law? Too many to count.

Today would be different for Coeffield King, however. He would not sit within the railing as a participating attorney; he would sit behind the rail with Sarah and Elijah, but still close to the young district attorney, Milton Ward. They had talked for hours, and he thought that the young DA was ready to prosecute the state's case against Hap Tyson. He was confident that the weight of the evidence would destroy the defendant, although he was troubled by the possible testimony from his granddaughter. She had avoided his gaze as he made his way through the people on the steps leading into the courthouse, and she did not respond immediately to his outstretched hand as he walked past her. After all these years, could it be that they were on opposite sides of some critical issue or event?

Hap had observed these few moments from the other side of the courthouse steps. It seemed that she wanted to touch her grandfather's hand, to seek the strength of his grasp, to find some calm amid the turmoil. Finally, she took his hand.

If she deserts me, I'm doomed. I'll hang. My God, I'll hang from the Medusa Tree.

Coeffield King continued to exchange nods and subtle waves with several spectators as he headed into the courthouse with Caroline on his arm. After getting her seated in the witness room, he found a front-row seat with his family and leaned forward to pat Milton Ward, the district attorney, on his shoulder.

King leaned back and gazed upward at the elevated dome above his head. The Edgecombe County Courthouse reminded him of the old Roman basilicas whose ceilings brought gasps when first observed. This copious space above his head seemed to house the spirit of God, but King felt that the spirit of the law soared as well.

Chapter 46
Day One, Two, and Three

The courtroom was imposing with its polished dark-paneled walls. The height of the ceiling awed Hap, and as they made their way forward back to their table and chairs, he stumbled slightly behind his lawyer while looking up. In a few moments, the bailiff called the courtroom to order.

"Oyez, oyez, oyez, all rise," the bailiff called out. "This honorable court being held in and for the County of Edgecombe is now opening and setting for the regular dispensing of business with the Honorable Hamilton Barnes presiding."

Everyone stood up when the judge entered. The silver-haired man strode through the rear door and up to his bench, his black robe rippling from the window's breeze. Turning dramatically, he smiled at those in the courtroom and nodded to the bailiff to proceed.

"God save the state and this honorable court... Be seated. The State of North Carolina versus Thomas Rolland Tyson, otherwise known as Hap Tyson," the bailiff announced.

Hap winced at each word and felt the weight of each punctuated syllable. He had not heard his full given name since his first day in school. "Please, just call me Hap, ma'am," he had said to his teacher.

Day One proved slow and tedious with the seating of the jury and opening statements by each opposing lawyer.

"Not guilty" was Hap's plea to the bailiff's question, as Linc Connors stood beside his client.

"Thank you, Mr. Connors. We'll hear Mr. Ward's opening statement first and then yours," Judge Barnes said.

Milton Ward stood and outlined the prosecution's case with such eloquence that many spectators might have thought they were hearing Coeffield King speaking. Ward spoke with firmness and resolve, offering a kind of rhetoric that made Linc Connors think that the old cuss had schooled him well, maybe too well. Scolding himself, he knew that he would focus on the weakness of the circumstantial evidence that would be used to convict on the charge...of murder.

On the second day, the prosecution began weaving the fabric of character assassination to enclose Hap Tyson, just as Linc suspected. After the first few sentences, however, he rose to object to the line of questioning and the answers from inconsequential witnesses.

"Your Honor, what relevance does my client's past, his childhood, have to do with the present situation?"

Milton Ward immediately rushed to stand before the judge. "Your Honor, I am establishing a pattern of behavior by the defendant, leading up to Will Cromwell's death."

Barnes allowed the district attorney to continue, but with a stern warning. He, too, seemed lulled by Ward's dramatic words. It was almost as if the judge wanted to hear just how far the DA–and perhaps King–would go. Linc Connors threw up his hands in frustration. A parade of witnesses testified throughout most of the day that even included reference to the incident of Miss Morris's poor cat. Linc Connors objected time and time again.

"Your Honor, testifying to this litany of events is ridiculous and can only serve to unfairly prejudice the jury against my client. Excuse me, sir, but is dipping Miss Morris's cat's tail in fuel and lighting it relevant to this case? Especially when no one has clearly established that my client perpetrated the deed? Please, Your Honor."

Judge Barnes turned to the young lawyer and with a slight smile said, "Point well taken, Mr. Connors; however, remember this is a case of violence and the jury is entitled to hear of the defendant's propensity for violence. Objection overruled. You may continue,

Chapter 46

Mr. Ward, with these sordid tales of the defendant's depravity."

With murmurs in the courtroom, the judge banged his gavel for order in his court.

The third day brought forth the first important witness to take the stand, George Edmundson, Elijah Cromwell's best hand and manager of the field labor. His loyalty ran deep. Linc had prepared his strategy for this witness, as the DA, with the master at his shoulder, took his turn. Ward glanced back at King with a slight smile.

"Please identify yourself for the court by name and profession," Ward began.

"I–I'm George, George Edmundson. I work for Mister Elijah and Miss Sarah Cromwell. At Shiloh. Yes sir, I do."

"Explain just what it is that you do for the Cromwells, Mister Edmundson."

George's eyebrows shot upward. Nobody in such an official capacity had ever called him Mister Edmundson; it scared him to hear the sound. The seriousness of all this legal proceeding chilled him to the bone. His stomach churned. The water glass shook as he drank before he spoke. It was hard for him, but he looked the young DA in the eyes and answered.

"Well, sir, Mister Ward, I look after the field labor and the crops."

"Oh, then you have a very responsible position at Shiloh, correct?"

"Well, yes sir, I do," he responded as he sat up straighter in his seat.

"Mr. Edmundson, on the day in question, November 26 of last year, you were on horseback down in what is called the lower 40 on Shiloh, is that correct?"

"Yessuh."

"And as you moved into this grassy area, you saw three people, did you not?"

"Yessuh."

"Objection, Your honor. The counselor is leading the witness. Please allow *him* to tell the details of what he saw and the events."

"Overruled. Mr. Connors, you know full well that the jury wants to get to the quick of it. Mr. Ward is only expediting the process. Please proceed, Mr. Ward."

"Of course, Your Honor. May I remind the court Will Cromwell was very close to the witness. I considered it appropriate–."

"No explanations, Mister Ward. Just continue."

Ward took a quick glimpse at Linc and marked his frown. He looked quickly at Coeffield King who nodded ever so slightly. In half a second, Ward turned to George, who nervously twirled his hat in his hand.

"Continue, Mister Edmundson. Tell who and what you saw in the area in question."

"I–I saw Miss Caroline on her pony, riding down toward the lower 40. With all the crops in, I'd been riding the upper land close to the main house, just checking things out. For some reason, I followed her, 'cause I thought I'd seen somebody in those parts before. I came to that grassy area and there they were, going at it."

"And who are 'they'?" Ward asked.

"Why, Master Will and Hap Tyson."

"And what exactly do you mean 'going at it'?"

"I reckon they was fighting, Mister Ward."

"Did you see the blow that knocked Mister Will down to die?"

"Objection, your honor!" Linc Connors said sternly.

"Overruled. Mr. Connors, do you suppose that this jury does not know that this is a murder trial? Sit down, sir."

Linc Connors turned to see a smile on Coeffield King's face. *The dirty old codger.*

Confident that the jury heard all of these inferences in the objections, the DA hid a smile behind his hand and cleared his throat.

Chapter 46

"Now, Mister Edmundson, give the jury and this court your eyewitness account of this altercation between the two men, between the deceased and the defendant."

"We-ll, I could not see much but their two bodies goin' against each other. I did see arms flying, but I'm not sure whose was whose."

"Mister Edmundson, what happened as a result of this skirmish? This fight?"

"That–that Mister Will died."

"Yes, that Mister Will died as a result of the fists of this defendant, Hap Tyson, the meanest scoundrel in Edgecombe County," Ward's voice reached a fever pitch before the gavel fell and Linc's fist hit the table.

"Objection, Your Honor! This is outrageous!"

Judge Barnes glared at Linc.

"Young man, take your seat and do not–I say again–do not let me hear your fist hit that table again or I will hold you in contempt."

Ward's smirk did not escape the judge's notice.

"Not so fast, Mister Ward. You know better and do not let me hear another outburst of this nature."

He looked at both lawyers. Then, he rose and leaned over and spoke with a grimace. "Have I made myself clear?"

Ward bowed low before the judge and apologized.

Oh boy, thank you, Coeffield King. You sly old fox. You know all the tricks.

Linc also nodded, but he could not believe the theatrics and how quickly it had happened. Linc concealed his anger at such a brazen display of unethical behavior, and he knew Coeffield King was behind it all. But now it was his turn.

Before he rose to ask his questions, Judge Barnes spoke to the jurors.

"Members of the jury, you are reminded that you are to try this case based on evidence presented from the witness stand, and not from any inflammatory language used by either lawyer."

Turning to Linc, the judge said, "You may proceed, Counselor."

Connors approached George Edmundson with the softest look that he could muster. He did not want the man to think of him as an enemy.

* * *

Willie Pridgen had come late to the courthouse. She was fearful of the outcome. She knew how difficult it was for anyone to go up against Coeffield King in this court. As she found a seat at the rear of the balcony, she had seen Maggie and Fate, touching as mother and son. She could not take her eyes off of them. Shaking her head, Willie leaned against the back wall of the balcony, barely hearing what went on below, but she frequently saw Fate grin and strike his fist into his palm. Her heart sank, for if he was happy, then her other son was not doing so well.

Oh, Hap, this cannot be happening to you.

Maggie turned at that moment, and the eyes of the two women met in recognition. They nodded. The trial continued as Linc Connors's voice rose into the dome of the huge room.

"Now, Mister Edmundson, tell us exactly the position of the fallen tree from where you stood." He paused as George frowned and cocked his head. "You look puzzled. Let me rephrase the question. Was the log facing you so you saw the log in its full length, from one end to the other, or were you in a position to see just one end of the log?"

"Oh, I came up on the backside of the grassy area, so I was seeing just the side, Mister Connors."

"Just the side." He turned from George and looked at the judge. "Your Honor, may I beg the indulgence of the court to set up a drawing for the jury and for Mister Edmundson?" After a nod from the judge, he continued. "Thank you, sir."

Linc set up an easel brought from the back of the courtroom to prop up a poster, showing a simple picture of the grassy area and log

Chapter 46

as had been described by Hap. During the setup, George looked nervously over at King as if to beg his help. Linc Connors turned also, only to see King scowling at him and his prop. Linc turned to face the witness.

"Now, Mister Edmundson, does this sketch look like the grassy area in question and the fallen log? Would you say that this is the scene you saw from where you stood?"

A hesitation... "Mister Edmundson? The court is waiting."

Milton Ward jumped out of his chair so fast that it fell over. His fist hit the table as he shouted his objection. Everyone—judge, jury, spectators—appeared to jump at the same time and turn toward him as one. Coeffield King's knuckles were white as he clutched the railing. He wondered if his coaching was paying off too well.

"Your Honor, how do any of us in this courtroom know the authenticity of this drawing? A rough and approximate sketch actually could be distorted. There is no proper foundation for this sketch."

The judge's eyes rolled toward the ceiling.

"Mister Connors, every first year law student learns that you must lay a foundation before using a picture. Ask the witness if this is a fair representation of the scene of the crime on the day in question."

"Thank you, Your Honor. Mister Edmundson, would you say that this is a fair representation of the area where you saw the two men?"

"Yessir. I been down there many a time, and that's how it looks."

"And would you say that your view was the side one? Correct?"

"Y-yessir."

"Now, with the time of year, after Thanksgiving, the leaves were mostly down and the shrubs and undergrowth were sparse, were they not? So, you would not be looking through foliage?"

"Objection."

"Sustained. One question at a time Mister Connors," said the judge in a tone generally reserved for dull school children.

"Yesssir." George nodded as he agreed, though cautiously, as if he were expecting to be tricked.

Linc read his mind, "Mister Edmundson, I assure you that all I want is for you to tell this court exactly what you saw. And, nothing more."

"Mister Connors, please, move along. I am sure that Mister Edmundson understands," Judge Barnes interjected.

The smile froze on Linc Connors face, before he straightened up quickly and faced the judge. "Yes sir, your Honor." Slightly bowing to the bench, he turned back to the witness.

"Now, Mister Edmundson, would you point and mark on the poster where the two young men were confronting each other?" George did as he was told. "How far away would you say that you stood from the two young men in question? A few feet? Twenty, thirty–?"

"Oh, I'd say 'bout 25 or 30 paces."

"In feet, sir, if you please."

"We use paces in the field, Mister Connors. I can't rightly say in feet."

"Well, with the court's permission, Your Honor, can the witness demonstrate for us the length of a pace?"

"The prosecution will stipulate that a pace is three feet."

"Thank you, Mister Ward."

"Your honor, the witness' pace may be longer."

"Do you really want to do this, Mister Connors?" said the judge with an exaggerated gesture of approval.

"Yes, Judge Barnes, I do. Mister Edmundson, the floor is yours."

George got up from his chair and stood at attention. Then, he took a lengthy step, a distance of about three feet, stopped, and turned to Linc.

"That's a pace, sir."

"Thank you. Let the record reflect that Mister Edmundson's pace is approximately three feet long. Now, if you will, while you're standing, point to the place where you stood at the scene."

Chapter 46

"Well, I'd say about here," he said, his forefinger tapping the poster.

"Are you sure, Mister Edmundson?"

"Yes sir, I'm sure," he said.

"Will you mark on the poster where you were standing?"

"Yessir." George did so and returned to his seat.

"If I calculate correctly, a pace, according to Mister Edmundson, is approximately three feet. Then, if you were here," he said, also tapping the poster, "you were probably seventy-five or so feet away. Speaking of feet, could you see their feet clearly as they stood on the grassy area?"

"Hmmm. Yessir, I-I think so," George added as beads of perspiration formed on his forehead.

"Mister Edmundson, if you could see their feet, I would assume you—"

"Assumption? Your Honor, I have to object," Ward interrupted.

"Sustained."

"Sorry, Your Honor. Mister Edmundson, could you see the arms, hands, the entire bodies of these two men?"

"Yessir, but I was pretty excited, 'cause they was going at it. I was also worried about Miss Caroline's safety."

"Mister Edmundson, did you see Mister Tyson strike Mister Cromwell?"

A hush fell over the courtroom. Every fan stopped. Every mouth closed. No breathing sounded. George felt that he was dying up on the stand. He stuttered and stammered until Judge Barnes advised him to answer the lawyer's question...and clearly.

"Yessuh. I'll try. You see, Mister Connors, arms were swinging every whicha way. I-I reckon I saw blows going both ways."

"Either you did, or you didn't, Mister Edmundson. Which is it? Did you actually see the defendant strike Mister Cromwell? With his fist?"

"Objection, badgering the witness."

"Sustained."

"OK. Did you actually see the defendant strike Mister Cromwell?"

"Yes, sir."

"With his fist?"

George sucked in the heavy air and bit his lip, but he did not look at Linc or the DA. He raised his head, his eyes riveted to Maggie in the balcony, who returned his stare, with a deep furrow on her brow.

"Mister Connors, I can't say for sure about a fist, but I did see a head butt from the defendant. Everything happened so fast, you see." George's head dropped briefly.

"And did Will Cromwell fall down as a result of being struck by Hap Tyson's head?"

"I can't say for certain. Things was happening so fast, I told you. I think so. But I'm not sure."

Murmurs rumbled through the courtroom, with the judge's gavel falling once more.

Linc started a new line of questioning. "Mister Edmundson, where was Miss Caroline during this ruckus?"

"Lemme see. She was...on the...grassy area," George dragged out his words.

"We understand that, but where in relation to the two men?"

"Uh—not too far away."

"Mister Edmundson, with your Honor's permission, now look at this drawing and point, then mark the location of Miss Caroline as she stood watching."

George looked at the judge who nodded his approval. He stood again, strode to the drawing, and pointed to the left side of the fallen log. Caroline had stood behind the two, yet still in full view of George.

"Mister Edmundson, how many paces was Miss Cromwell from Will Cromwell and Hap Tyson?"

"Hmmm... 'About four, sir."

Chapter 46

"And how many paces were you from the scuffle?"

"About twenty-four or twenty-five."

"So, it is your testimony that Miss Caroline Cromwell stood approximately four paces, or about twelve feet, from Mister Tyson and Mister Cromwell?"

George nodded.

"You must answer verbally, Mister Edmundson."

"Yes, Twelve."

"Once more, how many paces were you standing from the confrontation between Mister Will and the defendant?"

"Twenty-four or twenty-five," George answered.

Coeffield King sat behind the rail and scrawled notes on a piece of paper.

"In feet, the calculation would be approximately seventy-five feet, for the record, Your Honor. Thank you, Mister Edmundson, no further questions."

"Rebuttal, Mister Ward?" Judge Barnes looked at the DA over his spectacles.

"No, Your Honor, Mister Edmundson has answered sufficiently."

Chapter 47
The Surprise Witness

As George climbed down from the witness stand, the door opened in the rear of the courtroom. Litch Bagley stood in the doorway and handed a note to the sheriff's deputy, who brought it to Milton Ward. The district attorney read the note quickly and stood.

"Your Honor, may I ask for a brief recess? There seems to be a new witness for the prosecution."

"Granted. This court will recess for twenty minutes. Bailiff, take the jury to the jury room and sequester the new witness."

With that direction, the gavel fell, and Judge Barnes went into his chambers.

Linc and Hap bumped heads.

"Who is this fellow?" Linc asked, his scowl indicating his displeasure with this latest development. He did not like surprises.

"Litch Bagley," Hap whispered. "He was a friend of Will's up at the university and the family's. I think he's in love with Caroline."

"Uh-oh. You mean you think he might say anything to get her away from you?"

"I don't know, but one thing I do know, I do not want to put the trial off. I want it over, no matter what."

"Hap, don't be foolish—"

"Mister Connors, I have caused so much pain for so many people. I know the risk."

He choked on the next words. "I-I could hang. Oh God, I really could." His head crashed on his arms.

Chapter 47

"Hap, sit up! Now!" he hissed. "Don't dare let anyone see you in this state." He looked around to see if anyone was staring at his client. "Get hold of yourself. We will have our chance. And, I don't mean to lose this case. Do you hear me?" Hap's head had jerked upwards as he quickly wiped the tears from his face. Looking down, he still did not project an innocent defendant. "Hold your head high, man. We've got a long way to go, but we can do this. I just have to find the cracks in the prosecution. Now, you let me do my job. No more talk about a rushed trial. Ya hear!"

A few minutes later, Hamilton Barnes came back into the courtroom. The bailiff brought in the jurors and called the court back into session.

Milton Ward stood and addressed the judge. "Your Honor, may I ask my esteemed colleague to approach the bench with me?"

"Yes, but let's move this along, Mister Ward."

Both lawyers approached and stood.

Milton Ward spoke softly to the judge, "Your Honor, a most unusual thing has happened. Mister Litch Bagley, a guest of the Cromwells during the time in question, has come forward to testify that he saw the altercation between Will Cromwell and Hap Tyson. He is a credible witness and I would like to call him to the stand with Your Honor's permission."

"Mister Ward, why did this witness not come forward before? This seems very irregular," he growled back, irritated with another wrinkle in the trial. He liked his court to run smoothly and not be peppered with irregularities.

"Your Honor, I think I can clarify this issue in examination."

"Well," he sighed heavily, "I see no reason at this point not to have him say his piece. Do you have any objections, Mister Connors?"

"This is highly irregular, Your Honor. We should have been advised of everyone on the prosecution's witness list," he retorted with irritation. "Frankly, your Honor, we have been blindsided, but may I offer a suggestion?"

"What, Mister Connors?" he asked with his own continued irritation.

"Sir, why not have the witness heard out of the presence of the jury? Then—"

"Really, Connors?" he practically sneered. "I think not. Mister Ward, put your witness on the stand. Let's move this trial along."

"Judge Barnes!" Linc Connors wailed.

"Watch it, Connors. You're close to contempt." Hap's lawyer threw up his hands and walked back to his table. Things were not going well for Greenville's rising star.

"Thank you, Your Honor," Ward said, with a smirk on his face as he walked back to his own table. "The prosecution calls Litch Bagley to the stand."

The Bailiff opened the courtroom door and Litch Bagley straightened himself up tall and erect and walked down the aisle, then through the gate, glancing quickly at Hap Tyson before he took his oath and then his seat.

"Would you please identify yourself to the court, sir?"

"My name is Litchfield Jacob Bagley. My family lives in Raleigh and presently I am a junior at the University of North Carolina. I am a friend of the Cromwell family."

"Why are you here in this courtroom today, Mister Bagley?" Ward asked.

"I felt it my duty to come back to Tarboro today and testify in this case. I knew Mister Edmundson could be a witness, and I trusted his account of events, should he be called to testify. However, my conscience led me to come back and add my view to the evidence. At the time of this, this tragedy, all I could think about was getting to the house and being of some comfort to the family."

Chapter 47

Linc never objected to any of the statements. Hap's grip on his arm let him know to allow it, but why? The young man was on trial for his life. He should want Linc to grasp at any straws to clear his name. And his objections couldn't hurt a growing reputation, could it?

"Mister Bagley, where were you standing at the scene of the altercation between the defendant and Will Cromwell, and did you see Hap Tyson hit Will Cromwell with his fists?"

"Objection, Your Honor. Leading," Linc stood, even with Hap pulling on his coattails. He felt he had to do his job, even if Hap wanted no objections.

"Sustained. Rephrase, Mister Ward."

"Of course, Your Honor." Swiveling back to Litch Bagley, he asked, "Mister Bagley, you have come to contribute your testimony for this court pertaining to the altercation between the defendant Hap Tyson and Will Cromwell. Will you proceed to do so?"

"Of course. I stood behind the trees nearest to the grassy area of the lower 40. When I got there, Caroline was crying out for them to stop—Will and this Tyson fellow, but her cries were to no avail. They kept on. And then it was over. Mister Tyson's fists were balled-up. He was standing over Will, who lay sprawled on the ground with his neck on the fallen log. He was dead, Mister Ward. At the hands of that man." Litch quickly pointed at the defendant.

"Objection!" Linc Connors sprang to his feet.

"Sustained. The jury will disregard the last statement by Mister Bagley? As for you, Mister Bagley, you are to testify only the facts, in other words, what you saw, not your conclusions. Another outburst like that, and I will hold you in contempt."

"I beg the court's pardon. I have lost a friend, Your—"

"Mister Bagley, you are out of order. Are you through with this witness, Mister Ward?"

"Yes, Your Honor."

"Mister Connors, your turn," the judge said.

"Thank you, Your Honor."

Linc walked up to the witness stand and placed his hand on the rail.

"Mister Bagley, I am puzzled by your appearance at this trial, so I have to ask you to clarify your intentions to testify."

"Well, I had to get back to school to finish up my studies for the year. I was certain that George Edmundson would be a witness. I just thought it would be taken care of."

"You just thought? Mister Bagley, we have courts to decide how the laws should be carried out, not just your thinking on an issue."

"Objection, Your Honor, Mister Connors is badgering my witness."

"Yes, you are, Mister Connors, but I am inclined to agree with you. Mister Bagley, I will allow your testimony, but I find your coming forth at the last minute almost inappropriate. If Will Cromwell was such a good friend, why did you not tell the family immediately and let them know what you had seen?"

"I suppose I was not thinking straight. As I said, I was in a state of shock. I had never seen anything like this before in my entire life. I-I don't know what else to say. I suppose I do need to ask the court's pardon as well as the Cromwells'," he said, looking over at Will's family.

"Continue, Mister Connors," the judge instructed, scowling and running his fingers through his hair.

"Mister Bagley, what made you go down to the lower 40?"

"I discovered Will and Miss Caroline were not in the main house, so I thought that they were out riding and I wished to join them. We had ridden before to that grove where the grassy knoll is. I just guessed that might be where they were."

"You say that you heard Miss Caroline's cries. Did you hear

Chapter 47

either of the two men speaking?"

"I only heard grunts and sounds from struggling. No distinct words."

"Mister Bagley, did you see George Edmundson?"

"Yes, I did."

"Could you point out on this drawing about where Mister Edmundson was positioned, where you were, and where Miss Cromwell was?"

Litch pointed to a spot where he said he was, and then to a spot where he said George was. He pointed to a spot where he said Caroline was, which was closer to where Hap and Will were fighting.

"Please mark these spots with an O, not an X, so we will know your mark to be different from Mister Edmundson." A brief pause ensued. "Now, when you saw that Will was down, what did you do?"

"I fell back in disbelief. George, uh-Mister Edmundson, ran and picked Miss Caroline up off the ground and told her that he was going for help. I raced back to the house to assist the family in any way that I could. Evidently, it took George a little while to get Caroline to understand what he was going to do. Then he had to get back to his horse. By then I was pretty much ahead of him. I don't think he even knew that I was down there in the area."

"Your Honor, I just have a few more questions for this witness," Linc said, as he faced Litch with his most penetrating stare before he spoke, making the witness rather squeamish as he waited for the questions. "Mister Bagley, are you in love with Caroline Cromwell?" The courtroom seemed to lean forward as one body to hear the answer.

"Your Honor! The relevance!" Ward practically shouted. Judge Barnes waved him off with a look of curiosity spreading across his face.

Litch looked at the jury, at the judge, at the Cromwells, before he spoke. "Yes, I am."

"And, Mister Bagley, would you not like to see Mister Tyson handed punishment for said crime? Please answer, sir."

"Oh, Your Honor, I must object. One more time, Mister Connors is badgering my witness!"

"Mister Connors, do you think you can rephrase that question?"

"Your Honor, I know what I saw," Litch Bagley spoke, turning to the judge.

"What you saw or what you wanted to see?" Linc spoke loudly and continued quickly. "Your Honor, I ask that the testimony of this witness be stricken from the record. I frankly consider him a jealous suitor who would say anything to rid the competition."

"Mister Connors, you are out of order, now," the judge said, as his gavel fell hard. He continued, "Just a minute, Mister Bagley. I am going to excuse you from the courtroom at this time. However, I am suggesting that you get back to your horse or carriage, make your way to the train station in Rocky Mount, and go to Raleigh or the university or wherever you came from. You are excused."

Litch Bagley's face reddened as he stepped down from the witness chair.

"Any other witnesses, Mister Ward?" the judge asked.

"Just one, Your Honor," he answered, not sure whether his surprise witness had helped or hurt his cause. "Miss Caroline Cromwell."

A series of low murmurs erupted in the courtroom. Judge Barnes banged his gavel for silence.

The doors to the courtroom opened, and Caroline walked unsteadily to the gate.

If only Hap could have helped her, held her, loved her, but Ward's hand guided her through the gate and up to the witness stand. Never once could Hap catch her eye as she approached the

Chapter 47

stand and the questions from the D.A. Caroline placed her hand on the Bible, vowed to tell the truth, and settled as comfortably as she could in the chair. Her hand on the Word was serious business in the Cromwell family. How many times had Will said in their childhood days, "You're not supposed to swear, Caroline, but put your hand on the family Bible and you must tell the truth, the whole truth, and nothing but...that's what Coffie says?"

Finally, she looked out into the gallery at her grandfather's face, a face she had adored all of her life. Her lids fluttered and her head dropped slightly as she tried to contain her emotions.

"Miss Cromwell, please identify yourself and your relationship to the deceased," Mister Ward said gently.

"My name is Caroline King Cromwell. Will Cromwell...is, was, my brother," she said in a voice barely louder than a whisper.

"Now, Miss Cromwell, will you tell the court a little about your background with the deceased? Just a few brother/sister experiences you had together growing up on Shiloh."

"Will Cromwell was the nicest of brothers and the kindest one I could ever hope to have. He always looked after me for as long as I remember."

Blood is thick, but not thicker than the truth, Linc said to himself, hoping that he was not engaging in wishful thinking.

Thus, began the question-and-answer series that bound brother and sister so tightly that no one would ever doubt the lengths to which either would have gone to support the other. The looks between Caroline and her grandfather, who sat ever so still behind the rail, even amazed the cynical Linc Connors. He also watched the jury as each question built an unbelievable picture of family and loyalty.

Finally, Judge Barnes leaned over and suggested they move on with the case. Ward bowed slightly. "Miss Caroline, can you tell the court your reason for being at the area known as the lower 40?"

"Yes, the lower 40 has always been a wonderful place to go and reflect. I felt the need to be alone and riding Nellie is one of my favorite things to do."

"When you heard another horse riding the road from the big house, did you have any idea who it might be?"

"No, but it was Will. He said that we had not had enough time together and he was grateful that we could be just brother and sister for a few moments."

"Thank you. However, it has been established that a third party showed up on the lower 40. Who might that have been?"

The volume of her voice was barely a whisper when she said, "Hap Tyson."

Judge Barnes leaned over and mentioned that the jury and the court needed to hear clearly her answer.

"Hap Tyson," she spoke and looked straight at the defense table.

"Thank you, Miss Caroline. Will you please tell the jury and this court what you saw between these two men?"

"There was a scuffle and Will died." Her voice cracked, as she sobbed as quietly as she could.

"Your Honor, no other questions."

"Cross, Mister Connors?"

"Yes, Your Honor." Linc stood and fidgeted for a second. He could not hate himself for what he was about to do. It was his job, his duty to his client. The pendulum had swung. It was time to out the truth.

Linc knew the effect of crescendo in this next line of questioning. He knew he would surely lose the jury if he appeared to be badgering this lovely young girl. He guessed that he already was considered to be an outsider, someone from outside the area who was defending a known ne'er-do-well, accused of bringing harm to a member of a widely respected local family. Suspicious gazes followed him as he paced before the twelve jurors. But he

Chapter 47

planned to move methodically before his attack. *Velvet, think velvet,* he prompted himself as he turned with a smile and soft eye at the girl, who sat with her head bowed.

As Linc asked a few more general questions, Caroline thought the lawyer seemed polite and cordial, and perhaps she could get through the rest of this ordeal after all. At some point, however, and Caroline did not know when, she felt discomfort and nervousness in herself. She saw her grandfather's hand reach for the rail. The questions had become more personal and intimate. Linc Connors had set a fuse and, now, he struck the match.

"Miss Cromwell, did you intentionally plan to meet Hap Tyson at the lower 40 on the day in question?"

Her knuckles turned white as she squeezed her fingers in her lap; her head came up slowly. Her mind raced. Under the pointed question she didn't know what to say. With eyelids fluttering, she looked briefly at her grandfather, who now was leaning forward toward the rail.

"In fact, Miss Cromwell, are you not in love with the defendant, Hap Tyson? And further, Miss Cromwell, would you not have left your family and home if Hap Tyson had asked you to do just that?"

Linc fired the questions, knowing he was badgering her unnecessarily.

"Your Honor," Mister Ward finally said weakly as he stood to object.

"Well, finally, Mister Ward. I thought you had lost your tongue."

But the spectators shifted their attention to Coeffield King as he stood up waving his notes at Milton Ward.

Judge Barnes struck the gavel. "Mister King, you must sit down."

King slowly sat, his eyes never leaving his granddaughter.

"Uh, Your Honor, no objections," Ward stuttered, confused by the old lawyer's actions.

Caroline was frightened by her grandfather's actions. *What is he doing? What am I to do?* She was all alone now, just her and her vow to tell the truth. Her head began to nod.

"Miss Cromwell, you will have to speak up. I'm afraid you can't just nod. Is this the answer to my first question or all the questions?" Linc Connors asked.

Judge Barnes leaned down and gently said, "Miss Cromwell, you must answer each of these questions, if Mister Connors will repeat each, one at a time for you to answer." His voice ended in a growl when he addressed Linc Connors.

Meanwhile, Linc had turned slowly to focus on his opponent—not Milton Ward, but Coeffield King. *Why did that old codger make Ward quit his objections? Why? Unless...* Realization hit him. *King wants her to deny the first question and all the rest. In fact, if I quiet her, she won't disavow all the allegations from the questions, especially the one about loving Hap Tyson. Preposterous!*

Linc quickly turned back to the witness and the task at hand.

"Miss Cromwell, would you please speak for all the court to hear your answer for the first question? Are you not in fact in love with the defendant, one Hap Tyson?"

She sucked in her breath, then nodding her head, she said "yes," barely audible.

"And your answers to the other questions? Did you plan to meet my client on the grassy area?"

"Y-yes."

No objection.

A pause... "Miss Cromwell, would you have left your family and gone away with Mister Tyson if he had asked you to?"

No objection.

"I don't know," she mumbled. "Perhaps."

"Thank you, miss. Now, let us go on with the exact order of

Chapter 47

events of the day in question."

He wanted to look over at King and the DA, but he dared not, as he leaned slightly toward her. "On the day of the altercation–"

She looked pale, almost as if she were going to faint.

"Are you all right, Miss Cromwell? Would you care for some water?"

He looked into her face. "Miss Crom–"

But before he could finish her name, her head jerked back. Her face was contorted into a look of intense sorrow that shocked the spectators. Looking up as she struggled to contain her emotions, she wrung her hands. Slowly she stood and wailed in heart-felt pain. Her blood curdling scream stunned the courtroom.

"It was an accident," she railed over and over in front of the court. "It was a horrible, horrible accident. Hap never struck Will. He tried to stop him. And when Will knocked Hap to the ground, Hap had no idea that when he stood up, his head would hit Will's chin and knock him over. Oh my God, Will…Will…Will."

Her pained cries pierced the air. She choked on her brother's name until the only sounds she made were gagging sobs as she collapsed in her seat. She looked first at her parents, then at her grandfather. Tears streaked her face.

"Order in the court!" Judge Barnes' gavel pounded, as spectators stood, muttering and leaning this way and that to glimpse the witness.

Coeffield King sat dazed by her confessions on the stand. He had no idea that what she had said earlier to him was really the truth, and that she would testify this way under oath. No one really looked at him during the questioning. They were focused on the witness, but he began to move. Slowly, he rose from his seat and pushed open the gate. He extended an unsteady arm toward his granddaughter, but then staggered forward, only to stumble between the two tables. An expression of bewilderment replaced the look of compassion, as the old man fell over the defense table.

Chaos erupted, but not before Hap had gently lowered the old lawyer to the floor. Judge Barnes and the bailiff jumped into action. Hap moved toward Caroline to block her view with his shoulder, but not before she'd seen the glazed look in her grandfather's eyes. He reached to comfort her.

"Take your hands off my daughter," Sarah Cromwell hissed at Hap, showing her contempt for the young man. Elijah pulled his wife and daughter away and escorted them to the back of the courtroom and out the door.

Doctor Knight shouted orders for the care of Tarboro's favorite son, now fallen.

"Bailiff, clear the court! Remove the jury and get help for Mister King," the judge ordered.

The bailiff rounded up several men to help remove the old barrister. Rufus Knight did not like the looks of his good friend.

Hamilton Barnes leaned heavily on the defense's table, peered at the two lawyers and spoke, in a tired voice, but one as professional as he could muster. "Take fifteen, gentlemen, and pull your summations together, so when the jury returns, they can hear what you have to say. Afterward, I will instruct them about their options."

With those words, he trudged up on the platform and opened the door to his office.

Collapsing into his chair behind his desk, he mulled over what had happened to one of his best friends and legal colleagues down east. This travesty would wear on him for a long time. Nothing like this chaos had ever happened in a court of his. He was devastated for his friend, but also for his reputation as holding a tight ship in his courtroom.

Only two people did not obey Judge Barnes, Fate and Maggie

Chapter 47

Edmundson. Fate sat with his head in his hands and wept, agonizing over what he thought was a lack of justice for Will's death. Hap just could not walk free. Why, oh why, hadn't he let the wild boar finish her attack at the Medusa Tree? His fist banged on the wooden balcony railing.

"Let it go, son," his mother whispered as she patted his quivering shoulder. "It was just an accident, a terrible accident. You heard Miss Caroline. There's no better witness in this case than his own sister. Don't let this thing eat you up. You hear me, son?"

Everyone in the balcony had heard his scream as it resounded in the dome in tandem with Caroline's wails. The two voices rose in unspeakable pain. Those who watch trials might have heard anguish from one side or another during trials in the past, but none like that heard in the trial of Hap Tyson for the death of Will Cromwell.

Maggie and Fate left the balcony, both saddened for their loss. Maggie had loved Will like her own as he grew from infant to a young man. Fate had loved him as a brother as the two had grown up together on Shiloh. Sleep would elude both of them that night.

* * *

When the allotted time had passed, the judge summoned the lawyers into his chambers.

"On reflection, I want to hear from you both."

"Your Honor, the prosecution requests permission to argue that Mister Tyson is guilty of the lesser included offense of involuntary manslaughter. Clearly, the evidence supports the position that the defendant was reckless and . . ."

"Enough. I've got it," interrupted the judge. "Mister Connors?"

"Judge, the defense moves for a directed verdict on the basis of Miss Cromwell's testimony. In addition, we move for a mistrial."

"On what grounds?" growled the judge.

"On the grounds that the court declared the trial over before the defense could present its case. That's a violation of due process and every tenet of criminal procedure."

"Denied and denied. Anything else?"

"Yes," said Connors. "We request that the court charge the jury on the principles of self-defense. The deceased was by all the evidence the aggressor in this altercation and my client was only defending himself."

"I'll tell you what I'm going to do. I'm going to instruct the jury like King Solomon."

"Huh?" uttered Ward and Connors simultaneously.

"Yes, I'm going to allow the argument of involuntary manslaughter since the jury may conclude that Mister Tyson was reckless. And, I'm going to charge the jury that Mister Tyson's actions might be considered self-defense and allow acquittal on that ground. We reconvene at three P.M. gentlemen."

With the jury seated, a collected Judge Barnes called for the lawyers' summations.

"You first, Mister Ward."

"Judge and jury, we have had an unusual occurrence in court today, but one *fact* still remains. Will Cromwell is dead. That fact is indisputable. The evidence shows that in a fist fight, the defendant deliberately killed Will Cromwell, the beloved son of Captain Elijah and Sarah Cromwell, The grand jury saw fit to charge him with murder. However, after consultation with the Judge, we the People believe that there is sufficient credible evidence for you the jury to find the defendant guilty of involuntary manslaughter. Judge Barnes will explain what the elements of that are but it is enough to convict if you conclude that the defendant was reckless in a way that resulted in the death of Will Cromwell. The time has come for you the jury to do your solemn duty and find the defendant guilty so the community can

Chapter 47

begin to heal. Thank you."

"Mister Connors? Your turn."

"Thank you, Judge Barnes. Several eyewitnesses have each given their view of the incident between my client and the deceased. Except for one, these so-called eyewitnesses were too far away to see what happened or too clouded in their own biases to testify accurately. That alone should give rise to reasonable doubt as to Hap Tyson's guilt. However, there is one witness who was in the best position to see the tragic events from barely twelve feet away. I ask you to consider the testimony of the deceased's own sister, Miss Caroline Cromwell. Miss Cromwell had the best view of the three. You heard her say that it was a terrible accident and that Hap Tyson never laid a fist on Will Cromwell. In fact, she said that Mister Tyson tried to stop her brother. Will Cromwell used his fists and kicked my client on the ground. Little did Mister Tyson know that when he raised up he would chin butt Mister Cromwell, as testified by his sister. Don't let sympathy or emotion sway your judgment. If there is doubt, reasonable doubt, doubt that you in your everyday experience would consider sufficient to give pause, then you must find my client not guilty.

"I move for the acquittal of charges against my client, Your Honor, and gentlemen of the jury."

Judge Barnes turned to the jury and spoke clearly to the twelve jurors. "Gentlemen, you have two options before you. Murder, the deliberate taking of another's life which carries with it the death sentence. Or, involuntary manslaughter which is defined as an unintentional killing that results either from recklessness or criminal negligence. If convicted of involuntary manslaughter, the defendant may be sentenced to prison for up to twenty-five years. If you choose the option of involuntary manslaughter, I will set a date for the sentencing of Mister Tyson.

"If you choose the other option of acquittal, Mister Tyson will walk free out of this courtroom." He paused then looked over at the bailiff.

"The bailiff will escort you to the jury room at this time, and when you have discussed and figured out your decision beyond a shadow of a doubt, each one of you will vote and the foreman of the jury will make the announcement of the verdict from the jury box. I wish you well in your decision and we will wait for your decision."

The jury vacated the courtroom once more to determine the fate of Hap Tyson.

* * *

"Linc, it's been over an hour. What is going on? How could they not trust the word of Will's own sister?"

"I am in shock myself, Hap. Maybe someone seated in the box has some hidden loyalty to the Cromwells that we did not suspect. Look, just hang in there. They are discussing everything, so that takes time, especially if there are several who have opinions and they want to express themselves. Who knows?"

The sound of the judge's office door made both Hap and Linc jump. The bailiff called out for all to rise as the jury door opened and twelve men filed into the courtroom.

All faces were stoic. Nothing, absolutely no expression, revealed any verdict one way or the other.

The jury sat.

"Mister foreman, has the jury come to a verdict?"

* * *

The foreman read the verdict of Not Guilty. Hap Tyson duly cried like a baby in his lawyer's arms. Linc Connors reveled in victory at the moment, especially when the District Attorney had shaken his hand. It was the custom for opposing lawyers to do that, but...

Damn! I was ready to do battle...

With a bitter taste in his mouth, Linc Connors stood by the

Chapter 47

door on the upper landing of the courthouse and surveyed the empty streets. Everybody had crowded the wagon bearing Coeffield King to the hospital. He sighed, finally settling down on one of the steps. It was over before it had hardly begun. He felt empty. Where was his victory? Maybe he could savor the outcome later, but all he wanted to do now was to leave Tarboro and get back to Greenville. No one would believe him if he tried a hundred different ways to describe that court scene.

Chapter 48
The Aftermath

Coeffield King awoke three days later. His nose was buried in starched sheets with medicinal smells twitching his nostrils. *Where am I?* That was the question on his mind as his clouded memory slowly cleared. First, he heard his daughter's voice. *What was Sarah saying?* Her words faded in and out. *Home? Did she say home? Am I home?* He wished reality would catch up with awareness. Every joint and muscle screamed with pain and exhaustion. He'd never felt such weakness in his whole life. *What had happened to him?*

His eyelids fluttered. *What room is this* he wondered? Certainly not his and Jacksie's. *Maybe the hospital? What had happened–? My God, the trial! Caroline!* His back arched. Another pain burned in his chest. *My heart! My heart!* His fist beat slightly over the throb as if he wanted to expunge it from his chest. In exhaustion, he froze, inwardly begging for relief.

Please, God... Give...me relief. Just give...me...time to right my wrong. Please.

The old gentleman had never been incapacitated before in his life. His immobility disturbed him greatly, but at least clarity of thought was returning.

He remembered reaching out to comfort his granddaughter during her testimony, when everything hazed and darkened. How surprised he had felt as his body shut down, and he was powerless to prevent it. He, Coeffield King, Tarboro's favorite son. He also recalled the big, gentle hands lowering his body to the courtroom floor. He had to thank whoever helped him. Yes,

Chapter 48

he needed to do that... But what in the world had he done to his granddaughter? Where was his compassion for her?

Her anguished cries reminded him of his own when he had lost his beloved Jacksie; now he had selfishly closed his mind to the fact that the boy's story might be true. Where was his compassion for him? *I failed you, Jacksie, and the Widow Bowden. Even John Constable, and Nate Jones, and, now, Caroline, my own flesh and blood. I am one sorry soul...*

Darkness overcame him once more.

* * *

Rufus Knight bent over his patient and strained to hear his stricken friend.

"I want to see...the boy, Rufus," King whispered to his doctor. "Please...don't let any more time...go by."

Doctor Knight nodded and turned to the door. "He's right outside on the doorstep. He's been here every day."

"Every day?"

"Yes, Coeffield, along with your family."

Rufus Knight walked briskly to the door of the hospital room and stopped, only to tell Elijah, Sarah, and Caroline that the patriarch wanted to see Hap Tyson.

"No," Sarah barked, but Elijah held her back and nodded in silence.

"Sarah, whatever he wants," he said sternly.

The three looked at each other, not knowing what would happen next. The medicines seemed to be making the old man jabber out of his head. At times, he even talked to Jacksie.

Eagerly following Doctor Knight toward the doorway, Hap nodded hesitantly at the Cromwells but dared not linger. He tiptoed into the room, the same room where he, too, had suffered and agonized and recovered. The old lawyer's swift debilitation shocked him. Who was this man, chalky and cracked-lipped, lying shriveled in the same bed where he had lain? Certainly not

Tarboro's favorite son. There had to be a mistake. He glanced quickly around the room as if to expect the tall, stalwart gentleman to come out of the shadows. The steel man, who, through the District Attorney, had challenged his very existence in the courtroom.

"Boy? Come close...I want...to tell you...about compassion." The words slipped out in hoarse clips, barely audible.

The voice seemed familiar, but Hap was truly amazed at the stark change in Coeffield King, from resolute and proud to withered and humble. He leaned closer to hear the story of John Constable and Nate Jones and the vow the old man made at the site of the Medusa Tree.

"Son, those poor unfortunate souls never...had a chance...or received compassion. They...swung at the hands of a bloodthirsty mob for no good reason. My father and I... we tried to find the culprits...over the years...but we failed. Then my compassion got...buried...somehow, and stayed buried...in your case. I refused to acknowledge...your truth and...Caroline's. I'm so...sorry, boy, so very sorry."

Slowly, his hand crept out from under the covers.

"Sir, you don't-"

"Oh, but I do. I...could not live with...myself without righting...this wrong. Forgive...an old fool."

He jerked Hap's hand as if to wrench an answer from him.

"I do, sir. I do," Hap whispered back.

"Good. Good."

The tension in his face eased.

Hap's hand dwarfed the old man's, but King's grip still showed some strength. And then, King studied the young man's hands and knew they were the hands that had treated him so gently in the courtroom. He smiled.

"It was you, wasn't it? Thank you," Mr. King said, puzzling Hap even more.

Chapter 48

The patient's eyes closed, as he clasped the youth's hand. When he opened them again, he cocked his head with great curiosity, then broke into a huge smile, peeling years from his ashen face. He spoke again.

"Will? Is that...you, boy? I can't believe it. Bend down...son, your grandfather wants...to tell you something."

Hap's eyes widened. He was embarrassed but heard a soft murmur from Doctor Knight behind him. "Pretend. What can it hurt?" The door clicked shut.

As Hap bent close to the bed, the wizened old man whispered, "I love you, boy."

He pulled Hap's head down on his chest with his other arm. Never once had Hap known this kind of familial love, only the affection from Willie and a shy hug or two from the old doctor. He could hardly remember Pap, and he certainly remembered no affection. His eyes closed as he nuzzled in the bosom of a man who was supposed to hate him. He fell to his knees beside the bed as King stroked his head—not the blond head of his grandson, but the thick brown hair on Hap's head.

Soon, rhythmic breathing came from the sleeping patient, but even in sleep his grasp of the young man's hand never loosened. Hap slowly freed his hand and slid his head from under the arm and rolled around to sit by the bed. He allowed himself time to reflect and to revere the old lawyer who had confessed and apologized to him. Him. A waif. Him. A ne'er-do-well in the eyes of many. But this man had shown him dignity.

He stood up and turned to the sleeping man, who now had become a giant in his mind. Hap's words were slow and deliberate. Gulping down emotion, shaking as he stood, Hap made his own vow.

"I also will make my life one of service and compassion. Thank you, sir. Thank you." Bowing as he spoke these words, Hap Tyson wondered if he would ever see Coeffield King alive again.

Chapter 49
REDEMPTION

Wendell Tyson had not come to his son's trial. He knew about it–everyone in and around Tarboro knew about it–but he could not attend. What had he ever done to deserve Hap's love? After all, he had sent him away all those years ago. So, it was no small surprise to open his door the weekend after the trial to find this tall, lanky young man with big hands and a crooked smile, standing on the porch of his modest home. The boy's eyes questioned greatly, but the smile indicated a need for his *daddy*. Wendell Tyson marched into his son's arms and cried.

"Son, son, I'm so sorry. I can't begin to tell you... Oh, my Hap."

"Pap, I asked to live with Willie," he reassured his father, "but I'm here now. I'm here."

Wendell could not let go of his boy, as the years of guilt receded with each successive squeeze and pat on the back. How he could have let his own son go he would never understand, but looking at him now, he knew that Willie had done a good job. Some day he would thank her properly.

"I wanna go to school, Pap. I've made myself a vow."

"What kind of vow?" he asked as they sat at his kitchen table.

"I won't get into it now, but I want to prepare myself for a job to serve others. I don't know what it'll be, but I'll figure it out."

Wendell smiled and felt pride to see this kind of manhood and maturity before him. How strange and wonderful to be able to praise one's own flesh. The crooked smile no longer looked evil on his son's face.

"You want a summer job?" his father asked.

Chapter 49

"You bet," he said, "but I gotta finish my credits to get into a school."

"We'll do whatever it takes to make it work, son. Whatever it takes."

So, the son reunited with the father to work together in his spare time. Hap spent the rest of spring and his summer finishing his credits. He amazed himself, for learning came easy with desire and goals. His hopes were high. How could all of these good things be happening to the young man who once was the meanest scoundrel in all of Edgecombe County? Willie would say it was redeeming grace.

He just had to make it all work.

Chapter 50
ACCEPTANCE

Dean Perry stood in front of his desk and looked at the gangly young man standing before him. He had never in his entire career seen such a bundle of nerves. Well, he would discover if Hap Tyson had any backbone, and the sooner the better.

Rufus Knight had reminded Hap to shake the dean's hand and sit when invited. He forgot and sat first, but he jumped from his chair and grabbed Perry's hand. He was overcome by sheer panic as he stood shuffling from one foot to the other. His hat fell from his other hand, which he quickly tried to catch in mid-air. He failed and his hat landed on Dean Perry's foot. Blood rushed to his face. With a flicker of a smile, he scooped it up from the floor.

"Well? Sit down...again, Mister Tyson," he instructed Hap as he seated himself and peered over his wire spectacles, shuffling papers as he did so.

Congleton Perry's bald head shone under the light of his office in South Building. Rosy cheeks and a pug nose were prominent on his face, and his piercing steel gray eyes focused on the prospective applicant.

"Mister Tyson, I find your entry into our university most unusual."

"Sir?"

The Dean was a hard man when it came to admitting students into the University of North Carolina. He wanted the best student, but he also wanted to offer an opportunity to a youth who could perform, but often never had the chance to prove himself. This young man before him, as nervous as he was, appeared to be the perfect candidate for his philosophy. Rarely had he

Chapter 50

misjudged in all the years he had sat behind his desk.

"Your high marks at the Academy in Greenville last spring and this summer are most impressive, but can you tell me why your grades from Tarboro were so poor? In other words, Mister Tyson, why should we let you into this institution this fall?"

Leaning forward, he gave Hap his most concerned scowl and then leaned back to allow the youth either to stew or to salvage the awkward beginning of their interview.

As big as he was, Hap felt like a bug under the scrutiny of this pressing official. He thought he had bungled their introduction, and he needed no failures at this juncture. For one brief moment, his right hand covered his eyes to hide his uneasiness. With a sniff, he mustered courage and stared directly at this man across the desk and pled his case.

"Mister Perry, Dean Perry, you may not find me worthy of admission to this school, but you must know my feelings. My background is unusual, but my desire is as great as anybody else applying today. They have nothing, absolutely nothing, over my hope to better myself. Many of them have advantages; I will have to make my own. This university can help me do it, Mister Perry. It can."

Well, well, well, and so it can, Congleton Perry said to himself, as Hap continued his impassioned explanation.

"I look into your face, Mister Perry, and I do see a fair-minded man, just as Doctor Knight told me. But you do need to be concerned about me and I understand that. If you will let me, I would like to tell you a story...about compassion."

Hap paused and thought about his vow to Coeffield King.

"You see, I've made a vow to be of service and show compassion to people. Someone taught me that not too long ago. I believed him and felt it was right for my own life. I've been considered lowly and unworthy in many eyes, but the university is my chance to change all that. It's my key to bring myself up to have a better life and to show compassion for other people. Please, sir, I want to enroll this fall. I want to learn to be a servant and help people. I want to learn who Hap Tyson is and who he can become. Can I? I-I... that's all I have to say."

His eyes remained riveted on the man behind the desk, and it was Perry whose eyelids fluttered first. Clearing his throat, the dean shuffled through his papers once more, before he spoke.

"...Uh, Mister Tyson, the recommendations on your behalf are extraordinary. I do not think I have ever had such powerful support for an incoming student. Your Doctor Knight ranked second in his undergraduate class here and first in his medical. That man could have gone anywhere, made all kinds of financial advancements, but he chose to go back home and care for his people down east. There's no telling how many patients who have never paid him a penny. The heart and generosity of your mentor ranks extremely high, about as high as your marks at the Academy," he added, trying to relax the intense young man.

Once more, he coughed nervously and continued. Why was he nervous for God's sake? He was not the one on trial here. *Really, Perry, you are softening in your dotage.*

"And, then there's Coeffield King—"

"Coeffield King?" Hap sprang from his chair, tipping it backward as his knuckles hit the front edge of Dean Perry's desk. "Coeffield King." Hap scrambled to upright his fallen chair.

"From your reaction, I have to assume you did not know this."

"Doctor Knight handled that part for me. I-I'm so thankful."

He could not say anymore as his mind raced.

"I am well aware of what's happened to you, Hap, and what's happened to Mister King. Doctor Knight wrote the dictation from Mister King and he signed it with much effort."

Dean Perry did not even realize that he had called Hap by his first name. This young man had been rattling Perry's brain from all the letters logged from Rufus Knight over the past two years.

Chapter 50

The good doctor had been working on this application for a long time. Yes, he had wheedled Perry just right.

"Hap, do you know a Mister Michael Collins? He's your third recommendation."

Oh my God, Hap thought, *do I know Michael Collins? The tutor! How and why would he recommend me for admission?* His brow furrowed deeply.

"Michael is my wife's nephew. I sent a message to Tarboro asking if he knew you. In the return post, he wrote he had privately approached Doctor Knight and volunteered his recommendation. Rufus was elated not to have to solicit another person since his time has been consumed with his patients, especially his personal care of Mister King." He shook his head with his closing words. "Rufus needs to slow down. A man his age cannot maintain this pace."

Pausing briefly, he stood and walked over to his window. Silence swallowed the two.

"Hap, come here, son," Perry motioned to him. The young man walked over to stand beside him. Dean Perry pointed to the open quad that spread before them.

"Upon the shoulders of all incoming students rests the history of this institution. It will be your duty to carry not only its history but also its reputation of scholarship and ethics into the world. Congratulations, young man, I am positive you will make a fine Carolina gentleman."

He extended his hand.

Hap's spirits had risen with each of the words. The crooked grin spread quickly across his handsome face. Looking down the quad, he knew that he would be in good company. He was joining men who had walked these grounds and completed their studies since 1795.

Grabbing the dean's hand, he pumped it until the rather stoic gentleman laughed out loud at the jubilation of his new student, totally unaware that his wife's nephew would have sold his birthright to get Hap Tyson away from Tarboro and Caroline Cromwell.

Chapter 51
THE UNIVERSITY

*H*ap stared at his bed in amazement. Packing up for college proved to be quite an undertaking, as he selected clothing for fall, winter, and spring. The bulk of his clothes and belongings had to travel with him on the initial trip. His father's improved circumstances meant that Hap would have a wardrobe much better than the clothing he wore to finish school at the Academy in Greenville. Perhaps not the dandiest of wardrobes, but not the shabbiest, either.

"Son, we need to celebrate," Wendell Tyson said, as he stood with Hap looking at the piles of clothes on his bed. "You're the first Tyson who's ever gone to college."

"Pap, you don't have to go to that much trouble."

"It's done. I'm killing the fatted calf–well pig, that is. All your brothers and sisters are coming with children in tow. It'll be something for sure."

He stopped and put his hands on Hap's shoulders.

"Who'd ever believe Wendell Tyson's son would be going to the university and getting *edicated*. But, there is one thing I want you to do. Bring Willie. She needs to be here to celebrate."

* * *

The feast was quite an affair. They barbecued a pig and chopped slaw. Thin, porous, lace cornbread crunched between their teeth. However, one ingredient was missing from this celebration–Wendell's corn liquor, a vital omission.

And Willie had come. All the children that she had cared for all those years ago when Wendell's wife had passed made the most of her, laughing and telling their children all about *their*

Willie.

"Thank you, Hap. I cannot believe this is real. All these children now have children," she laughed as she squeezed Hap's hand, but when Wendell walked up to them, she froze.

"Hap, do you mind if I speak to Willie?"

"Of course not, Pap. Willie, I'll be over by the pink lemonade." He hugged her one more time as he moved away to allow his father some time with her.

"May I sit down with you, Willie?"

"Of course, Mister Tyson."

"Wendell, please," he murmured.

"W-Wendell." The name was hard for her to say, but she did.

"I, first, have to apologize to you for my bad behavior all those years ago. You know I'd been jugging, especially after my wife died. I have put that part of my life away, but I also need to thank you, Willie, for taking care of Hap as you have. He's become a fine young man, and it's because of you."

"Thank you, W-Wendell. You blessed me with a son, you know. I have to thank you for bringing him down Station House Road." They sat and watched *their* son as he re-acquainted himself with all his siblings, plus his nieces and nephews.

All the Tysons enjoyed that day in Wendell's backyard, never suspecting that their boy with the crooked smile still had remnants of the black cloud over his head.

* * *

In Chapel Hill, Litch Bagley's senior year at the university began with sipping brews with friends and studying new faces on campus. The younger students usually sought the upperclassmen for advice about curriculum, fraternities, and even the local girls. A significant difference for Litch in his final year, though, was the presence of Hap Tyson on campus. Quite accidentally he had heard his name mentioned in South Building. Surely, his ears deceived him.

Chapter 51

"Miss Lowe, did I hear Dean Perry say we have a new student, a Mister Tyson?" Litch asked.

"Why yes, he's from down east. Do you know him?"

"I might."

"Dean Perry spoke highly of him. You just don't hear the dean rave about a new student, but he's impressed."

Litch thought that he had nothing to fear from Hap. The relationship with Caroline was over, or was it? Something nagged at him. Tyson merited his scrutiny.

* * *

Hap lived off campus in a boarding house, but he loved the quad and spent much time there, lounging, reading, and people watching. He knew that seeing Litch on campus would be troublesome. At the moment, all they were to each other was just a passing glimpse at his trial. That was in the past, yet he knew their inevitable meeting was going to happen.

The back steps of South Building with its clear view of lush lawns and academic buildings were the site of many student gatherings over the years. One particular day, as the leaves stirred on Polk Quadrangle, Hap approached a crowd, listening to two young men debating their political views.

Pulling on a neighbor's sleeve, he quietly asked, "Who are these fellows?"

"Litch Bagley's the tall fellow and..."

Litch turned around just as Hap heard his name. He could not take his eyes off the young man. Litch's voice rang above the other.

"These carpetbaggers have depleted the South's coffers, already deflated from the war. I'm telling you this reconstruction process is just about as bad as the war. We're in a mess, and they're not helping."

"Just a minute, Litch. Sure, some of them were looking for opportunity, but many came to help former slaves become useful citizens," the other student countered.

"But they've made such radical changes in North Carolina and they've stolen political power from our own native sons. It's disgusting."

Hap was impressed that Litch knew so much, but he was a senior. He should know more. He's striking, too, just as Hap remembered at the trial, as he stared at Litch's fashionable clothing. Looking down at his rough pants and loose cotton shirt, he felt homely. The differences between the two were stark.

"Listen to me," Litch's opponent argued. "You've admitted to me and these other fellows that slavery is wrong, was wrong, and never should have been. This new state constitution confirms that and puts us back in the Union. What's wrong with that?"

"Dawson, you're right, but our native sons would have done it themselves. Maybe slower, but still..."

As Litch scanned the crowd for support of his issues, his eyes locked in on Hap's. His conversation faltered for a second, as he spied the new student. Hap smiled and nodded as if to say, I remember you. Litch nodded back ever so slightly, determined, though, to keep his focus on the debate at hand, picking up his rhetoric with an impassioned fervor. Hap faded into the background and headed for his room, leaving Litch and the others to continue their sparring.

Apparently, the back steps of South Building is the place to be seen and heard, he thought.

* * *

Days later, Hap lay sprawled under his favorite elm on Polk Quad, using its prominently exposed roots as armrests, as he read an assignment and jotted down notes.

"Excuse me," a voice boomed above him. "Are you not Hap Tyson from Tarboro? Over in Edgecombe?"

Hap looked up and squinted into the overhead sun at a shadowy figure looming over him. Dropping his book and notes,

CHAPTER 51

he scrambled off the ground to see who spoke, although he knew it was Litch Bagley.

"I just decided to get this over with, Tyson. There is no way that we can avoid each other since our enrollment here will not allow us to hide. I'll tell you what my intentions are, as soon as I graduate."

The two tall young men looked eye to eye. Hap was not about to back off. His hands clenched in his pockets with each word from his adversary.

Litch's words came out softly yet firmly.

"'Just want you to know that I intend to marry Miss Caroline Cromwell." Then, his voice hardened. "You know, Tyson, if you had tended to your own business last year, a life might have been saved, and much heartache for Miss Caroline would have been avoided. I warn you, sir, keep your distance from Shiloh. I intend to be there during the year to court her. Never try to see her again. The Cromwells want no part of the boy who killed their son. By the way, Tyson, Miss Caroline and I will have a passel of children, heirs for the Cromwell family. Are we clear on all I've said?"

Litch glared, turned slowly, and swaggered away, not even allowing Hap to make a reply. Hap's mouth opened and closed, as he became just another bumbling freshman in the sight of a suave senior. Grabbing his book and papers, he ran to class, but he never heard one word of the lecture.

*   *   *

Coeffield King had suffered a series of small strokes over the spring and early fall, becoming more infirm. He had reluctantly given in to a life in his chair under Jacksie's portrait, as he would listen to his granddaughter read Poe and Cicero.

"Coffie?" Caroline called out to him one day.

The old man looked up at his granddaughter. He smiled as she held up the worn, suede-covered book of Poe and the brown leather-bound book of Cicero.

"Which today?" she asked. He lifted a bony finger toward Poe. "Ah-hah, I feel Annabel Lee coming forth from these pages."

His dry laugh brought her close to kiss the top of his head. He would dream dreams and speak a word or two once in a while, but other than that, his life seemed to be one of waiting to join his beloved Jacksie.

Back at Shiloh, Elijah and Sarah had not heard a word from Caroline's tutor. It was as if he had fallen off the face of the earth.

"Elijah, Michael Collins is gone," Sarah said one day after a visit to town and Mrs. DeBerry's Tearoom. "Now, why would he just disappear without so much as telling us good-bye?"

She turned to Caroline.

"Darling, do you have any idea?"

Caroline innocently shook her head and shrugged her shoulders.

"By the way, my dear, we have a letter from Litch. He wants to come after Christmas and stay a few days at Cromwell Hall."

Her mouth curled into a slight grin.

"Surely, you don't think he's coming to see Elijah or me?"

Caroline half-smiled back.

"I'm not sure I want to see Litch Bagley. I am not sure if I am ready to see Litch Bagley. Mother, you two certainly want to plan my life. Thank you very much, but I do feel this need to look after Coffie, and I don't need other distractions."

"I understand that, dear, but you must consider this long trip he's making just to see *you*. It's only decent that you entertain him. After all, he's such a charming young man, with intelligence and grace. Don't lose this moment, darling," her mother prodded, pushing her daughter's curls away from her face.

"You do not want to question yourself later, do you?"

"I suppose not," she said in a hushed tone, only looking up quickly to add, "unless Coffie comes to Cromwell Hall for the entire holiday season. I know it will be hard, but I will do

Chapter 51

everything to look after him and make him comfortable. You don't have to worry."

Walking to the door of the sitting room, Caroline turned and smiled at her parents as they busied themselves with their holiday plans.

Why can't you two just let me live my life the way I want to?

Chapter 52
CHRISTMAS

Fall semester at the university passed quickly. Studying occupied much of Hap's time, but he was determined to spend his holidays at home in Greenville. And Willie? He knew sometime he had to visit her in Tarboro at least once. He reached over and picked up her last letter, envisioning her trek to the box at the end of Station House Road to find his letters.

Dear Hap,

How are you? Are you still enjoying the university? I hope your family is doing well...

"Trying to cut the apron strings, eh, Willie?" he said aloud, as he tapped the edge of her letter. "You think Greenville's my home now? Well, we'll just see about that."

Grabbing a pen, he dashed a return letter to her.

How strange to Hap that his new life in Chapel Hill had begun to dull the old. He now had a home in Greenville, but he still had Willie in his life. And Willie meant Tarboro. His mind began to wander as he posted her letter.

I wonder if I'll see... No! I've got to stop thinking about her. Litch will probably be "acourtin'," like he said.

* * *

"He's coming. Oh, my gosh, he's coming."

Willie crushed Hap's letter to her bosom. She danced around in her modest cottage, trying to imagine his presence filling it. She would have to scrub everything, make new curtains, cook his favorite meals. She sniffed, as she smoothed out his letter, tucking it into a chest with all the rest.

"Thank you, son."

CHAPTER 52

He was going to spend time with her after Christmas. He had not been in Tarboro since the trial, nine months before.

* * *

Chapel Hill sparkled for the Christmas season. The villagers had garnished the lampposts with red ribbons and greenery; the shop owners had filled their windows with decorated trees and toys. Crèches nestled in corners of several storefronts, intriguing the children with the animals surrounding the baby in the manger.

For the first time, Hap reveled in his shopping for all his long-lost siblings, as he figured out who would get what special gift for the holiday. He fingered his hard-earned money in his pocket, grateful for the few odd jobs he had found on campus to provide him with money of his own. This Christmas would be his first in Greenville, since he had gone to live with Willie as a four-year-old.

Unbelievable how life changes, he thought, as he entered the festive shops to make his purchases. And when he saw the toiletries lined up on the counter in a sundries shop, he thought of Caroline. If he were purchasing something for her this day, he would definitely pick out a fragrance—not just any fragrance—but her fragrance. His eyes closed as he remembered that day in Carver's Mercantile when she flung open the door and stared up into his face with those unruly curls flouncing. Her fragrance, he would never forget.

Slowly, he picked up and sniffed each bottle until he found the one with the scent of gardenias. Motioning to the clerk, he asked her to wrap his choice. Then, as if startled from a dream, he grabbed his purchase and scooted through the door.

Lying in bed at his rooming house, Hap removed the little perfume bottle from its wrapping, opened it, and breathed deeply its sweet smell. He lay motionless for an hour, unable to focus on anything. *Spare me,* he mumbled, over and over, but his visions of her overpowered him.

He saw her at the lower 40, as she would ride through the clearing on Nellie. Or sitting on the fallen log, smashing her crop on the rotting bark. Or holding her in his arms as they practiced dancing for her birthday celebration. And he would never forget how she fingered the lavaliere he had given her at her birthday celebration. Where was it now? Thrown to the wind? The ache in his heart was real. He buried his head in his pillow, punching it with each deep sob. When would it be over?

Chapter 53
Christmas at Cromwell Hall

Cromwell Hall teemed with Christmas spirit. Sarah could not believe that her father would be in her own home for the holidays. Every year after her mother's death, she had begged him to come for the entire festive month, but he had always declined.

"Sarah, you know I will come for Christmas dinner, but all the other celebrations are for your family. I'll be fine. Trust me," he would say every year, as he would hug her and kiss her forehead.

Now, here she was watching her own daughter achieve what she had never been able to do. She would harbor no ill feelings, but she felt a twinge of jealousy at the depth of the relationship between her father and her daughter.

Well, if she can give Coffie something I can't, then so be it.

* * *

Caroline had been right. Moving Coeffield King to Cromwell Hall was no easy task.

"We cannot leave Poe or Cicero," she declared, holding up both worn books for him to see. Both shook their heads, for neither would have dared leaving them behind.

They made the trek to Cromwell Hall with his two literary friends, along with several cartons and trunks.

"Coffie, here's your room just as you asked," Sarah said, as they stood in the doorway of the downstairs guest room where Will had lain dead.

As painful as it was, Coeffield nodded and slowly shuffled to the chair by the window with Elijah's help, then watched as his belongings transformed the room into his own. How strange, the family thought, that the old patriarch had insisted upon staying in that room. No one in the house dared to dissuade him; it's what Coeffield King wanted.

The old man did not speak much these days; he mainly listened.

"Father," Sarah said one evening, "we'll have a visitor after Christmas for a few days. He's a family friend that we met on vacation a while back. His name is Litch Bagley. He's from Raleigh."

Caroline had entered the room, noticing a slight frown had crossed Coffie's brow. He searched her face for any hint of feelings for this young man. *What did Sarah say his name was? Litch? Litch Bagley?*

He felt the faintest hint of jealousy that anyone would dare vie for his granddaughter's attention when he needed her so desperately. Then he cursed himself.

Jacksie, what an old fool I am? How can I deny our granddaughter a love such as ours?

* * *

The Christmas festivities cheered the old man. He wondered why it had taken him so long to find his way down the road for longer visits. His daughter's numerous invitations whirled in his head. Frankly, he felt guilty about Sarah. Maybe he had neglected her, since Caroline had become his close companion. He would try to rectify that over the holiday.

But, oh, sweet Caroline, you are so like your grandmother. You keep her alive for me.

* * *

Litch Bagley arrived two days after Christmas with a grand flair.

"You two, ladies, are...are...simply beautiful, and I come bearing gifts," he said to Sarah and Caroline, holding up his index finger and turning to a loose leather bag. From it, he produced a package with velvet ribbon in profusion on top.

"For you, Miss Sarah."

Chapter 53

"Litch, you shouldn't—yes, you should have."

They both laughed. He turned and pulled a small package wrapped in red foil with a white file bow.

"And, for you, Miss Caroline, please accept this with my deepest affection."

"I don't know what to say," she mumbled, embarrassed at his familiarity.

"A thank-you is sufficient," he said, turning to laugh with Sarah again.

"Thank you," she murmured, still quite uncomfortable.

"Well, open them up, ladies. Christmas is past."

As they busied themselves opening their presents, Litch slipped over to Maggie.

"And to the other lady of the house," he whispered, handing her a box and smiling at her, as she frowned at him.

But her jaw dropped when she held up a shawl knitted from aquamarine yarn.

"Mister Litch, that's my favorite color. How did you know?" she whispered back. He grinned widely. *How did that man know?* she wondered.

She cut her eyes at him and shook her head.

"Litch, it's beautiful," Sarah said, as she admired the silver bangle she had already put on her wrist.

Caroline stood speechless as she stared at a delicate filigreed lavaliere, in the shape of a dogwood blossom, with a small diamond nestled in the center. She thought of Hap's gift for her 16th birthday, tucked away in a bureau drawer.

"Here, Miss Caroline, let me help you with the clasp," Litch offered, relishing the task of being so close to her. He turned her toward the mirror.

"It's lovely," she said, as they looked at their reflection.

"We make a handsome couple," he teased.

"Litch, please," she whispered nervously.

Sarah smiled as she watched the two.

"And for you, Captain Cromwell," Litch said, as he reached into the leather bag one last time, "a box of the finest Havana cigars."

"Why thank you, Litch. Maybe we can share one or two before your return to Raleigh."

"I would be honored."

"Come sit in the parlor," Elijah said, extending his hand to the young man. "Sarah's father is spending the holiday with us. You'll meet him later."

When Litch realized that Coeffield King resided in the house, he was beside himself. Now, he had an additional factor that could help persuade Caroline that *he* was the choice to carry on the bloodline. Excitement brimmed in his eyes as he began to contrive what he would say in his meeting with the family patriarch.

* * *

King heard a slight knock on his door. He struggled to focus as Caroline's head appeared.

"Coffie, I have someone here I want you to meet. May we come in?"

She saw him nod slightly from the chair by the window where he sat for much of his day, anticipating occasional visits from family, friends, and visitors. When Litch Bagley came close enough, the old man saw him glance at Caroline.

Oh, my God, he's in love with her.

"Sir, it's such an honor," Litch said, his eyes filled with enthusiasm. *Maybe this man can purge her feelings for Hap Tyson?*

The old man extended his hand shakily and surprised himself with his own grip. The young man's was firm. He liked that.

Jacksie, I've got to let her go. Mister Bagley just might be the one.

Chapter 54

QUESTIONS

*B*attered by weather and overgrown with weeds, the old Station House appeared more dilapidated than Hap remembered, even though he had been away for less than a year. Looking down the road, he smiled, recalling the church ladies of Tarboro coming with shoes and clothing for the "poor little chirrun." He relived his first glimpse of Caroline and her mother in their carriage and remembered how he was taken by her in the streaming sunlight. He closed his eyes as he savored the memory—how long ago that seemed. He continued down the road at a slow pace, flooded with other memories of the road.

Hap reined his horse when he saw Willie standing on her porch. She seemed so small to him, as she clung to the porch post, smiling, then covering her mouth to catch a sob.

"Son," she called, running down the steps to the edge of the yard. She clutched her shawl as the breeze billowed her calico dress.

"I see you been out sweeping the yard, Willie, but the leaves ain't on the ground in December."

"Just wanted everything perfect for you, Hap."

"You're perfect for me, Willie," he said, dismounting and walking toward her, "and a blessed sight for my eyes, ma'am."

"So are you, son. So are you."

She stood on tiptoe and hugged him the best she could.

"Are you sure you haven't grown a bit? I declare I could hug you better than this before you left," she said, patting his plaid flannel shirt under his thick denim jacket.

He laughed, lifting and swinging her. Her squeals pierced the air.

"Put me down or we'll never have lunch."

"What'd you fix for your starving son?" he said, removing his brimmed felt hat. He bowed slightly. She gave a brief curtsy.

"Everything you could possibly want. Then, maybe we can talk."

She hooked his arm and gathered her shawl together in the December chill.

* * *

After lunch, Hap settled in a rocker by the fireplace.

"Well, catch me up, Willie. What's been happening around here?" he asked her as she handed him apple pie for dessert. "These apples from Shiloh?"

"Yes, the Captain's so generous."

"Wood from Shiloh, too?" He nodded toward the neatly stacked red oak on the hearth.

"Yes," she answered with a curious look on her face. "But I want you to tell me about you. What's it like up there at the university?"

"Awww, shoot, Willie, it's just studying, studying, and more studying. But I do have a question for you, a serious question," he said, wolfing down another mouthful.

"What?" she asked, her mouth opened slightly.

"Why do you stay here with such painful memories haunting these old walls?" he asked, his arms motioning toward the inside of the shack. "This road's been good and bad to you over the years. Haven't you ever thought about moving?"

"Why, no."

"Your momma and daddy are gone. You got no family in Tarboro. Or close friends. Do you?"

"But, Hap, I've lived here all my life, except that time I lived with your family."

How could she tell her adopted son that her natural-born child was right over that bridge in Tarboro? How could she tell him her feelings for Elijah Cromwell? A smile flickered.

"Maybe this old gal was just too blamed lazy to find another place," she joked.

Chapter 54

"Seriously, Willie, why don't you move? You could even go live in town. Nothing or nobody's stopping you. Right? It might be good for you."

"Maybe I will. Maybe I will."

Wanting to change the subject, Willie smiled widely and took his plate.

"Why don't you go into town? Look around. Walk the streets. Stretch those long legs."

"Only if you'll ride with me."

He jumped up.

"Come on."

She felt the blood rush, as he pulled her out the door. They ran to the barn to saddle her old bay. His horse still stood patiently at the hitching rail. Even with all the troubles that followed him through the years, Hap always seemed to say the right things to her.

* * *

"Willie, why didn't you ever get married?" Hap asked as they rode toward the bridge.

"Married? Pshaw. Who'd want to marry me?"

She was quiet for a moment.

"Although I was in love once."

"Ah-hah."

"But the young man was not free."

"Oh," his voice dropped.

"And, I just never found anybody else," she said with a shrug.

"Is this person in Tarboro or Edgecombe County? Now?"

She did not answer but looked curiously at him.

"Willie, you would have made someone a very good wife. Not many came courting, so I always wondered if there ever had been– Darn, Willie, was it by any chance Elijah Cromwell?"

Chapter 55
Release

"I insist! Tea at Mrs. DeBerry's and I've been thinking about one more present," Litch said, looking at Caroline across the table at lunch the next day.

"Nonsense! You've spent a treasure. No, Mr. Bagley."

"Now, Caroline, tea would be lovely. Litch has not seen the Town Common," Sarah said, finishing her last bite.

"Sure, Caroline, take Litch and give him a tour of the town," Elijah said.

"All right, I will go, but Coffie wants me to pick up several fresh shirts. I can't believe it. We must have packed half the clothes in his house, but he insists he needs them. It won't take long, Litch. I promise. His house is on the green not far from Mrs. DeBerry's."

* * *

Coeffield King looked out the window as the young couple crossed the porch of Cromwell Hall to the carriage out front. He chuckled.

Litch Bagley is in for quite a surprise if he ventures into my parlor.

* * *

Caroline had actually enjoyed Litch's company this holiday, probably because he had visited among the family and not just showered only her with all his attention. She was glad they had no driver this day so Litch would keep his hands to himself. She wanted no emotional confrontation. So far, everything had gone smoothly. Their conversation was light and carefree, until they were a short distance from town.

"What do you know, the first live creatures we see are right out

Chapter 55

in the middle of the road. What do you think, Caroline, shall I run this horseflesh right through 'em?"

"Don't be...silly."

Her voice slowed to a strange cadence. She had recognized Hap and Willie as the two riders moving out of the road and back into the yard of the old Station House, out of the carriage's path. Her face flushed. What could she do? Smile? Wave? Nod? *Oh, God in heaven...*

But Litch's face lit up in recognition, and putting the reins in one hand as the horse trotted quickly, he slipped his other arm around Caroline's seat and claimed both possession and position.

Are you looking, Tyson? She's mine, brother.

Caroline could only stare, frozen, her eyes locked with Hap's as they had at the courthouse during the trial. Then they had passed, over the bridge. Only then did she notice Litch's arm, and that caused an unbelievably sinking feeling.

It's over. Why should I ever dare to hope? It's over.

* * *

"Are you all right, son?" Willie asked as they gave the carriage time to pass. "We can go back if you want."

He shook his head.

"Absolutely not. Willie, I assure you I'm fine. Why don't we race across the bridge like we used to?" he challenged.

Smiling, she pushed the bay off in front of him.

"Hey, I didn't even say 'Go!'"

His voice disappeared with the wind.

He caught up with her, as they reined their horses at the first rail and trough on Main Street to begin their walk, mother and son remembering earlier times, feeling a rekindled closeness with each other.

When they came to the Town Common, they noticed the Cromwell carriage in front of the King house. It was empty.

They wandered into the Town Common and sat on a bench,

each silent, lost in thought, comforted by the presence of the other. Willie was grateful that Hap had forgotten the question he had asked earlier. She knew he would ask her again, and she knew she would never lie to him.

Hap stood up and pulled Willie up to him.

"Willie, I'm not your flesh and blood, but you'll always be my mother," he said as he patted her hand.

"Let's go home, son. It's been a long day."

They strolled toward Main Street, turning their backs on the Town Common and a past life. Only once did Hap glance toward the carriage that slowly moved from the King house to Mrs. DeBerry's Tearoom.

Chapter 56
The Proposal

Pitch leaned over, his hand waiting for the key for Coeffield King's front door.

"I can manage, thank you," Caroline said, clutching her small velveteen bag.

"Please, I insist."

Shrugging, she accepted his hand as he helped her down from the carriage and turned to climb the steps of the stately Georgian house. He stopped her on the stoop in front of the massive door.

"Caroline? Have you ever thought of all the people who crossed that green or climbed these steps to see your grandparents?"

She smiled.

"Almost every time I come."

He took the key and slipped it into the lock. The big oaken door swung open. White sheeting covered the furniture throughout Coffie's house.

"Why's everything covered up?"

"Leota still spends her mornings here, but we thought it best, just to keep the dust down while Coffie's at Cromwell Hall. Stay in the parlor. I'll only be a minute."

Leaving him in the sitting room, she went to gather the shirts from her grandfather's chifforobe.

"I can't believe it! Caroline, come here."

The excitement in his voice brought her running.

"What? What's the matter?"

She dropped the shirts by the coat rack.

"The matter? My God, you are the spitting image of your

grandmother."

"Oh, good grief, Litch, you scared me to death."

"The resemblance is incredible," he exclaimed, walking from side to side before Jacksie's portrait, eyeing her from all angles.

"Thank you for letting me come in. The house is grand, but that portrait is grander."

He quickly reached for her hand, and before she could pull it away, he kissed her palm, lingering a moment too long for her comfort.

"Litch, please. We shouldn't even be in here alone."

"Caroline–," his voice broke with emotion. He would not let go of her hand. "Please, just listen to me. For God's sake, listen."

He paused and swallowed, still holding her hand. "I love you!" he blurted out.

Caroline stepped back.

"No! Don't stop me." He raised his hand, as she tried to pull away. "What I have to say *must* be said. Just listen to me."

Caroline tugged again to pull her hand away, but to no avail. She frowned.

With a deep breath, he continued gently, "I've taken the liberty of telling your grandfather of my intentions."

"What? How could you?" Anger laced her voice. "*We* have not even broached the subject."

"I know, but…"

"You know, but-what? How could you be such a presumptuous–no, *pompous*–ass?"

"I know," his voice rang out. "But I couldn't help myself." His voice dropped. "Remember the day I sat with your grandfather, while you and your mother visited the Engles?"

She nodded.

"Well, he wrote the question down on paper and asked me about my feelings and intentions. *He* asked *me*, Caroline. And, he approves."

Chapter 56

His eyes softened; he smiled. He still held her hand, and once more he raised it to his lips and pressed deeply.

She was stunned. Her grandfather had initiated such a conversation?

"Grandfather? Coffie?"

Her voice sounded disbelief.

Litch took advantage and clasped both her hands in his. He dared to proceed.

"He wants this marriage. He does. He gave me his blessing. Look at that portrait. He knew I'd see it."

With that declaration, he kissed her cheek. Her soft skin and fragrance intoxicated him, but somehow Litch pulled away and walked to the door.

"Shall we have tea at Mrs. DeBerry's?" he asked, holding out his hand to her.

With her mouth still opened, she numbly followed, as Litch gathered the unnecessary shirts for Coeffield King.

The carriage moved slowly around the green to the tearoom. Two small figures on a bench caught Caroline's eye. She knew it was Hap and Willie. Numbed, she peeked over Litch's shoulder, as he reminisced about the holiday. She watched the figures get up from the bench and walk away. Only once did Hap Tyson look back. Caroline turned back and stared at the young man beside her.

How was this possible? Could Coffie be right? She had always respected Coffie's feelings, his opinions, but could he be right this time? Hap was seeking a new path. Maybe she should as well.

* * *

"It's agreed!" Sarah clapped her hands and spoke with assurance. She bent over her father and kissed the top of his head. Only his desire and wish for his granddaughter had pulled off this *coup*. And now it appeared that Caroline King Cromwell would marry Litchtfield Jacob Bagley in early summer after his graduation from the university in late spring. Sarah was beside herself. A June wedding! Tarboro had never seen one like the one she would plan. Mrs. DeBerry and Maggie would help her prepare food and decor that the townsfolk would talk about for years to come. Jacksie Thrash had taught her daughter well.

Litch had worked on his parents, eventually convincing them that Caroline was truly the young woman for him and that he loved her dearly. They even had come once with their son to renew their acquaintances with the Cromwells. Litch returned to Cromwell Hall several times, weather permitting through the cold winter months to see Caroline and to secure their wedding plans.

Oh, God... She is truly mine...

Chapter 57
The Announcement

Spring approached Chapel Hill with its annual signs of rebirth. Shrubs and trees wore tinges of green and red, as leaves unfurled and swollen buds burst forth. Once more, the quad behind South Building burgeoned with students as the cold winter subsided. Hap's first semester's performance pleased him. With high spirits, he had plunged into his work, savoring his successes and knowing his efforts had prevented emotional despair. Only one course had given him a shock, but his chemistry professor, Atticus Sims, had saved him.

"Master Tyson, I need me a summer lab assistant. How about it?" Doc Sims asked.

The young man laughed out loud. "That's rich. You wouldn't have asked me last fall, now, would you?"

"Absolutely not," Sims said, lighting his pipe as they sat on a bench outside the chemistry building. His shaggy white hair hung over his rumpled white collar; his sweater vest showed signs of wear and more than one small hole from falling pipe tobacco ash. Doc Sims had taken Hap under wing, after sensing great possibilities. He had never seen any student demonstrate such tenacity in overcoming ignorance.

"Son, we've worked enough together for me to know you're a good risk, as long as you don't blow up my lab."

"I promise," Hap said, relieved that his slim wallet would get some padding. Wendell Tyson had sent him money, but he wanted to hold his own as best he could.

"Son, I do need you a few extra days after exams to help me with some personal work." He paused, then smiled, "Are you sure you're pleading your cause with such hopelessness last semester wasn't a ploy to get on the good side of old Doc Sims?"

"Sir? No," he said, then returned the smile. "But I must confess that you saved me."

"I could not resist the challenge of such a pathetic plea. All you needed was a little prodding. It worked, didn't it?"

The old professor smiled and patted his protégé's shoulder.

* * *

Why he loved the old elm on the quad, Hap did not know. Feeling its strength against his back just seemed a steadying force. He wondered how many other students had claimed this spot fifty, seventy-five, or even one hundred years before? To him, it was a most special place, one where he could sit and read and soak up the pleasant surroundings, but one day Litch Bagley interrupted his serenity for a second time, arriving with a group of his cronies, guffawing and pumping each other's hands.

"...Fellows, I cannot wait for you to see her at graduation, then you'll know all my bragging is true. She's the most beautiful woman I've ever seen...yes, we've finished all the plans...this June after graduation... Fellows, I still cannot believe I'll be a married man in just a few short months."

Then, Litch spied Hap over the shoulders of his friends. He smirked. Savoring this moment, he swaggered toward Hap, sitting under the knurled old elm and spoke loudly, enough for his friends to hear.

"My dear Master Tyson! By now, you've heard about my good fortune of claiming the hand of Miss Caroline Cromwell. I believe you know the young lady...from Tarboro...in Edgecombe?" He extended his hand. "Come now. Congratulate me on our impending marriage in June."

Hap's head remained bent over his book. There was no graceful escape with all the onlookers. Slowly, he got up and looked at the extended hand with disdain. He did not offer his

Chapter 57

hand in return. Never uttering a word, he strode away to fading words, "...in June, old man, we'll be sure to send you an invitation."

The other fellows drowned Litch's laughter as they buzzed around him. Hap fumed, not so much at the news, but at the malice of this young man. These goads made it even harder to forget her.

Caroline, what are you doing?

Chapter 58

GRADUATION

*T*he spring flew by.

"Caroline, we need to pick up Litch's graduation present from the jeweler. The engraving's been done, and I know he'll love it."

"Yes, Mother," Caroline answered listlessly as she had been the last three months. Maybe all wedding details and frills are for mothers, and not for brides? Frankly, she did not care and was thrilled when her mother handled these matters.

The parties and entertaining had proceeded without pause. Everyone wanted to entertain Tarboro's darling girl, the granddaughter of its favorite son, Coeffield King. Litch had returned during spring break for one round of parties. He'd been charming and gentle. Maybe this marriage was possible, she thought. Coffie seemed happy; she could not spoil his joy at seeing his granddaughter married before he died.

"Child...you do...my heart good," he would barely utter, while thinking to himself, *Jacksie...Jacksie...she reminds me so much of you...if you were only here...now...with me...*

* * *

For his graduation weekend, Litch reserved rooms for the Cromwells at the Patterson Hotel on the corner of Franklin and Columbia, convenient to the campus and village. He had overlooked one small detail: Hap's rooming house was only a block away from the hotel.

The train jostled Caroline and her parents as it headed toward Carrboro. Sarah leaned over and patted her daughter's hand.

"Are you excited, darling?"

Chapter 58

"What? Excited? Yes, Mother. Litch is graduating with honors."

"No, Caroline. I mean your wedding."

"Sarah," Elijah interrupted, "of course, she is, but let's enjoy a little peace. I'm sure things will pick up, if I know Litch."

Litch had arranged a dinner at the hotel for his family and hers upon their arrival on Friday. After pheasant and all the trimmings, the diners' lively conversation continued past eight o'clock. But when the old grandfather clock in the corner gonged on the half-hour, Jacob Bagley stood up.

"Ladies, please excuse your gentlemen. We're going to retire to the veranda for cigars and brandy."

"Of course, Jake, we'll have coffee here and then really retire. Litch, it's been a wonderful evening," his mother said, as she blew him a kiss.

"It has, Litch. Hasn't it, darling?" Sarah turned, her eyes encouraging her daughter to speak out.

"Yes, it's been lovely."

Litch beamed, as he walked over to kiss her cheek. She blushed as he followed the men out through the French doors onto the porch.

The ladies chatted and sipped their coffee, and Caroline wandered around the charming room, looking at paintings and the impressive collections of porcelain. She walked from the private room to the hall door and gracefully slipped away to get a breath of fresh air, but something on the registration desk caught her eye, an interesting leather book lying at the end of the counter. Her eyes were riveted on the engraved words: Student Directory.

Looking over her shoulder, she turned back swiftly and thumbed through the pages. Tyson. Tyson. Tyson. Her fingers stopped. Thomas Rolland Tyson, 102 Cedar Lane.

"Sir," she said to the hotel manager. "Where's the 100 block of Cedar Lane?"

"Just go out this door and it's the next street over. It's a short street with mostly boarding houses. May I help you find someone?"

She tried not to look startled at his answer.

"Sir? Oh no, no thank you."

Hap lived one block away. She did need fresh air, then. She stood, gazing toward Cedar Lane from the inn's huge porch and saw a lone figure scurrying along.

"Hap," she said aloud. "Hap."

Stop this, she scolded herself, never taking her eyes off the disappearing figure.

* * *

Hap could not sleep that night. Doc Sims had kept him late in the laboratory, until both pleaded exhaustion.

"Ahhh, protégé mine, a late supper is your reward. A good compensation?"

"Of course," Hap smiled, but too many brews prompted an early ride home for the elderly gentleman. Hap watched as his professor's carriage creaked away, the horse's hooves clopping on the cobbled street.

Walking from the village, Hap passed the Patterson. Only then did he think about graduation. Somewhere in the village, the Cromwells must be staying for the big occasion. He walked faster to shake his mind from the sounds of laughter and festivities coming from the hotel.

Hap's room at the back of the boarding house had its own private entrance, giving him convenient access these late nights. He could not get through the door fast enough, but his mind raced to thoughts of the Cromwells and Caroline. Grabbing a book, he sat by his light, hoping for sleep. An hour passed.

The knock was so slight that he almost ignored it, thinking it might have been a pop in the timbers of the old house. He turned back to his book. Another light tap. *Doc Sims?* he thought. Tossing the book aside, he scrambled to his feet.

Chapter 58

As the door swung open, a shaft of light from the porch lamp haloed the golden head he had loved for so many years. Her head slowly came up. She stepped around him into his room, never saying a word. He closed the door. Stunned by her appearance, he could only stand mute, a puzzled expression on his face.

She smiled nervously, her eyes darting around his room, and then, she walked to his desk. She touched his books, his papers, his pens, everything on it. Letting her hand trail over all his things, she seemed to be reliving all the moments he had sat and studied and written, catching up on his life that she had missed.

Slowly, without saying a word, she moved around the room, as if wanting to touch all that he had touched. She smiled at the pictures on the bureau of his family and looked into eyes that she did not know, but who knew him with love. She came full circle back to him with her hand resting on his bed.

He had watched her with such curiosity as she had covered his room. Drinking in every move she made, he prayed he could remember each second, totally captivated by her presence. He turned slightly when she had reached the bed, a furrow between his brow.

In an instant, she covered the few steps between them and buried her face in his chest. He inhaled her fragrance as if it was sustenance. Her arms had locked around his waist so quickly and hard that he immediately felt desperation in her body. He lowered his long arms and draped them ever so slowly across her shoulders, as he sensed his own body losing control.

For minutes they refused to release the other, each fearing reality to break the moment. Finally, her head lifted to his and invited a kiss that he had craved for years.

She had forgotten the fullness of his mouth, but his kiss electrified her as much as the first time in the lower 40 at Shiloh. How many years ago? It felt like yesterday to her. She could feel the rhythm of his heart beat and knew hers matched it.

He had forgotten how small she was. She seemed lost in his arms, but her fragrances had never changed and still excited him.

She broke from their kiss first. Looking up at him with her sparkling azure eyes, she softly spoke for the first time.

"Love me, Hap. Love me as your wife."

He lifted her high above his head and slowly lowered her, absorbing each inch of her body with his own. Swinging her up into his arms, he gently laid her small frame in the center of his bed. He stood looking down at his bride with the loving eyes of the bridegroom.

I, Thomas Rolland Tyson, take thee, Caroline King Cromwell...

Yes, this night she would be his bride and he, her groom. A tear formed in his eye, which he dabbed with his sleeve. Slowly, he unbuttoned his shirt and laid it neatly on the back of his chair, his chest rising and falling with desire for the young mistress of Cromwell Hall.

She held outstretched arms to him, inviting him into the bosom of her soul. He had longed to hold her for so many months that he could hardly believe that she was really here and the moment was, too. In his heart as he looked into her eyes, he knew that their time together was closure and not a fresh beginning. Another tear started to trail down his face. This time, she caught it before it got too far.

"I know, my love, I know..."

*　*　*

His eyes flew open; he knew she was gone, not just from his bed, not just from his room, but from his life. He rolled over and sobbed as he had so many nights trying to forget her.

Chapter 59
THE GRADUATE

The graduation weekend festivities began with a brunch at the hotel and then on to Memorial Hall for the exercises. Litch stood so impressive in his robe with all the honorariums hanging from his neck. The women oohed and aahed, forcing acclaims from Caroline. Litchfield Bagley would have believed anything that anyone said whether they meant it or not. He was having the time of his life, and in one month that joy would be even greater. He could not have been more in love with Caroline than he was at this moment.

"We must have some time together tonight," he whispered to her after the ceremonies. "The night should be perfect for strolling to the village or on campus. Please, let's just excuse ourselves from these adults. They can handle themselves all right without us," he implored.

"Litch, the day's been so fu–"

"Don't refuse me, sweetheart, you know we'll go back to Raleigh until the wedding. I won't see you, dearest, for an eternity. We'll just get up from dinner and go."

She couldn't refuse him. After all, she would be his wife in only four more weeks. Could she go through with this wedding? Could she?

Oh, Hap, what am I doing?

The dinner went faster than Caroline could imagine. As the waiter removed the last plate, Litch jumped to his feet.

"Well, family and family-to-be, you'll have to excuse the young lady and me. We need some time together. You know I won't see her for a while before the wedding. It's been the most perfect day and I cannot thank all of you enough for coming to this grand occasion in my life."

Jacob Bagley leaned forward.

"No, Dad, not another toast! Just excuse us."

With no further ado, he whisked Caroline out of the dining room. As soon as they were down the walk, he steered her onto the grounds of the inn toward a secluded bench. He pulled her to him and kissed with a passion she had known only once. He engulfed her; she lost resistance. This man *was* to be her husband. She *had* to love him. Didn't she?

"Oh God, I love you more than I would have ever believed," he said and squeezed her tighter. He ran his fingertips lightly over her curls and continued. "You are truly the most beautiful woman to me." He kissed her forehead. "Here," he pointed to the bench. "Come sit. I have a gift for you." He removed a long, slim box from his breast coat pocket and opened it for her.

Her mouth dropped open. Her face questioned the contents.

"This necklace was my grandmother's."

"It's, it's exquisite."

Her voice was only a whisper.

"I want you to wear it with your wedding gown. Here, let me fasten the clasp."

Caroline could only obey as her will diminished. She felt unworthy of this treasured gift, but how could she protest? She would soon be his wife.

Oh, Hap, what am I doing?

Chapter 60
THE NEW LIFE

Hap sat on the steps of South Building, staring down the quad of Polk Place. It was June and the first summer session had begun. His eyes glazed over, totally unaware of the bustling students, rushing across the green to find their classrooms and meet their professors. Classes would begin in a few days. In fact, Hap had been in South Building to get his new dormitory room assignment, but this afternoon, no one seemed to bother with the young man staring dreamily at the campus trees and buildings as they scurried past. A distant toll of a bell stirred him, bringing him back to life.

A faint smile changed his expression from one of lethargy to relief. He finally was beginning to sort out his feelings about his life, even about Caroline. Not once did he think he would not see her again in his dreams, but now he knew it would be different. He would see her as a life-long friend, which she was. He would see her in their youth, at the lower 40 on Shiloh. He would see her as his first love, never to be forgotten. A part of his heart would always be hers, but at this point he glimpsed survival in his life, not from the past, but in the future. He glimpsed relief in his soul, a lifting of his spirit.

Caroline was an important ingredient of his youth. He had learned so much from her, especially how to have a real relationship with a young woman. He had been so naive and ignorant in the affairs of the heart before meeting her. She had taught him the gentler side of life that he had never known. He had the street smarts, but she had extended the good life to him. Yes, he had learned much and he would never forget her.

Perspective was the key.

He sighed and smiled once more, the crooked smile that many, at one time, had deemed evil. But this smile showed no malice, no evil. It just was a curious expression, now his natural expression.

Hap Tyson realized how much he had been blessed in his life. In his more recent years, he felt himself being lifted up from a pit, the pit of being a scoundrel in the streets of Tarboro. He thought of Pap and realized his father's struggle in leaving his youngest son on Station House Road with Willie Pridgen. And he thought of Willie, who was forced to take a small child, not even her own blood kin, and how she struggled to bring him up right, as if he was her own blood kin.

I forgive you, Pap, I really do. All you've done for me of late has redeemed your leaving me. In fact, you did me a favor and Willie, too. We needed each other. I needed a mother; and she, a son. Yes, I forgive you, Pap...

And I thank you, Rufus Knight, for being my second father. I knew you were someone so special when you talked to me as a four-year-old on my way to live with Willie. I look at my leg and cannot imagine the condition it would be today, if you had not used your unbelievable skills to save it. Importantly so, I could never have gotten here to the university without you, either. Thank you, my friend... I will not fail you...

Ahhh, then there's Coeffield King and my vow. You, kind sir, set me on my path, a path of compassion and service. Never will I forget your asking me to forgive you in not believing my innocence in Will's death. You made me feel worthy and not as a n'er do well, as you knew me in my youth. My heartfelt thanks, sir...

And then, there's my sweet Willie. How you put up with me for all those years. I will never know. Me, the "meanest scoundrel in all of Edgecombe County," but you loved me as your

Chapter 60

own, unconditionally. No matter what happened to me, you picked me up from the mire and made me feel special and treasured. Oh, my Willie, how I love you, my mother...yes, my mother.

Then, his thoughts faltered. His eyes fluttered as the most important person in his young life came into view...again.

Caroline. My God, you are lost to me, and yet I'm not going to pieces anymore. I have pulled myself together, held my head high, and steady...and I am ready for whatever comes my way. I cannot believe this has happened. Never would I have believed this would happen. Never... You will always be my first love. No one can ever take that away from me. I wish you well. I do! I do! Take care... I lo—...

Suddenly, Hap jumped up from the steps and looked toward the autumn sky. His chest rose over and over again, filling his lungs to the fullest. He felt as if his ribs would crack. My gosh, he was going to survive, even though he had no idea what tomorrow would bring. But whatever it was, he would be ready.

Once more he looked down the quad. He thought of all who had walked that green before he had. Actually, he felt that he owned a part of that lush grass lawn that linked all the buildings of learning, the places that had secured a life for many others before him and would secure his future as well.

What an opportunity he had and he would not waste it, not one iota. He would fulfill his vow to others and to himself. Of this he was absolutely certain. A tear spilled down his cheek, over his crooked smile.

Suddenly, the back door of South Building opened. Dean Perry stepped out.

"Ah, Hap, how are you?"

Hap made a feeble swipe at the errant tear.

"Son, are you all right?"

How could I have forgotten Dean Perry?

"Oh, sir, I am so fine. Fine indeed."

"Good. I assume you've received your new room assignment?"

Hap nodded, unable to speak.

"Very good." He gently slapped his young protégé on the back and whistled as he walked down the steps. He turned, winking at Hap and saluting him, as if they had a secret between them. He moved on toward Gerrard Hall for a meeting, all the while looking around Polk Place as if claiming that hallowed ground as *his* own. Hap smiled.

He turned briefly and looked up at the window of the dean's office, recalling his conversation about being a Carolina gentleman and upholding the standards of the University. His smile turned into laughter as he remembered how adamant he was about wanting to enter the University. When he swung back around, Dean Perry had entered the arched doorway of Gerrard and disappeared, as the heavy door clanked shut behind him.

Then Hap mimed his mentor, whistling as he skipped lightly down the steps of South Building. Once more, he marveled at how he had survived the black cloud that had chased him all the way to Chapel Hill, but the University was going to save him; he was certain of that, as well as all the people who kept nudging him down the right path. He clenched his fist and shook it at whatever spooks haunted Polk Place.

At last Hap Tyson felt the freedom he had coveted for so long. No more tears fell as he strode down the walkway. Only the familiar crooked smile covered his face, the curious smile, not the mischievous one of the *meanest scoundrel in all of Edgecombe County*.

Willie would say "Glory."

Chapter 61

Point, Counterpoint

The morning of Caroline and Litch's wedding, Hap Tyson woke with a start. The last sermon of the minister of First Presbyterian Church in Chapel Hill flooded his mind. His words were impassioned, charged, with ways mere mortals could overcome their troubles. *Overcome* was the way and hope to which Hap would cling.

First, on the agenda, he *had* to move from the boarding house. Everywhere he turned in his room, he saw Caroline. Each move she had made that night was imprinted in his brain. How could he ever forget! After hours of unrest, he conceded the rightness to change his surroundings. To change not just his boarding house room, but he needed a break from Chapel Hill, from school, from Tarboro, and he knew where the answer lay. After the first summer session, he was going home. To Pitt County. To Pap.

But, second on the agenda that very day, he had another important task to deal with, the perfume bottle. He had found it tucked away in one of his valises. At that moment, he turned and looked at it on the bedside table. He got up, dressed quickly, and began organizing his move from the boarding house. Mid-afternoon he would take care of his other task.

The University laundry was within walking distance from Hap's room. A creek and a bridge clustered behind the building, a perfect place to dispose of the bottle. Quite ceremoniously, he stood on the bridge over the creek. As he held the tiny perfume bottle, he watched the stream, entranced by the gurgling sounds and sparkling rivulets. Unscrewing the top, he poured the contents over the railing, only to have the breeze lift the intoxicating aroma to his nose. Staggering, he hurled the bottle into the water below and fled blindly down the street. Over and over he ran his fingers through his hair in frustration, only to realize that residue from the cap remained on his fingers. Rushing through the door of his room, he poured water from his pitcher over his head to rinse the fragrance–and her–away. No, he could never return to this room. He looked at the clock in his room and knew what was happening that very moment in Tarboro. The vows.

"Litchfield Jacob Bagley, wilt thou have this woman, Caroline King Cromwell, to thy wedded wife..." and so the ceremony began in Calvary Episcopal Church in Tarboro, North Carolina, on June 15, 1882. Sarah Cromwell was correct in that Tarboro had never seen such doings in many years. The interior of Cromwell Hall was transformed into ethereal gardens, decorated with magnolia leaves and every white flower the nursery in Wilson could find, gardenias, lilies, and the palest of roses. The floral perfume filled the air.

The profusion of greenery and candles on garden tables dazzled the eyes of all the wedding guests. And the food from the hands of Mrs. DeBerry and Maggie stunned everyone's taste buds from the shavings of smoked ham to the fondant icing on the cake. It *was* the wedding of the decade.

Coeffield King could not have been happier, appearing ten years younger. He had lived to see his precious granddaughter married. What more could he ask of life? He knew he'd be with his Jacksie soon. This gift truly humbled him.

A father's pride is no greater than at the birth or marriage of his child, Elijah thought, as he walked his daughter down the aisle. Nothing could have made *him* any happier, except perhaps having his son there to share the joy.

"Caroline King Cromwell, wilt thou have this man, Litchfield Jacob Bagley, to thy wedded husband..."

"I will."

Chapter 61

Oh, Hap, what have I done?

* * *

Oh, Caroline, what have you done?

Acknowledgments

My father Connor Eagles must head the acknowledgement list! Why? For years, he dragged his two young daughters, along with our mother, to every museum, battlefield, fort, and historical home that loomed on his radar. Little did I know that he was instilling the love of history and the preservation of it in my heart and soul. Thank you, Daddy!

Thank you, Mother, for having family in Tarboro, North Carolina, who endeared themselves to our family and filled the first ten years of my life with wonderful experiences in that historical village.

Thank you, Cromwell family members, for providing the backdrop for the first book of The Edgecombe Trilogy, **Frozen Angels.** I have tried to find living Cromwells in the area, but have been unable to locate anyone. The Cromwell cemetery is abandoned where many of the ancestors reside.

A big shout out to the ladies of Sheppard Memorial Library in Greenville, who never knew what question or help I might ask of them. They were always accommodating.

A special thank you to Betsy Allen who read the long version of the manuscript before it became three books. To a writing group who pushed and prodded in uncomfortable ways at times, but I thank them for their honesty.

A big thank you to Steve Row, who aided in editing the first manuscript, and, along the way, taught me a thing or two about writing.

ACKNOWLEDGMENTS

Thank you to Albert Coates, whose signed book on Chapel Hill, *A Magic Gulf Stream in the Life of North Carolina*, and Hugh Lefler and Albert Newsome's book on North Carolina which provided bountiful details and pictures of eastern North Carolina.

Thank you to Carteret Historical Research Association for their bicentennial book, *Historic Carteret County North Carolina*, edited by Mrs. Fred Hill and her associate editors. (1976).

Thank you to the Episcopal Church for putting together a Prayer book, which I used countless times for scenes in Calvary Episcopal Church in Tarboro, North Carolina.

Newspaper articles, magazines, and, yes, even on-line subjects that would come up during writing jags, all contributed to push the storyline along.

With all the previous thank you's, my loudest must go to the Edgecombe County Bicentennial Committee (1976) for their book *The Edgecombe Story*.

And I cannot forget my two new best "lawyer friends" who got me straight on all legal logistics in the book, as well as some good editing suggestions. Thank you, Frank and Rho, the publishers of Simply Francis Publishing Company.

To conclude, thanks to all who have provided input and did not even know it for **Frozen Angels**. I appreciate every life who has touched mine to give me material, whether to lace my storylines or provide historical facts.

And, yes, I even asked Siri a question or two. Thank you, Siri.

Joanne Eagles Honeycutt

ABOUT THE AUTHOR

Joanne Eagles Honeycutt graduated from the University of North Carolina in Chapel Hill in English Education and received a Masters in Reading at East Carolina University. She taught in the Pitt County Schools and Pitt Community College before retiring.

In 2016, Joanne received the Sallie Southall Cotton Award from the City of Greenville Historic Preservation Commission for her continued dedication to preserving eastern North Carolina history through the Eastern Carolina Village & Farm Museum. For years, she has volunteered for this open air museum, a project of her father's, Connor Eagles.

Her regard for history prompted her to write *Frozen Angels*, Book 1 of the Edgecombe Trilogy. Watch for the upcoming sequels to her first novel.

Joanne and her husband live in Greenville, North Carolina, along with their son Mark and his family.

Made in the USA
Middletown, DE
21 March 2024

51420377R00157